Meditating Murder

Ann Saxton Reh

Prospect Street Press

Ann Saxton Reh/Prospect Street Press
www.annsaxtonreh.com

Publisher's Note: This is a work of fiction. Names, characters, incidents, and places, including the town of St. Judith, are products of the author's imagination. Locales and public names are sometimes used for atmospheric purposes. Any resemblance to real persons, places, incidents, or organizations is entirely coincidental.

Cover design by Karen Phillips / www.PhillipsCovers.com

Thanks to Lourdes Venard of Comma Sense Editing for pointing out road signs and potholes on those long, last miles.

Meditating Murder/Ann Saxton Reh. -- 1st ed.
ISBN-13: 978-0-9996259-0-3

To Don and Erica,
the center of my world

In memory of Bruce

And with gratitude to the women writers
who nurtured me through it all

Chapter One

People traveling up California's Mendocino coast in the late 1980s always wondered about the Victorian mansion that sat alone on a bluff near the town of St. Judith. In spite of its lavish garden and expensive renovation, the house had the bewildered look of a thing much praised, but seldom loved.

The same might be said of the Hon. Gerald Fitzwilliam, who on a Friday afternoon in late August sat in his study on the ground floor of that house, reading a newspaper. His distress grew each time he read the headline, "Antiquities dealers arrested in New York. Officials renew efforts to stop looters."

Gerald crumpled the paper and hurled it at the dark leather wingchairs facing his desk. No doubt a dozen looted artifacts were upstairs in this very house.

Swiveling angrily in his chair, he caught sight of his official portrait on the paneled wall. A sense of doom engulfed him. Soon, that round, congenial face might be staring back at him under the headline "Former U.S. ambassador implicated in antiquities trafficking."

It wouldn't matter that he'd never owned an antiquity in his life. It would all be blamed on him. People would say he should have noticed when his wife Kassandra stopped buying old pots in bazaars and started acquiring valuable artifacts. If he'd paid attention, he'd have been able to intervene before this crook Michael Blaine-Poole had moved into the house and wormed his way into Kassandra's starry-eyed trust.

"If I were still in the State Department, I'd have this jerk shut down in five minutes!" he told himself. Then, he sighed. Dwelling on "ifs" was pointless. The great diplomatic machine had stopped working for him after he left active service. That was a fact of life in any profession. Within a few months, colleagues were too busy to return phone calls. Friends faded like lights along a desert road.

He got up and went to look at the twenty-four photographs in matching frames arranged on either side of the official portrait. His career—his life—in neat rows. There he was, young and thin, clasping the hand of a prime minister. And there, the odd, gray-suited one, in a line of Arab sheiks. Here, in the last picture on the top row, this undistinguished man who had plodded his way through the ranks was presenting his credentials to a king.

The telephone's ring startled him. He reached across the desk and grabbed the receiver. "Gerald Fitzwilliam," he said, dropping automatically into his professional tone.

"Hello, Mr. Ambassador!" David Markam's voice came through the wire like warm, familiar balm.

"David!" Gerald shouted. "Oh, it's so good to hear from you. How are you?"

"All things considered, not bad. The doctor released me yesterday. Now, I can get out of Washington. This muggy heat's worse than Jeddah in July. I may go up the coast to Maryland, maybe lie on the beach for a few days. I've got some serious thinking to do." The casualness in David's voice sounded forced, as if he were trying to be stronger than he felt.

"You just need a good rest; that's all."

David swore. "I need to get the hell out of this business. I'm forty-two years old. I need to do something else while I can. No way I'm going to spend the rest of my life behind a desk in this town!"

Gerald did not answer at once, knowing too well what the attack by terrorists three weeks ago in Istanbul had probably done to David—to both his body and his psyche. The thought sickened him. He had mentored David, regarded him almost as a son.

A desperate inspiration came to him. He didn't dare to examine it closely. "Are you up to traveling a bit farther?" he said. "How about coming out here? We live on a coast. We have a beach. We even have an excellent cook! You can rest for a few days, and we can talk things over. How about it?"

It took some more persuading, but David finally said,

"Well, I've always wanted to see California. If you're sure it won't be an imposition, I can probably get a late flight out of Dulles tonight."

"Good, good. You'll have to spend a few hours in San Francisco, but there's a small plane that ferries people up the coast early in the morning. I'll reserve a seat for you. We'll have breakfast waiting when you arrive!" He paused. David had to be told what he was really in for. "There's just one worm in the ointment I should mention."

"Is there a problem? I can make other plans."

"Oh, no! You must come. It's just that some of Kassandra's friends are also staying with us. They're a bit of a nuisance, but they'll be leaving next week."

"Anybody I know?" David sounded wary.

"Possibly. But you'll hardly see them. They're working with Kassandra on the book she's writing about her antiquities collection. We have plenty of room. It will be fine, I promise you." He closed his eyes, hoping it was true.

When he hung up the phone, he brooded for a while. What he was doing to David was contemptible. But what choice did he have? As besotted as Kassandra was with Blaine-Poole, the only thing that might stop her from making her collection public was proof that he was dealing in looted artifacts.

David was the man who could find that proof. His phone calls to Washington would be answered. He had access to all the resources of an international network. More importantly, he was the only one who could be trusted with the sensitive aspects of the matter.

Gerald went back to the wall of photographs and studied the picture of himself and David, taken on the steps of the Embassy in New Delhi the day David arrived for his first Foreign Service assignment. With his light olive skin and dark eyes, David looked at home anywhere from the Mediterranean to South Asia. Even then, he had the poise and self-possession that made him such an effective diplomat.

Beginning to feel more optimistic, Gerald decided that he'd made the right decision. With Michael Blaine-Poole still here in the house, David could see the situation firsthand and do something about it. Of course, he'd be able to rest here, too. They'd talk about old times, maybe go sailing. It was certain to work out quite well.

As long as Kassandra didn't decide to object. He felt his neck muscles tighten. How he loathed the confrontations that happened so often these days! She would be angry that he hadn't consulted her first, as he usually did. But this was his home, too. Even if she did own the house. He glanced once more at his official portrait to steady himself and went to tell her David was coming.

Reaching the staircase in the central foyer, he heard the clatter of cooking pans and the muffled closing of a door in the kitchen. He looked at his watch. Only an hour before the houseguests would be clamoring for cocktails. How nice it would be simply to put on his jacket and stroll through the garden, perhaps all the way to the edge of the bluff to look at the ocean.

Long practice had taught him how to neutralize his emotions. When he reached the top of the stairs, he felt calm. From an open door on the right of the long hallway, he heard his wife saying, "Is it the original pigment?" Her voice was loud, as if she were talking to someone across the room.

Blaine-Poole answered her. "Difficult to say absolutely. This red ochre could be original." The British inflection in his voice was more pronounced than usual.

"I need certainty. I refuse to write 'may be original pigment' in the description!" Kassandra insisted.

Gerald stepped into his wife's large, high-ceilinged bedchamber, blinking against the late afternoon light that, despite the cloudy day, streamed through the tall windows facing the ocean.

On the other side of the room, the light was absorbed into the surface of an eighteen-foot gray wall, pierced by rows of softly glowing niches. Gerald looked with distaste at the display. In each niche stood an ancient piece of stone statuary or a bronze Hindu deity in tense posture of repose or ecstasy.

He struggled to keep his expression neutral as he glanced up at Blaine-Poole, who was kneeling on the platform of a wide library ladder, peering through a magnifying glass at a massive stone statue of the elephant-headed god Ganesh.

Blaine-Poole was a big man, in his late forties, with a beefy virility polished by expensive tailoring. He tossed off a casual two-fingered salute in response to Gerald's greeting, and the charlatan detector Gerald had acquired in three decades of diplomatic negotiations kicked into high gear.

Kassandra sat at a card table between her bed and the sitting room beyond. She put her pen down and frowned when she caught sight of her husband. "What is it, Gerald? I can't deal with anything now. We're days behind schedule."

Automatically, Gerald tried to think of a way to placate her, but no words came. His gaze fastened on her face, seeing, as if she were a stranger, how the light from the windows emphasized the paleness of her skin, the thin, pointiness of her nose. How deceptive that air of delicacy was. How utterly infuriating that petulant expression.

He sat down across the table from her. "I've just had a call from David Markam."

She stared at him, then picked up her pen and held it poised as if she were anxious to get back to her work. "What's the matter with him now? Isn't his recovery going well?"

"It's going very well. In fact, he just needs a place to rest for a while. I invited him to come out here to visit with us." He said it easily, as if he anticipated no resistance from her.

Kassandra's mouth tightened. "I don't suppose he'll be up to traveling across the country for several days."

"No. He's coming right away. He'll be here tomorrow."

She leaned closer to him and said in a low, angry voice, "You know it's not convenient now! Tell him to come next week."

Glancing over his shoulder, Gerald saw that Blaine-Poole was still bent over the arm of the Ganesh statue, apparently paying no attention to their conversation.

"It's too late to stop David now. He'll be en route to San Francisco tonight," Gerald said, not bothering to keep the satisfaction out of his voice.

Kassandra fixed him with a withering glare. "Why doesn't he stay with his family in Washington? His father lives across the Potomac in Arlington."

"He might not be comfortable going home to his parents, Kass."

"They're divorced."

"Who?"

"David's parents. They divorced four or five years ago. His mother lives in England—in a village somewhere. But surely his father could put him up for a few days."

"Where did you hear all of this?" Gerald demanded.

"That girlfriend in Georgetown might take him in," she went on, "the college professor he practically lived with before he was sent to Turkey."

Gerald wanted to shake her. "How could you possibly know these things about David's life? He wouldn't have told you he was . . . his personal business. He never mentioned to me that his parents were divorcing."

She looked up, and they stared at each other. Then Kassandra smiled, and, in spite of his frustration, Gerald grinned. "My God, you're a formidable snoop."

"I know."

For a moment, they held each other's eyes. Then Kassandra turned toward Blaine-Poole and said in a loud voice, "What shall we do about that pigment?"

Gerald sat where he was, hating this habit she had of dismissing him like a child when her mind flitted to something else.

"Can't say, luv," Blaine-Poole said carelessly.

Kassandra wrote a few words and turned again to Gerald. "I still can't imagine why you asked David to fly all the way across the country. He must need medical care. And he's probably in a precarious mental state."

She paused and her eyes went to the wall of niches. Looking thoughtful for a moment, she said, "I hope you don't have any silly ideas about enlisting him to interfere with *my* project."

"I just thought he needed a place to rest," Gerald said. "It seemed like a good idea."

"You know very well it wasn't."

The squeaking of the ladder announced that Blaine-Poole was coming down. He stepped back from the wall and squinted up at the statue. "We may have to leave this one on his own for a bit." He smiled at Kassandra and rolled his hefty shoulders. "What do you say we carry on after dinner? My old back is speaking to me rather rudely."

Pompous ass, Gerald thought.

Kassandra smiled indulgently and stood up. "Have a soak in the pool in my meditation room. Those warm bubbles are wonderful for aching muscles." She moved next to him. "Before you go out there, let me have just one more peek at the new piece." Blaine-Poole crooked his arm. She linked hers through his, and they left together, talking softly.

Gerald got up and walked back and forth in front of the display wall, glaring at the lighted niches. Disgusted, he picked up a small clay pot. How was Blaine-Poole getting away with transporting these things? He must know about the recent prosecutions of dealers who bought looted artifacts. Was he planning to decamp after he finished the work here and leave Kassandra to face the consequences?

"What are you doing with that pot, Gerald?" Kassandra demanded from the doorway. "You're squeezing it! That's a four thousand-year-old treasure. Put it down before you break it!"

Gerald replaced the pot with exaggerated care. "How do you know it's that old? It might have been stolen from some ancient site, or it could be just a fake." He stopped when he saw the indignation in her eyes.

"How many times have we been over this, Gerald? If you weren't such a Philistine, and if you had any respect for my education and ability, you wouldn't say things like that. Every piece I own has been authenticated by a reputable museum, not to mention vetted by Michael."

"That really isn't the point, Kassandra."

"And you certainly don't have any right to insult his qualifications. He's a proven expert at sorting out the genuine from the fakes. In antiquities, at least."

There was a heavy silence between them.

Before Gerald could think of a response, she made another one of the mercurial mood changes that kept him off balance. Like a gloating child, she flopped onto her bed and lay back against the pillows.

"The new piece he brought me is gorgeous! I do think it will be the most beautiful thing in my collection." She smoothed the skirt of her dress, her expression growing smug. "You'll never believe where it came from! He told me he had trouble getting it out of the country," she said complacently.

Whether she was more pleased with the treasure or with imagining Blaine-Poole battling Indian bureaucracy on her behalf, Gerald couldn't be sure, but the look infuriated him. She was completely unprincipled! Looting another culture's heritage didn't matter to her at all.

Clenching his teeth, he said, "How much are you paying him for this one?"

Kassandra picked up an auction catalog from a stack on her bed and leafed through it. "Never mind what it cost. You know I never talk about prices."

"Never talk about them? Didn't I hear you bragging last year that you spent nearly $100,000 for that stone elephant god? The thing is obscene, not to mention hideous!"

She looked defiant. "That was nothing. Cheap by comparison!"

"So this new piece is even more?" He pointed at the small blue valise on her nightstand. "Don't tell me you've got over $100,000 in that case. Oh, no, Kass!"

Her hand moved to cover the valise protectively. "You know I pay cash for everything I buy, so don't bother to say anything else. The trouble with you is that you're jealous, Gerald. You've had your glory. Now you begrudge me this one chance for recognition. Besides, it's my money. I do what I want with it." She tapped the case with her knuckles for emphasis.

Once again, the stifling feeling crept upon him as it did so often these days—rage at his impotence to stop her, then a massive sense of alienation from her that seemed to choke off all feeling. He turned and walked toward the other end of the room.

"You shouldn't have invited David without telling me first," she called after him. "And you'd better not be bringing him here to interfere with my plans. It won't work, Gerald."

He kept walking through the sitting area, into the long, sterile bathroom. His face, when he caught sight of it in the mirrors, looked flushed and alien.

The warm paneling and English colonial furniture in the small bedroom beyond closed him in familiar comfort. He'd gotten used to having what Kassandra called his dressing room in every house since she had insisted on separate rooms because of her insomnia. He had to admit that he seldom missed having her next to him, but, on occasion, the loneliness of his bed overwhelmed him.

Quietly, he closed the door and went to the window. Over the ocean, the clouds were the color of cinders.

Pine trees at the edge of the bluffs swayed. This odd storm, so unusual for August, seemed part of the disorder that had engulfed him. Early retirement had been a terrible mistake. Leaving Washington for this exile with Kassandra, a disaster.

Moving closer to the window, he watched the fog coming in. Inexorably, the mist drifted over the garden, blending flowerbeds, bushes, and tall yew hedges into hazy masses. Would his memory of the place be blurred like this when he thought of it years from now? After Kassandra was gone?

Chapter Two

It was after 7:00 before Gerald made his way downstairs. Dreading the evening ahead, he had taken longer than usual to change his clothes. Even here, in what he thought of as the hinterland of California, he tried to keep up his standards. Putting on a jacket and tie when there were guests for dinner still seemed right to him.

He paused in the doorway of the cavernous living room. After three decades of diplomacy, he instinctively gathered the mood of a room before he entered it. Surprisingly, the atmosphere seemed almost pleasant.

A fire was burning in the towering corner fireplace. Kassandra, Theo Greg, and his wife, Holly, were sitting in the upholstered chairs and couches grouped around it, talking. Across the room, Christine Moreland and Ken Laird stood by the Victorian sideboard, their heads close together, their expressions serious.

Even in a sports jacket and open-collared shirt, Laird looked like the soldier he was. Gerald liked this young army officer who shared his interest in the Middle East. But he did not like the intensity with which Laird held Christine Moreland's gaze.

They saw him and stopped talking as he approached. Christine, slender and elegant in a pale blue dress, smiled her reassuring smile. "How are you this evening, Gerald?"

"Uncommonly well," he said heartily. He picked up a crystal decanter among the bottles on the sideboard. "You two look very solemn. I trust nothing's wrong."

Christine hesitated and laughed lightly. "Just talking shop. You know how I get carried away."

Not sure what she meant, Gerald poured a glass of sherry, giving himself time to sort through his emotions.

Christine moved a step closer and touched his sleeve. "We were really talking about Kassandra's reception on Sunday," she said softly.

Relieved, Gerald said, "Frankly, I'm dreading it more than I can tell you." He raised his hand to stop their protests. "You don't need to spare my feelings. The whole project is deplorable." He glanced toward the fireplace, where his wife and the Gregs were talking. The room was very large, but Kassandra had excellent hearing, as he had reason to know. Lowering his voice, he said, "I might as well tell you now. I've decided to put a stop to it."

Their faces showed the surprise he expected. He swallowed the sherry, fortified by its smoky burn in his throat, and put the glass down. "It's too late to forestall the reception, but this whole business of the book and the donation must *not* go forward. I've asked a friend of mine to come here. He's arriving tomorrow—sooner than I anticipated, but if anyone can do something about this madness, it will be David Markam."

"Markam?" Laird said sharply. "He was in that attack on the Consulate in Istanbul last month. I heard he'd been wounded—"

A bellow from the other side of the room interrupted him. "What's going on over there? How about letting us in on your secret!" Theo Greg shouted, waving his glass. Wine sloshed over the side, and he licked the dribbles among the black hairs on the back of his hand.

Kassandra said, "It would be nice if you could join us, Gerald."

With a rueful look at Christine and Laird, Gerald donned his famous diplomat's smile and said, "My dear, we would like nothing better!"

He reluctantly took the chair next to the couch where Theo Greg, as round-bellied as Kassandra's Ganesh statue, sat caressing a glass of red wine. The bottle of his special Cabernet Sauvignon on the table at his right was already half empty.

Gerald's opinion of Theo Greg alternated between awe and disdain. Who could deny that his exploits as a photojournalist had taken incredible drive and audacity? Knowing what he had been in the past made it even harder to put up with the drunken bore he had become.

Theo's wife, Holly, perched next to him in a dress

apparently made from dozens of greenish-brown scarves, had her usual air of intensely focused intellect. Her hard, watchful eyes were fixed on Christine.

Before Gerald could think of something to say, they heard Melanie laughing in the hallway. She and Michael Blaine-Poole burst into the room arm-in-arm.

"We thought we'd drop by for dinna," Melanie said in a mock Oxford accent.

Gerald regarded his only child with dismay. His pride in Melanie's glowing beauty gave way to embarrassment when she draped herself into a chair as if posing for a perfume ad in her gold *lamé* dress. She motioned for Blaine-Poole to sit on the wide arm of her chair and threw a taunting smirk at Ken Laird sitting across from her. Laird's deep-set eyes narrowed, and Melanie giggled.

What was happening to Melanie? Gerald thought. Certainly, she'd been unhappy since her divorce, but she was almost thirty, not a reckless teenager. He ground his teeth when she turned to whisper something to Michael Blaine-Poole, who bent over her, smiling. This outrageous flirting must be some silly game she was playing to make Laird jealous.

But it was Kassandra who seemed most upset. Glaring at Melanie, she said, "Now that we're all finally here, I want to be sure you understand how important the reception on Sunday is. We must bring the museum trustees around. Your enthusiasm will make them see how a magnificent collection of South Asian art could make St. Judith a cultural destination!"

Gauging the group's reactions, Gerald saw amusement, apathy, even resentment on their faces. Except for Christine Moreland, who was sitting in a chair slightly apart from the others, her long hair tied loosely back, her gray eyes distracted. In the soft light, she had a look of transcendent serenity.

Theo slammed his empty glass down. "Waste of time sucking up to a bunch of trustees. You can't depend on people. Just like that time I was down in Tamil Nadu covering a famine—or maybe it was an assassination—something big," he said.

"I'm traveling with this group of journalists in two cars. Not a mile out of the city, a gang of bandits waylays us. In broad daylight! The goddamn bastards in the car behind us just pull away and take off. Leave us sitting there with our asses hangin' out. Lost two of my best cameras. A week of work! Can't depend on people." He turned and pointed at Gerald. "'Course if the Embassy had been on the ball, it never would've happened."

Gerald barely listened. The previous evening with these people had drained and depressed him. Sitting through the rest of this one would be torment. The silence from the others told him they were waiting for his response to Theo's absurdity. He shook his head. "We did warn you journalists there were *dacoit* gangs in that area."

"You guys are always issuing warnings. Paid any attention to those, I'd have nothing but pictures of the geraniums in front of the Embassy." Theo glanced at

Kassandra, who sat woodenly impatient.

"Speaking of pictures," Holly said, reaching for the knitted handbag at her feet, "the college is sponsoring an exhibit of Theo's work next month. "The *Examiner* did a feature story on him." She rummaged through the bag and brought out a carefully folded newspaper clipping. "It's very well done," she said, handing it to Kassandra. Theo refilled his wineglass and drained it nonchalantly.

"A one-man exhibition—why, that's brilliant!" Blaine-Poole exclaimed, grinning.

Melanie laughed and Theo's eyes widened. Holly opened her mouth in indignant surprise. But the explosion Gerald had expected didn't come. Theo poured the last of the wine into his glass and sipped it.

After an awkward pause, Kassandra held the clipping out to Gerald. He rose, took it, and scanned a few paragraphs. In fairness, he knew that a Pulitzer Prize-winning photojournalist who had taken a picture in Vietnam that made him universally known by the single name "Theo" would still be a celebrity on the college campus where he taught his art.

He smiled at Holly. "This is quite impressive. I can see why you're proud of him."

Holly looked satisfied. "The pictures for his new show are stunning! Starkly modern, but with huge emotional impact."

Gerald gave Melanie a warning frown when he handed her the clipping, but she passed it to Blaine-Poole without looking at it.

"Black-and-white trees—*tres passe*," she said.

Holly put her glass on the coffee table and squared for battle. "What do you know about art? You're—"

Grasping her arm, Theo said in a strangled voice, "Don't. Let it go."

Melanie raised her eyebrows in amused contempt.

Gerald searched frantically for a comment that would defuse the tension, but he was relieved of the necessity by Kassandra, who rose and stood in front of the fire as if she were about to give a benediction.

"We've had enough of this. These squabbles are distracting us from our focus. Now, before we go into dinner, I want to tell you the most important news. Christine knows a publisher who will be just right for the book!"

Christine looked startled. She said, "As I told you this afternoon, what you want may not be possible."

Kassandra seemed less than pleased with the response, but she sailed ahead. "Oh, I'm sure it will work out. For now, as I said, we must be prepared for Sunday. The brochure Melanie designed will be ready tomorrow. I'll go into town myself to pick it up from the printer. I want to be sure it's done correctly."

She frowned at Theo. "It pains me that it's such a rushed project. If you had finished the pictures sooner, I'd be much happier with it."

Theo stared at her morosely. "You're the perfectionist, Kassandra. It wasn't my fault you wanted to retake every other shot."

"Why fret about it, luv?" Blaine-Poole said. "I've had

a look at Melanie's design. It's brilliant. Bound to give those trustees a flutter!"

Kassandra's attention was distracted by a young blond woman who had just come through the door. She was dressed in a frilly blouse and short skirt, and they all watched in silence as she lifted a pitcher of orange juice from the tray she was carrying and put it on the sideboard. She started toward them.

Kassandra held up a hand and said hastily, "No need to collect the glasses, Ellie. Will you ask Mrs. Sawyer to come in?"

The girl scanned the group as if she were amused. "Yes, ma'am," she said and turned to go.

As soon as she passed through the doorway, Melanie said, "Looks like she's got a date tonight. You'd better let the handyman off early."

Kassandra glared at her repressively.

The housekeeper, flushed and harassed, hurried in, wiping her hands on a dishtowel. She listened intently while Kassandra spoke to her in a low voice.

"Yes. I'm sorry," the woman said. "I was checking on the dining room and didn't realize she'd come in here. I'll take care of it. Dinner will be ready in about ten minutes, ma'am."

As Gerald anticipated, the dinner was a tedious continuation of the hostilities. Even Kassandra seemed strained by the bickering. As soon as the meal was over, she rose and said, "We'll have coffee in the living room. There are still so many details to go over. I'm sure you're all tired, but we have to do this tonight. Most of

you won't even be out of bed when I leave for town
tomorrow."

Blaine-Poole took Melanie's arm and said smoothly,
"Since we've done our bit, we'll be off to that marvelous
hot tub of yours. You will excuse us, won't you,
Kassandra, my luv?"

Rigid with fury, Kassandra watched them go and left
the room. Ken Laird also left without a word.

Gerald was embarrassed. He walked with Christine to
the back door, wishing he could go all the way to her
cottage. But, out of the corner of his eye, he saw Theo
and Holly standing in the hallway. He followed them
into the living room.

Kassandra was waiting for them. As soon as the
Gregs sat down in their usual places near the fire, she
started issuing instructions for the next day's work.
Holly took a stenographer's pad from her bag and began
making notes. An occasional grunt indicated Theo was
listening.

Gerald looked at his watch. Ten o'clock. Theo
wouldn't last much longer. Soon, Holly would help him
up to bed. Presumably, Melanie and Blaine-Poole would
have enough sense to get out of the hot tub before
Kassandra went out there for her ritual hour in her
"meditation room."

He went to the sideboard. So near the window, he
heard a gust of wind buffet the house, sending a whisper
through the shadowed oak beams overhead. He poured a
cognac, retreated to his study, and closed the door.

For a few minutes, he stood in front of his wall of

photographs, picking through memories. Then, he checked to be sure his jacket was still hanging on the coatrack in the corner. Leafing through a pile of unread magazines on his desk, he selected the latest issue of *Foreign Affairs* and sat down in one of the wingchairs to read.

Melanie and Blaine-Poole ran swiftly across the wide lawn to the octagonal wooden building out on the edge of the bluff. Inside the warm, moist room, they shed their sandals and robes and sank into the bubbling water of the Jacuzzi.

"I thought I'd freeze on the way over here," Melanie said, shivering.

Blaine-Poole slid down into the water and reached for her hand. "Come here close to me; you'll soon warm up."

Resting her head on the edge of the pool, she looked up into the rafters of the domed ceiling and shivered again. "What an awful place this is!" The soft light on the cedar walls made it feel romantic, but the vibration from the waves crashing into the cave under the cliff unnerved her.

"Does wonderful things for me," Blaine-Poole said. "No wonder Kassandra comes out here to meditate every night."

"Meditate? Ha! All she ever does is think up new ways to make us suffer."

He caressed her shoulder. "Why let her worry you, luv? Just relax and be happy as I do. We have a fine cook to feed us, and your father keeps a first-rate wine cellar." Scanning her body appreciatively, he whispered, "Did I mention the company is rather tempting as well?"

Melanie wiggled her toes, intrigued by the interesting combination of coarseness and sophistication she saw in this man. A skilled hairdresser had managed to minimize the semicircles creeping up his broad forehead. The big, sunburned hands had the finish of a professional manicure. His body, too, was toned. And the black Speedo he was wearing left no doubt that he was well endowed.

He had begun flirting with her the evening he arrived, and she enjoyed it. Not that she really wanted to make Ken feel bad, but it was delicious fun to infuriate Kassandra. And being desirable was always sweet.

"You must not be suffering overmuch if you're stopping here so long," Blaine-Poole said, running his forefinger down her arm as if to counter any hint of criticism.

Caught between pleasure in the physical sensation and annoyance at what he was implying, Melanie shifted away from him. "I'm not staying here for my health, you know. As soon as I finish doing the layout for her ridiculous book, I'm leaving."

Blaine-Poole hauled himself into a more upright position, rested his arm along the edge of the tub, and massaged her neck gently. "Why did you commit yourself if you weren't keen on doing it?"

"It's just a business deal," she said defensively. "Kassandra is going to lend me the money I need to open my shop in San Francisco."

"Oh, right! She did mention she was putting up the funds for your new venture."

Melanie sat up. "What? That's just like her to take all the credit. She's not 'putting up the funds.' It's an investment in my ideas. We'll both make a profit."

She glared at him when she saw a skeptical glint in his eyes. "Don't laugh at me! I've contracted with some wonderful young artists to design my line of accessories. I'm going to set trends. This may be my first business, but I know what I'm doing!"

He raised his eyebrows at her seriousness and grabbed her hand when she flicked water at him. "You don't have to convince me. With your looks you could own the whole bloody world!" He kissed her palm.

Melanie made a hiss of self-derision, pleasure surging through her anger, but she pulled her hand away. In the art of flirtation, she knew exactly how to proceed.

"What about you? How can you criticize me for staying here? You can get good food and wine anywhere. Why don't you hire a courier service to deliver those hideous things you buy for Kassandra? Why bother to come in person?"

"I had to be here in person to meet you, didn't I?" He swung his arm around to embrace her, but drew back, listening. In the noise of wind and surf was the sound of a thump on the wooden steps outside.

The door opened and Rob Covelo, the handyman, stopped in the entrance, apparently not expecting to find anyone there. He waited for a moment, his stocky young body tense with hostility.

"Do you want something, Rob?" Melanie said, shaping her tone to emphasize his employee status.

Rob held his ground. His long, flexible mouth curved into a half-smile, delivering a message Melanie both resented and liked. "I wondered why the motor was running. Didn't know a party was going on in here."

"Well, either come inside or go away. You're letting the wind in," she said lightly. She felt Blaine-Poole's grip tighten around her shoulders. To have two men vying for her attention was familiar territory, and she knew her power in these little dramas.

Rob stepped in and closed the door. He sat down on the padded bench that stretched halfway around the room and stared at the floor.

Melanie watched him, wondering why he had been kept on as handyman for nearly two years. According to the housekeeper, he did his work begrudgingly and disappeared from time to time with no explanation. But he seemed devoted to Kassandra. That, of course, was the answer. She knew how to inspire devotion. And she was a weaver of dreams.

Rob glanced up. Meeting her eyes, he jerked his gaze away. "Mrs. Fitzwilliam will be out here in a few minutes. I'm s'posed to see if the tub's okay. She always wants the pH level tested before she goes in," he said sullenly.

Melanie opened her mouth to tell him what
Kassandra could do with her pH level and then decided
the comment didn't fit the image she wanted to project
at the moment. Rob looked unhappy, and she realized
how young he must be. Probably not more than
nineteen. Seeing his scarred and work-toughened hands,
she felt a flicker of compassion for him. He was shackled
by Kassandra's chains just like they all were.

She heaved an exaggerated sigh. "I guess that means
our time is up. We certainly wouldn't want to interfere
with her little fetish, would we?" She glanced at Blaine-
Poole, but he was gazing at the ceiling as if he were
bored.

Another sound, the thin wail of a cat, trickled
through the wind outside. The door flew open with a
gust of cold air and a white Persian leapt into the light.
Behind it came the blond maid, Ellie.

Unlike Rob, who made pathetic attempts to keep his
dignity, Ellie flaunted her contempt for them all. She
slammed the door and stood with her hands on her hips,
glaring. Melanie guessed that she must have expected to
find Rob there alone.

She was dressed in a tank top and shorts, her legs
and bare feet caked with patches of sand as if she had
been on the beach down in the cove. Goose bumps
covered her arms, and the nipples of her breasts were
hard under the thin cotton. Rob stared openly at her.
Michael, with a fascinated but slightly embarrassed
expression, was also staring.

The cat rubbed against Ellie's legs and she picked it up, cuddling the reluctant animal and kissing its nose. "Mrs. F's looking for you," she said, her words muffled against the cat's fur.

"What does she want?" Melanie said.

Ellie shrugged. "I don't know, but she's pissed. She said you better get up there."

Melanie's face burned. She felt a sense of humiliation out of proportion to the absurd situation. How dare Kassandra send a servant ordering her to come! Surging out of the water like Venus rising from sea foam, she reached for her robe and jammed her feet into her sandals.

She paused, waiting for Michael to follow. He sat with his arms spread along the rim of the pool, his face patient and amused. "She hasn't sent for me. I think I'll just enjoy myself here a bit longer."

Melanie plunged outside. The wind seized her, chilling her wet skin and snatching at her heavy hair. She hurried up the path to the house, seething.

Kassandra was sitting at the table in the breakfast room, wearing a pink satin robe over her bathing suit. She was writing in a bound ledger, bills and receipts spread out around her. Looing up, she took off her reading glasses.

Melanie shivered. Feeling like a child in front of the headmistress, she pulled out a chair and sat down. The scent of cinnamon-apple tea from the cup at Kassandra's right hand irritated her. Defiantly, she met her stepmother's eyes.

"Well? What was so important that you had to send that little pig after me?"

At first, Kassandra kept her eyes on the ledger with the air of bearing an offense selflessly. Melanie folded her arms, determined to wait.

Picking up her pencil, Kassandra began drawing tight little circles on a piece of scratch paper. "I don't see why you say such unkind things, Melanie. Your welfare is my only concern."

"You'll forgive me if I find that hard to believe." Melanie waited for her response, reluctantly fascinated by the hand clutching the pencil, so pale and blue-veined under a sprinkling of brown spots.

Kassandra's face reflected none of her agitation. The eyelids were half closed, her expression fixed and bland. She began connecting the circles with sharp parallel lines. "Your behavior this evening was a disgrace. Your father and I have been discussing it, and he agrees," she said. "You simply are not ready to handle the responsibility of running a business."

Melanie tried desperately to think of some defense against what she sensed was coming.

"You have been given so many opportunities," Kassandra went on. "But we can't recall a single one you did not squander. That's the only word to describe it."

"What are you talking about?"

"A fine education; a wonderful marriage—"

"How would you know anything about my marriage or my education?"

When Kassandra did not respond, she leaned across the table. "Are you actually threatening me? You're saying you *won't* put up the money for my shop? You can't do that, Kassandra! I've already contracted to buy merchandise. I've gotten licenses. I've negotiated a lease on a store space."

Kassandra gave her an angry look, put down her pencil, and folded her hands. "I am too tired to continue this discussion tonight. I've told you repeatedly that you will inherit a considerable amount from me eventually."

"But you promised I could have it now! You said if I came here and did the design work for you, you'd write the check next week, Kassandra. It was a business agreement. You can't just change your mind!" Melanie heard the hysteria in her voice and hated it. "What am I supposed to do? Put everything on hold until you die?"

"It isn't a good investment, Melanie. Your past mistakes have shown that you're irresponsible, but your attitude the last few days has proved how immature you are. And cruel as well."

"Cruel? What are you talking about?"

Kassandra's mouth tightened. "You were inexcusably rude to the Gregs this evening."

Melanie laughed. "That's ridiculous. Theo and Holly don't care what I think about them."

"And your treatment of Ken Laird is shameful. He was here a few minutes ago, looking for you. I didn't want to tell him you were still out with Michael."

"Why not? Did you think he'd find us having sex in your precious hot tub?"

Red blotches heated Kassandra's pale cheeks. "I have no idea what he might have found you doing. I thought you had matured beyond this kind of adolescent display, Melanie, but you seem unable to resist making a spectacle of yourself."

"No, that isn't what's really bothering you, is it?" Melanie said. "You're jealous because your darling Michael likes to be with me instead of you."

Kassandra sighed. "That remark is just what I'm talking about. I've told your father he must let you face the consequences of your actions."

"What actions? What do you mean?"

Avoiding her eyes, Kassandra said, "If your father knew what you did last year, he would be hurt deeply."

Melanie stood up. She was trembling, her throat tight with rage. "You don't dare tell him. You don't dare!" Clinching her hands to keep from slapping Kassandra, she ran through the kitchen and out into the night.

The wind tore at her robe and stung her eyes to tears. Hugging herself, she ran across the terrace and onto the grass. Above her, the bright half-moon rode in and out of cloud streaks. Once she reached the garden, where tall yew hedges blocked most of the wind, she slowed to a walk, swinging her arms to warm herself and settle the chaos in her mind.

How could she have been so stupid? She knew what Kassandra was like. Why had she believed her? Hadn't she learned from the past how that honey voice flowed around you, and went on and on, stirring excitement, promising unbounded help, until your fears were drowned and you completely forgot how treacherous she was?

Standing very still, Melanie realized this betrayal was not completely unexpected. It had always been a possibility that Kassandra might change her mind and jerk away the gifts she had promised. She had done it before.

But this threat to tell Père what happened last year was something new. And terrifying. She hadn't really been sure Kassandra knew about it. There was none of the usual hinting.

She began to walk again. Somehow, the desperation she felt seemed to be generating a new kind of strength. By the time she reached the house, she felt calmer. Going in, she closed the door quietly. The kitchen was dark except for the glow of the hood lamp over the stove. The humming of the refrigerator and the click of a quartz clock gave substance to the silence. She looked into the breakfast room to be sure Kassandra was gone.

Curious, she walked down the short hall beyond the kitchen where the housekeeper and maid had their rooms. Pausing outside Ellie's door, she heard faint sounds from a television. Rob might be in there with her. More likely, he'd finished and left her drinking herself to sleep.

With a small hope that her father would offer comfort, she looked into his study and found it empty. She climbed the stairs and moved along the hallway lit by dim wall sconces. There were slits of light under the doors of all the occupied bedrooms but no sound came through the thick walls. Kassandra's door was open and the room dark, since she was still out doing her precious meditation.

In her own room, Melanie stripped off her bathing suit and burrowed under the duvet. Ken might come to her later. She was not sure whether she wanted him there or not. For now, she needed to be alone with this new sense of strength, to understand what possibilities it held for her. For a long time, she lay in the darkness, thinking.

Chapter Three

David Markam woke from a doze when the small plane began its descent for landing. He looked down at the rectangle of gold-brown dirt gouged into a dense pine forest and watched, fascinated, as the plane glided toward the tiny strip of runway.

When it had shuddered to a halt, he could see Gerald waiting outside a chain link fence, his usually affable face anxious, as if he were a little embarrassed to be seen where he was.

David did not move until the other two passengers had left. He was tired, bone weary, but the pain in his wounded arm had settled into a bearable burn. He stepped out, pausing to adjust his sling, and drew in a breath of cool, resin-scented air.

Gerald came hurrying toward him, his hand already extended for a handshake. He clasped David in an awkward hug. "You've made it. I'm so happy to see you.

We just can't afford to lose the good ones like you." He brushed away a tear.

"Mr. Ambassador," David murmured, disconcerted by Gerald's effusiveness but warmed by the genuine feeling he knew was behind it. He pulled his hand away gently. "You're looking pretty fit. California must agree with you."

His former chief had taken off some weight and added a leathery tan. In an open-collared shirt, he seemed younger than his sixty years.

"Oh, I work at it, believe me. It's part of the lifestyle here—the illusion of being able to move faster than time. Which bags are yours?" he said, bustling over to where the pilot had unloaded the luggage. David identified his two suitcases and reached for one of them, but Gerald seized them both. He stowed the bags in the trunk of his Volvo parked just outside the fence, and they got in.

Aware of an odd feeling, David pondered it for a moment and then said, "You know, I just realized, I've never seen you drive."

Gerald nodded. "I suppose that's true. Either we had a driver, or you were behind the wheel. Well, times change. Perhaps not always for the better."

Though he heard the shift in Gerald's tone and sensed that he was brimming with the need to talk, David resisted the appeal. He'd had enough of other people and their problems. He had no emotion left to give.

Hoping to keep the conversation uncomplicated, he

said, "How's Kassandra?"

"She's fine. Fine. Busy organizing and arranging things as usual. She's rather driven these days. I knocked on her door to let her know I was leaving for the airport, but she apparently got up early and went out. I'm sure she'll be waiting for us when we get there."

Knocked on her door. So Gerald and Kassandra still occupied separate bedrooms. Now, as in the past, he didn't want to speculate about the arrangement. It was not the way he and his own wife had lived. But the Fitzwilliams' marriage had lasted a long time. And Layne had left him just before their third anniversary.

Three years. The time when his life had been whole. Regrets he had tried to bury began to stir again. The terror of Istanbul had done more than mangle his arm and exhaust his mind. It had given new life to old grief, burdened his sleep with dreams that left him hollow and dazed.

Gerald began to talk about 19th century Russian exploration along the California coast. David wanted to listen, but the words grated on his nerves. He let his eyes rest on the towering trees with early morning mist still lingering in their branches. When the road reached the highway and they turned north, there were glimpses of sparkling Pacific Ocean between stands of pines and meadows of tall dry grasses.

They drove for a while in silence, passing a small cluster of restored Victorian houses that suggested New England, but this country was newer, rawer than the Atlantic Coast. It suited David's desire to touch something rural, unhurried, after the chaos his life had been for the past month. Gradually, he began to regain a sense of balance, to feel grateful that Gerald had urged him to come.

"This is beautiful country, but not the kind of place I ever expected to see you living in," he said after a while. "I always thought of you as a city person."

"So did I. This was Kassandra's idea. Retiring in California was her dream. She bought the house years ago and leased it to some people who used it as a B & B. When I began to think about retiring, she had it remodeled for us. It was quite pleasant, in the beginning," he added.

David still resisted the pull of the distress he heard in his voice.

Gerald said, "Well, it's a great place to relax. No negotiation tables, no crises. We've got a superb cook who'll put some pounds back on those long bones of yours."

His expression sobering, he glanced at David's wounded arm. "Damned bad business in Turkey. I called the State Department as soon as I heard that the Consulate in Istanbul had been attacked. I couldn't believe it when the desk officer told me you were one of the wounded. I thought you were working in Izmir."

"So I was, until a few days before. Instead of going straight back to Washington, I decided to detour though Stamboul. A Turk I know was arranging a trip down to the ruins at Catal Huyuk for me. I just happened to stop by the Consulate that day to see a friend. Strange karma."

Gerald shook his head. "The press blamed it on a local militant group. Personally, I'd have bet it came from that bunch we've been watching the past decade."

"You'd be right—grown bigger and better funded. Probably a new splinter group, but definitely related. We'd been sending urgent reports about them to State for at least four months. But you know how that is."

They exchanged a familiar glance of frustration. After days of debriefings and report writing in Washington, David was ready to answer the questions he knew were coming. But Gerald had read the newspaper accounts of the attack on the Consulate in Istanbul, and he'd spent nearly half his life in Foreign Service. He needed few details.

When David had given him a bare outline of events, Gerald looked pained. "Incredible. Senseless," he said. "I can't imagine anyone wanting to destroy that beautiful Palazzo Corpi."

"If there's any good news, that was it. They had explosives, but they were stopped before they had time to use them. The damage was pretty well confined to the Annex building where we were. That appeared to be the primary target."

"Six killed."

"Yes. Two Turkish security police. The rest Americans. Bill Ralston was sitting next to me."

They were silent for a while. Then Gerald said, "The aftermath is hard. The atmosphere that settles over a diplomatic post after an attack is unnerving. We're a breached fortress in hostile territory. Even the illusion of safety is gone. And everybody's trying to carry on as if nothing unusual has happened." He cleared his throat. "Well, I'm glad you're out of it for a while. We'll make sure you have a rest."

Relieved to move on, David said, "So! Tell me about this memoir you're writing."

"Not much to tell yet. I keep starting and getting bogged down. I need a new perspective. I was hoping you'd inspire me."

"I'm probably not your best source for that. My perspective is a little askew these days. By the way, I've been trying to figure out what you were talking about in your last phone call. What was that cryptic reference to illegal antiquities all about?"

Gerald threw him a rueful glance. "That, as they say, is a sore point. I'm embarrassed to admit it, but that's what I really need your help with." He shook his head. "I never should have involved you in this mess."

I wish you hadn't, David thought wearily. Immediately, he regretted the feeling. How many times had Gerald come to his aid over the years? Taken his side when he'd rebelled against policy, saved his hide when he'd been on the verge of being ousted from some country as *persona non grata*?"

"You may as well tell me about it," he said. "Does this have something to do with things Kassandra brought back from overseas?"

When Gerald nodded, David said, "Not sure what I can do to help. I really don't know much about artifacts."

"Ha! That I don't believe! You've been to every ancient city in South Asia and around the Mediterranean."

David was used to teasing like this. He knew people called him Markam of the Ruins behind his back. He never tried to justify his fascination with ancient places. How could he?

Ruinenlust, the Germans called it. The compulsion had seized him the first time he saw Leptis Magna, the Roman city in Libya, when he was fifteen. Only those who shared the condition could understand how those marble columns, magnificently desolate against the blue Mediterranean, had imprinted his senses.

Some of his interest was intellectual—a yearning, as he walked across a broken mosaic floor, to see the stoneworker setting those tiles in place. But it was his emotions that were most ineffable. Each time he encountered a ruin, a craving overtook him for something he could not name, and it mingled with a transcendent wonder at being part of all time.

"I still have a few left to see," he said. "All I know about the artifacts from those sites is what I've read in books or on label cards in museums. I've never dealt with antiquities trafficking. Maybe once or twice we did some liaison with other agencies when it came up in a matter we were handling. That's about it. So, tell me what's worrying you."

"No, no. I don't want to go into it now. I invited you here to relax. Undisturbed. That's all I want you to do,"

Gerald said hurriedly.

David waited until his irritation with Gerald had lost its edge. Then, he said, "Did Kassandra buy most of her pieces in India?"

"I guess so," Gerald said. "She did spend an inordinate amount of time in the shops and museums in Delhi. I have to admit, I didn't always pay as much attention to her activities as I should have."

Stopping for a red light, he tapped his fingers on the steering wheel distractedly. "I thought she had lost interest in the collecting when we first got to St. Judith. We were the typical nine-day wonders here. Invitations came in, requests to sit on boards of directors. Very flattering, but exhausting for me. Kass thrived on it.

"Things changed when we went down to San Francisco to hear some symphony performances. She spent an entire day at the Asian Art Museum, poring over the Avery Brundage South Asian collection there.

"I could tell she was excited afterward. She worked for weeks getting the paperwork ready to offer her collection to that museum."

"They turned it down?" David said.

"Flatly. I've never seen her so distraught. Since then, she's been obsessed. She had a whole wall of her bedroom reconstructed to display her pieces. Floor-to-ceiling lighted niches."

David could see how upset Gerald was, but he wasn't sure why. "Displaying them in her bedroom seems pretty harmless. Do you think she has some illegal pieces? Is that it?"

Gerald grimaced. "I don't really know. She wouldn't admit it if she had."

"I doubt that any foreign government has made a claim against her," David said, beginning to sense the depth of Gerald's alarm. "We'd probably have heard about it if she were mixed up with anything really bad."

"I suppose so. It's just that she's gotten involved with this agent—this Michael Blaine-Poole. He's an expat—a Brit, I think. He claims to have contacts with government agencies, eases Ministry red tape—you know the type. I don't trust him. All my instincts tell me he's the worst kind of weasel."

"What does Kassandra say about your concerns?"

"She thinks I'm a Philistine."

David chuckled. "I'm not sure I want to get into the middle of this debate."

"Perhaps I am prone to overreacting on occasion. Still paranoid after all those years of living on the tightrope. But she's spending enormous amounts of money. And she is so secretive about it. I think she's dealing with something she doesn't understand the implications of—that could have ramifications."

Lately, David had been more than usually aware of the particular brand of paranoia one developed in Foreign Service. It was a hypervigilance that had become as much a part of his life as the clothes he wore. But he had known Gerald too long not to respect his instincts.

The light turned green, and they surged forward.

"I've tried to make Kassandra see how serious this

is," Gerald went on. "Everything I say generates hostility. Not that she listens to me, anyway. I can't even object on the grounds of expense. She has her own money. The house we live in is hers!"

David guessed that the part about the house was a very sore point with Gerald. "So she's now buying antiquities from this agent—Blaine-Poole, is it? Does he get them in the U.S. or overseas?"

"He claims that he buys the pieces from 'original sources.' Mostly in India."

"I've never heard of him. He's probably one of those well-greased individuals we have trouble keeping track of. But it doesn't sound good to me. 'Original sources' could mean the artifacts have been looted."

"Exactly. He and Kass have had an arrangement for over a year now. I don't know how she found him, but she's completely besotted. She tells him what she wants. He acquires it—allegedly has it all documented properly—and transports it to the U.S."

"If this has been going on for over a year, why is it coming to a head now? Has something else happened?"

Gerald threw up his hands and then quickly grasped the wheel again. "It's escalated to absurdity. She's decided to donate the collection to the local museum here. And she's found a publisher in San Francisco for the book she's writing about the damned thing!"

Seeing the anxiety in Gerald's face, David began to realize what the "implications" and "ramifications" of Kassandra's decision might be. "You mentioned the book on the phone yesterday. I had no idea you were talking about anything like this. If there are looted artifacts in the collection, it probably won't be long before somebody starts making waves."

"And I'm in the boat that will be swamped!" Gerald said. "I feel like I'm already dogpaddling in rapids, David. Kassandra has become ruthless, unreasonable. I don't even know her anymore."

David said nothing. The depth of this emotion made him uncomfortable. He realized that in spite of all the years they'd worked together, he knew little about Gerald's personal life. Even less about his wife. When she and Gerald first married, she'd had no experience of Foreign Service life, and she'd been much too eager to make use of the status she thought Gerald's position conferred on her. Aside from being bossy, she'd also been adept at manipulating people and dividing loyalties.

Now, whether he liked it or not, he would be getting to know Kassandra well.

Chapter Four

Well, this is it," Gerald said, turning off the highway onto a narrow lane. A few yards along, the road was barred by a high wrought iron fence. Gerald pressed a remote to open the gates. They drove in silence along the eucalyptus-lined road.

David lowered his window, filling his lungs with the trees' pungent scent. After about a quarter of a mile, the trees ended abruptly and the road curved to the right, leading to a wide circle of gravel driveway.

The house, with gables and a massive turret at each end, looked more like a late-Victorian hotel than a home. A long, two-story garage lay beyond it, but Gerald parked at the steps of the front porch. Inside, they passed through a paneled foyer that opened into a living room of vast and grandiose proportions.

In the dimness, David could make out red silk
drapery, heavy furniture, and a towering rock fireplace,
rising to the black beams of the ceiling. The stifling
opulence and the acrid scent of wood smoke in the air
made him glad to cross the room quickly.

They stopped in a central hallway, and Gerald
pointed to the broad staircase on the right. "What will
it be? Upstairs to your room first or a cup of coffee and
some delicious pastries?"

"Food and drink," David said.

"We'll leave your cases here." He put them down and
led the way to a door on the far side of the hallway.
They went into a breakfast room that was bright with
morning sunlight. Its semicircular wall on the ocean side
indicated they were on the ground floor of the house's
left turret. Scattered newspapers and used coffee cups on
the big round table made the room feel casual and
welcoming.

David looked out the windows at the flagstone
terrace, bordered by purple flowering bushes. From the
terrace, a smooth lawn stretched fifty yards or more to a
luxuriant garden with trees and sculpted hedges that
obscured the view of the ocean beyond. He and Gerald
helped themselves to coffee smelling of vanilla beans
from an urn on the sideboard. Hungry for the first time
in weeks, David took a cinnamon pecan roll from the
silver platter.

They sat down at the table. Gerald sipped his coffee
and looked toward the windows, frowning. "I can't
imagine where Kass is. She stopped by my study last

night on her way to her meditation and told me she wanted to show you the garden herself before anyone else got hold of you. I was certain she'd be here waiting for us."

"I didn't know Kassandra was into meditation."

Gerald shrugged and looked a little sheepish. "Oh, we're very New Age these days. We started Tai Chi several months ago. I kept it up. Practice every day." He made a graceful s-curve with his hand.

"Kass does a little yoga but she is very diligent about what she calls her meditation. She had a building with a jetted pool built out on the edge of the bluff." He gestured toward the windows. "You can't see it from here. It's on the rim of the gully. Terribly inconvenient. Nearly seventy yards from the house.

"Every night at eleven, she goes out there and stays until midnight. It's become a ritual. And no one else is allowed near the place while she's there. Bit strange, I suppose," he added.

"Christine—Dr. Christine Moreland, our lodger in the cottage out on the headland—introduced us to meditation as a way to relax. She used to be a practicing psychologist."

David was not quite sure how to react to these radical lifestyle changes in two people he'd always considered the epitome of convention. Meditation? Hot tubs at midnight? A resident guru? Was it his imagination or had Gerald's cheeks reddened when he mentioned Christine Moreland?

The door from the kitchen swung open, and a tall,

frazzled woman in her early fifties stood in the doorway. Wisps of her hair stuck out at angles from her narrow face. She was flushed and the brown eyes were angry.

"Oh, it's you, Mr. Fitzwilliam." Surprise momentarily replaced the anger. She glanced at David, then began again, subdued but determined. "I thought Mrs. Fitzwilliam would be down here by now. Things are just about to go to pieces. She has to tell me what hors d'oeuvres she wants for the reception on Sunday so Rob can go to town to buy the groceries. And that young man has disappeared, too. Ellie says he left in his old pickup and didn't come back last night."

Gerald rose and in his smoothest diplomatic tone said, "Mrs. Sawyer, this is David Markam, our old friend. Mrs. Sawyer is the extraordinary person I've been telling you about who looks after us. She is the creator of these wonderful pastries."

The woman was clearly embarrassed. "I knew we were expecting you, sir. I'm sorry to be carrying on like this in front of a guest." She wiped a section of the table with a dishtowel.

David acknowledged the introduction. "Excellent coffee," he murmured, discreetly withdrawing to the windows to be out of the line of fire.

"Of course, you must have some help with all of this work," Gerald said. "You say Rob's truck is gone? Do you suppose he drove Mrs. Fitzwilliam to town to buy the food?"

She looked shocked. "Mrs. F. would never set foot in that old wreck of his!"

"No, I suppose not. Perhaps she drove in herself."

An emphatic shake of her head disallowed that possibility. "Her car's in the garage. I checked there right off."

"And Ellie doesn't know where Rob is?"

The housekeeper's look of disgust indicated that the question had opened an even deeper vein of annoyance. "She might know, but she says not. I tell you, Mr. Fitzwilliam—" She hesitated, glancing at David, and lowered her voice, as if to spare an outsider the unsavory details of the household's domestic life. "Ever since Mrs. F. gave Rob that room over the garage, I've had a devil of a time with those two. He's out there asleep half the time, and Ellie's jealous because he got the room. I don't know which one's worse. And that Ellie—well, you know, sir."

Gerald looked distressed. "I didn't realize you were having problems like this," he began.

Mrs. Sawyer ignored his discomfort. "I don't care what she says, I know she was out there in Rob's apartment last night. I heard her sneaking in late. Very late."

Putting his cup down, Gerald said briskly, "We'd better get Mrs. Fitzwilliam to help us out. I'll go upstairs right this minute and let her know how much she's needed."

He rolled his eyes in David's direction and hurried away. After an awkward moment, Mrs. Sawyer went to the sideboard. "I'd better bring out more pastries and some fresh coffee. Mr. and Mrs. Greg should be coming in before long."

When he was alone, David relaxed, bit into his pecan roll, and chewed it thoughtfully. The scene he'd just witnessed reminded him of countless others he and Gerald had been through together. Maybe irate diplomats instead of frantic housekeepers, but the dynamics weren't much different.

The door from the hallway opened, and Gerald came in frowning. "Kass isn't in her room. It looks like she must have gotten up early and gone out."

Mrs. Sawyer appeared in the kitchen doorway. "I'm sorry, sir. I forgot to tell you something." She touched her forehead with the back of her hand. "I've been so busy. Anyway, Dr. Moreland was here looking for you early this morning. I told her you were in your study. When she didn't find you there, I realized you'd already left for the airport. She wanted to speak to you, so I said I'd let you know when you got back."

Looking pleased, Gerald said, "Thank you. I'll see her as soon as I can. It just occurred to me that Mrs. Fitzwilliam is probably in the garden. She was looking forward to showing David around. I'll bet she's out there already."

He turned to David. "What do you say to a walk up the garden path? We're bound to run into Kass."

David thought of many things he'd rather do. Unpacking, taking a nap, getting away from the tension he could feel was building in this house. But he knew from long habit how to generate enthusiasm when necessary.

As they were going out the back door of the large kitchen, Gerald paused and said to Mrs. Sawyer, "I'll tell you what. If Rob hasn't appeared by the time we get back, I'll drive to the market myself to get what you need. Try not to worry. Everything's going to be just fine."

Walking across the flagstone terrace, Gerald turned to David with a rueful grin. "That reminds me of the time I said the takeover of the embassy in Teheran wouldn't last more than a week."

Chapter Five

Kassandra's garden was laid out for strolling along decomposed granite paths that meandered among tall yew hedges, beds of flowers, trees, and vines. The hedges looped and circled, creating sheltered garden "rooms" for benches or pieces of sculpture.

Pointing to the stones of a dry streambed, Gerald said, "Kass intends to have water piped in to make a little creek there."

"She's done all of this in the few years you've been here?" David said.

Gerald grinned. "Well, you know her; she's never done a small project! Actually, the previous owners created the original three-acre garden. Kass—to put it modestly—expanded it. She also wants to have a fence and walking path built around the perimeter of the bluff. Lately, though, these projects have been overshadowed by her plans for the museum exhibit."

At the far edge of the garden, they strolled through a stand of pines, their shoes crunching layers of dry needles that littered the ground. As they emerged from the shadows of the trees, David saw two men in sweat suits jogging toward them on the bare, rocky stretch of headland between the garden and the bluff's edge.

Gerald called out to them. "Ken! Michael! Good morning! David Markam's here. We just got back from the airport."

"You ought to let them go on with their run. I can see them later," David murmured.

Gerald glanced up at him with the *have I made a faux pas?* expression that David knew very well really meant *too late now, my friend.*

He introduced Michael Blaine-Poole, who looked David over and said, "Right! Markam. Hero returned from the wars, we hear."

David let the remark pass. Blaine-Poole was about what he'd expected—arrogant, shrewd. He looked like the kind whose audacity would make him memorable. If he was doing some illegal antiquities trafficking, his trail might not be too hard to pick up.

Ken Laird shook his hand. "Good to see you, David. It's been a couple of years, hasn't it?" A grin momentarily transformed his chiseled features.

"Something like that," David said, remembering the last time he'd had occasion to visit Lt. Col. Ken Laird at the Pentagon. He was a quiet, serious man, and highly efficient at what he did for a living.

"Have you seen Kassandra?" Gerald said. "We seem

to have several domestic crises brewing at once."

They shook their heads, and Gerald's eyes grew more troubled. "I wonder if she could be at Christine's cottage."

"Christine's car was gone when we went by her place," Laird said. "Maybe they're out together."

"Perhaps that's it," Gerald said. He looked unconvinced. "Well, we won't keep you. She's bound to be around here somewhere."

David watched the two men enviously when they started off again. He thought he'd take a walk along the same route as soon as he'd had a chance to change his clothes. He needed the exercise. It might help him generate some tolerance before Kassandra got hold of him.

When they reached the house, Gerald stopped by the breakfast room for more coffee. He pinched off half a · muffin, crammed it into his mouth, and grinned guiltily. "Sweets are still the one vice I'll never overcome." He gulped his coffee. "Why don't I show you where your room is?"

Climbing the wide polished staircase, he said in a low voice, "I don't think the Gregs are awake yet. They probably won't be down for a while. My God, it seems like a hundred years ago that we first met Theo in Delhi. I think he was covering the riots we had. What year was that? My life seems more and more like a living memoir these days."

Listening with a kind of detached nostalgia, David realized how much he'd missed Gerald. The tension of the past weeks began to ease a little. Maybe coming here was the right thing after all.

Gerald showed him to a room near the top of the stairs.

"I'll be in my study when you're ready. It's the door past the breakfast room," he said.

Alone, David glanced around the room. Its curved outer walls told him he was in the turret on the right side of the house. Kassandra's touch was evident in the antique furnishings. A heavy brass bed, bow-fronted rosewood dresser, a large Victorian wardrobe in lieu of a closet. Folded at the foot of the bed was a thick duvet, its cover embroidered in a red and blue design of stylized leaves and flowers that he recognized as Kashmiri.

He pushed aside the curtains covering one tall window and was grateful that he could see the ocean. It was just a narrow view through the gap created by a gully between the bluffs, but it was enough. He knew he would look at it often.

The bathroom, also vaguely Victorian, was tiled in white, accented with blue-patterned Turkish tiles. He splashed water on his face and adjusted his arm sling. Considering the energy it would take to unpack his suitcase and the pain changing clothes would provoke in his arm, he decided against going out for a walk right away.

In the hallway downstairs, he heard Gerald's voice coming from the door of what was obviously his study. He was speaking rapidly into the phone.

David went in and sat down in a wingchair.

Gerald's eyes were worried when he hung up the phone. "That was the printer. He called to find out if Kass is still planning to pick up the brochures she ordered. I've already phoned several of her friends. They haven't seen her. Christine's back home. She hasn't seen her either. It just isn't like her to disappear this way."

"No one knows when Kassandra left the house?"

"She must have gotten up and gone out quite early this morning. I didn't hear her in the bathroom." He crossed his arms and frowned. "Well, I suppose it's silly to worry about it. She's bound to sail in here any minute! Make yourself comfortable, my friend."

David got up to look at the wall of photographs. "This is an impressive gallery."

"Entirely Kass's idea, of course," Gerald said. He came around the desk and stood beside him. "Gross self-aggrandizement. But some good memories, I admit."

David leaned closer to a large black-and-white picture and smiled. "I'll never forget the weekend we spent at that old Maharaja's estate! The peacocks kept us awake all night."

Gerald chuckled. "He was quite a character, yes. He died a few years ago. I met his son once at a party in Washington. Not much of a chip off the old block."

A door slammed at the back of the house. They heard shouts, then running feet. Michael Blaine-Poole burst into the office, panting, his cheeks maroon under his tan. "Gerald, listen! There's a body down off the cliff. You need to ring the police straightaway!"

Gerald froze, his pale eyes wide. "Who is it?" he said in a hoarse whisper. "Is it someone we know?"

Blaine-Poole put his fists on his hips, his large body heaving with exertion. "We couldn't be certain. You need to ring the cops, man! They must have a rescue squad or something. There's no way in hell we can climb down there."

Gerald blanched, but an expression of competence under pressure David had often seen took the place of shock. He picked up the telephone and punched in a few numbers. "This is Gerald Fitzwilliam. We have an emergency—an accident. Someone has fallen off the cliff."

He gave directions to his house, listened, answered a few questions in monosyllables, and put his hand over the receiver. "They want me to stay on the line. It will take them a few minutes to get here."

"Have you any binoculars?" Blaine-Poole said, looking around the room.

Gerald pointed to a drawer in one of the built-in cabinets. Blaine-Poole opened it and rummaged through office supplies and folders.

"Oh, no," Gerald moaned. "I let Theo borrow them. I suppose they're in his room."

Blaine-Poole turned impatiently. "I'd best go back out there."

Watching Gerald, David recognized a look of appeal he knew well. "I'll go with him," he said.

Blaine-Poole had run on ahead, and David decided to take the path that wound all the way around the garden rather than trying to find his way through the network of paths that wandered among the tall hedges and bushes. As soon as he rounded a stand of pines, he saw Blaine-Poole and Ken Laird standing farther along the headland, near an octagonal wooden building at the edge of the bluff.

When he came up to them, Laird moved a few feet closer to the edge. "You'll have to come over here. You can only see it from this angle."

David shaded his eyes against the reflection of sunlight off of the ocean. He planted his feet more firmly in the loose sand and leaned out as far as he dared. The bluff dropped steeply. About fifty feet below them, a body, dressed in a pink garment, was lying face down on a ledge of black rock that jutted out into the ocean.

He stepped back and studied the situation. As he had seen from his window, the bluff formed one side of a deep gully that widened into a strip of beach at the water's edge. A small boat was bobbing in the water, just out from the beach. The man steering it waved to them.

"Given the slant of the rock, that guy in the boat can probably see the body better than we can from up here. How did you know it was down there?"

Ken Laird said, "We didn't see it the first time we came by here. After we talked to you and Gerald next to the garden, we went up as far as Christine Moreland's cottage and turned around." He pointed along the headland that eventually curved away from the ocean and disappeared into a stand of pines at the far end of the garden. "When we came back this way, we heard the guy down there in the boat blowing his horn. We could see what he was pointing at as soon as we got to the edge of the bluff." He brushed the back of his hand across his eyes. "I don't think there's any doubt—"

Blaine-Poole squatted down. "No bloody way to get down this slope or on to that ledge from the beach."

In the distance, beyond the house, a police siren and the wail and honk of a fire engine reached them.

"I'll go back and let Gerald know," David said.

He walked quickly, then tried to run, but his balance was still precarious with his arm strapped to his left side by the sling, and his first jarring steps sent a stab of pain through the wound. The siren had stopped by the time he reached the terrace. Rumbling and hissing, a fire truck came to a halt on the access road that ran along the far side of the house.

Mrs. Sawyer met David at the kitchen door, her face flushed with anxiety. "What's going on? Is something on fire?"

Just then, Gerald came in from the hallway. Mrs. Sawyer turned to him. "I didn't know what to do, sir. I heard the sirens. When I realized they were turning off on our road, I pushed the gate button."

"That was the right thing to do, Mrs. Sawyer," he said distractedly.

Meeting Gerald's eyes, David saw his immediate understanding that the crisis was real.

The front doorbell began to peal, and Gerald said, "Oh, no. That's the police. Would you talk to them,

David? I want to get out there to see what's happened."

He started across the terrace but stopped. "Tell them the side road ends at Christine's cottage. There's a bare strip of land between her cottage and the garden. They'll have to take that to get out onto the headland. I don't want them rolling across the lawn." He turned and began to run toward the ocean.

David went quickly through the darkened living room. When he opened the front door, two sheriff's deputies stood on the steps, one small and wiry, the other tall and redheaded. "You reported an emergency, sir?" the shorter one said, pulling a radio from his belt. David told them a body had been seen on the rocks below the cliffs.

"Who found the body?" the tall deputy asked.

"Apparently, a man on a boat near the shore spotted it and got the attention of two houseguests who were out jogging."

"Have you been out there yourself, sir?"

"Yes. I saw her."

The deputy's gaze sharpened. "You said, 'her.' It's a woman? Do you know who she is?"

Drawing in a deep breath, David said, "I think it must be Mrs. Fitzwilliam."

After he had answered more questions and relayed Gerald's instruction, he closed the door and stood for a moment, sorting through his thoughts. How had he known with such certainty that the body on those rocks was Kassandra?

Walking slowly back through the living room, he was

startled by a sultry voice. "Well, I've heard of arriving in style, but how did you manage a police escort in St. Judith?"

He turned to see Melanie Fitzwilliam, in an emerald silk nightgown, posed artistically on the arm of a brocade chair.

Chapter Six

"*Mon Cher,* David, how are you?" Melanie threw her arms around his neck in an embrace that, had he not been so distracted, might have embarrassed him. Her skin was still the smooth tawny gold it had been when she was a teenager. She smelled of bed warmth and stale jasmine.

When he pulled away, she stroked his injured arm. Her eyes, smoky jade and fringed with thick lashes, were dark with pity. "Oh, David. Père told me you'd been wounded. I couldn't bear to think of it."

He caught her hand and gave it an avuncular squeeze. "I'm glad to see you, too, Melanie, but you should get dressed. The police are here in force and I imagine they'll be coming into the house soon. A body has been found on the rocks below the cliffs."

Melanie shrugged. "That happens all the time around here. They'll haul him up, and he'll be an instant celebrity for a day or two. Come and drink some coffee with me. Or I'll make you a Bloody Mary. I want you to tell me everything that's happening in the real world. You would not believe how boring life is in this wilderness."

"I said a body is down there, Melanie. Someone is dead."

The beautiful eyes grew wide. "You don't mean one of *us*? Who? Don't tell me old Theo finally stumbled off the cliff with his camera. Who is it, David?"

"I couldn't see well enough to be sure, but it looks like Kassandra."

He watched her face register several emotions in succession. "Talk about wish fulfillment," she murmured.

Another siren wailed from the roadway. Melanie ran toward the stairs. "I don't want to be part of this. If anyone asks, tell them I'm taking a bath." She blew him a kiss.

From the living room windows, David could see a sheriff's all-terrain vehicle coming along the side road. He went back to the kitchen.

Gerald was huddled with Mrs. Sawyer and a buxom young girl in the back doorway, watching the passing vehicle. All three turned when he came in.

"They wouldn't let me stay out there," Gerald said. "Those deputies ordered me back to the house. They're stringing up yellow tape through the trees to seal off the headland."

A loud buzzer sounded.

Mrs. Sawyer looked exasperated. "How many more times will I have to open those gates?" She hurried across the room to press the button that activated the front gates. In the next minute, they saw a truck with a winch mounted on its front making its way up the road.

".Just leave them open," Gerald said peevishly. "You should have sent Rob down there to direct traffic."

The housekeeper stared at him. "I told you, Mr. Fitzwilliam. He's gone. I looked for him this morning." She eyed the girl suspiciously. "You sure you don't know where he is, Ellie?"

The girl had gone to the refrigerator and was pouring orange juice into a glass. She shook her head slowly, as if she had a headache. ".Just like I said, he left early last night and I didn't hear his truck come back."

Mrs. Sawyer took the teakettle from the stove and went to the sink to fill it. "Well, I'm not sure you would've heard anything anyway."

She ignored the girl's glare. "Get some carrots and cucumbers out of there. We need to start a salad for lunch. Even with the place falling to pieces, people have to eat."

Gerald and David retreated to the breakfast room and closed the door. In a low, urgent voice, Gerald said, "They wouldn't let me near enough to see who's down there. It can't possibly be Kass, you know."

"Why not?" David said.

Gerald rubbed his palms together nervously. "I don't know where Kass is, but I'm certain it's not her. It must be someone who was hiking along the bluffs. Perhaps a tourist who got lost."

David began to refill his coffee cup but changed his mind and put the cup on the table. "It's a woman, Gerald. And dressed as she is—"

"Of course it wouldn't be easy to get onto the property," Gerald went on feverishly. "An intruder would have to climb over the fence and wade through brambles around the perimeter. There's not much access from the ocean side. It's very shallow near the beach, but I suppose somebody could have gotten a rowboat in there and tried to climb the bluff. Accidents do happen along the coast."

They heard footsteps outside in the hallway and a male voice bellowing, "This place is a madhouse. Kassandra! Where are you?"

Gerald rolled his eyes. "It's Theo Greg. I'd better head him off before he blunders into the kitchen and upsets Mrs. Sawyer even more."

The door flew open and Theo Greg, a mountain of wheezing indignation, lumbered in. He was dressed in a blue flannel bathrobe over rumpled, striped pajamas, his wiry gray hair standing up on end as if someone had grabbed it to pull him out of bed. He glanced at David. "What's going on in here? Where's Kassandra?"

"There's been an accident out on the bluffs," Gerald told him.

Theo squinted out the window. "What kind of accident? Looks like they've got the whole county out there."

He turned back to David. "Seen you somewhere

before, haven't I?"

"This is David Markam," Gerald said hastily. "He was working with me in New Delhi when you were there."

David moved to shake hands with him, but Theo lowered himself into a chair as if he were exhausted.

Watching him, David thought he would never have recognized the man if he'd seen him somewhere else. In the years since they'd met, he'd gained at least forty pounds. His once roguishly handsome face was bloated, his nose scarred with broken blood vessels.

"I think I remember you, Markam." He grinned maliciously. "Heard you had quite a show in Istanbul. If you people had any decent intelligence, you'd have wiped out those gutless rats before they left their holes!"

David and Gerald glanced at each other, mutually irritated at his attempt to bait them.

The door opened again and a small middle-aged woman drifted into the room. She ignored them all, went to the buffet, and drew hot water from an urn into a cup.

David turned to her. "You must be Mrs. Greg. How are you?"

Holly Greg blinked at him. "We thought there was a fire." It was unclear whether the tone implied alarm or disappointment. She sat down at the table and unwrapped a tea bag.

"It will all be settled shortly," Gerald said soothingly. "I'll ask Mrs. Sawyer to get you some breakfast."

Holly held out her cup and saucer. "This tea water's

barely warm. I told her I have to have boiling water to make tea." Gerald took the cup from her. Giving David an apologetic grimace, he went into the kitchen.

David stood at the window. His view of the main activity out on the headland was blocked by the trees and hedges of the vast garden, but he could see the tall deputy coming across the terrace.

Theo got up and filled a plate with coffee cake and sliced peaches from the sideboard. His chair creaked as he sat down at the table and began to devour the food. "The last thing I need is interruptions," he mumbled with his mouth full. "Kassandra's going to be nagging at me again if I don't finish the rest of the collection today. Probably won't have time to go into town to look at that cypress on the bluff, either."

"Everything takes forever in this house," Holly said. "I can't even get a cup of tea."

Mrs. Sawyer stepped in from the kitchen, carrying a teacup and a steaming kettle. "A deputy came to get Mr. Fitzwilliam. They want you to come out there, too, Mr. Markam," she said stiffly as she poured water into Holly's cup.

David followed her out the door, grateful to get away from the Gregs. Outside, the breeze, a little warmer than before, carried the heavy stink of diesel fuel.

As he crossed the terrace, he looked to his right and saw the young maid sitting on the wooden stairs that led up to the rooms over the garage, smoking a cigarette. She turned away when she saw him, and he wondered if Mrs. Sawyer's suspicions about her and the handyman were true.

He took the perimeter path again and stopped at the tape barrier that stretched from the building on the edge of the bluff into the garden. On the far side of the headland, two men who looked like gardeners and an attractive woman stood watching.

Inside the barrier, men worked among the assortment of emergency vehicles. The truck with the mounted winch was parked close to the edge of the bluff. Blaine-Poole, Laird, and some deputies stood nearby. David guessed they were watching others rappel down to retrieve the body.

He ducked under the tape and went to where Gerald was huddled on a bench near the building. A woman in a tan pantsuit was sitting beside him, as if she were trying to give him comfort.

She rose when she saw him. He introduced himself, and she shook his hand hastily. "Detective Perez. I'm in charge of this investigation." She appeared to be in her late thirties, competent and self-confident. Her warm, brown skin and honey colored hair gave her a kind of monochrome that made her face, with its square jaw and full lips, interesting.

Looking him over, too, she said, "You've been injured, Mr. Markam?"

"It happened a few weeks ago—overseas."

She nodded, the assessing gaze not wavering until her attention was caught by raised voices at the bluff's edge. "Excuse me," she said, hurrying away.

David stood behind the bench where Gerald was

sitting and put his hand on his shoulder. He heard him moan when the black bag strapped to a litter came into sight over the rim.

One of the deputies wearing a climbing harness unzipped the bag and appeared to be pointing something out to Perez. After a brief discussion, she summoned Gerald to identify the body. Following him, David caught a glimpse of Kassandra's ashen face, flecked with bits of black rock and plant slime. Like other dead faces, it looked neutral, incapable of having influenced another life or even of having lived its own.

Gerald identified his wife, his eyes distracted and his shoulders rigid. Watching him, David guessed that his strongest feeling was embarrassment at having to be the center of attention at this spectacle.

Chapter Seven

The trucks that arrived with noisy urgency began their slow, grinding way back down the access road. Detective Perez and a few of the deputies stayed behind. She came into the breakfast room where David, Gerald, Laird, and Blaine-Poole were sitting around the table waiting for her.

"I'd like to talk to each of you individually," she said. "I have to ask you not to leave the house. You can wait downstairs or in your bedrooms. We'll get through this as fast as we can. May I speak to you first, Mr. Fitzwilliam?"

Laird and Blaine-Poole got up to go. Perez glanced at David, but Gerald said, "Why don't we use my study? There's no need to inconvenience everybody even further."

After they had gone, David strolled out into the hallway, feeling restless. He glanced into the living room.

Theo and Holly Greg sat next to each other on the largest sofa, reading magazines. Theo was drinking what looked like orange juice, but was more likely a Screwdriver.

David wondered where Melanie was. He hadn't seen her outside. She might not even know for certain that Kassandra was dead. Climbing the stairs, he contemplated the seven closed doors and decided against knocking on any of them or calling her name. Even if nobody had told her, she would know soon enough.

In his room, he stood by the window, watching two deputies who were still methodically investigating the grounds. The part of the bluff where Kassandra had apparently fallen was hidden from view by trees and bushes. He looked at the stretch of ocean sparkling in the sunlight. Oceans never were affected by human tragedies. The water danced under the sun or tossed itself, gray and gasping, in a storm. Living and dying were irrelevant.

Irrelevant. It was a good word to describe how he felt about the world around him at this moment. His cognitive faculties were intact. He was thinking, understanding. Yet he felt no emotion.

Instead, he had a baffling, disagreeable sensation that Kassandra's death was part of his routine. Her body had become one of the bodies in that conference room in Istanbul. He was seeing them all with a kind of blank fatalism. Just noting and going on, with neither grief nor compassion.

So I'm irrelevant, too, he thought. Gerald no longer

needed his help tracking down Blaine-Poole's business. What did Kassandra's collection of antiquities matter now? Her death had eliminated any threat of scandal. If Gerald needed solace, Melanie was here to give it. Leaving after the funeral, he decided, would be the tactful thing to do.

Keeping his mind still, he began to unpack the books he'd bought just before he left Washington, D.C., studying the cover of each. He'd also brought along copies of *Cannery Row* and *Sweet Thursday* to reread because he was finally going to California. Ever since that summer in his late teens, when he'd discovered those books, he had longed to see the places in Steinbeck's stories. He might still rent a car and drive down to Monterey before he went back East. He hadn't driven since he was wounded, but he could probably manage it.

Selecting a biography of Churchill, just published in paperback, he stretched out on the bed and settled himself to read. A knock on the door broke his concentration. He cursed softly. Whether he wanted it or not, he still had to deal with Gerald's troubles.

He followed the tall deputy down the stairs and along the hallway. When he passed the living room, he saw Theo and Holly still in there. No one else was around. The deputy opened the door of Gerald's study and motioned for him to go in. Detective Perez was standing behind Gerald's desk.

She shook hands with him and said, "I'm glad to have a chance to talk with you, Mr. Markam. I just wish it weren't under these circumstances." She sat down, inviting him to take one of the wing chairs.

David wondered if she had used the chair behind the desk when she questioned Gerald. More likely her takeover had followed that interview.

She adjusted a lined writing pad in front of her on the desk and looked pleasantly encouraging. "You just got up here from San Francisco this morning, didn't you? This was a bad situation to walk into."

David cleared his throat and sat up straighter, trying to focus his attention. "Yes, that's right. I flew from Washington, D. C. last night; got here this morning. Kassandra's death was a shock. For all of us, I'd say."

"Mr. Fitzwilliam tells me you were wounded in that attack on the American Consulate in Turkey last month. I read about it in the paper. What an experience that must have been!" Excitement flickered in her eyes for an instant.

Unwilling to be enticed by her curiosity, David looked away.

She shifted in the chair. "You and Ambassador Fitzwilliam have known each other for a long time?"

"A very long time," he said, glancing at the gallery of pictures.

Perez did not miss it. She got up and looked at the picture of him shaking hands with Gerald. "You both worked in India? Sounds exotic."

He knew she was trying to establish rapport with him, but he was too numb to match her effort.

She sat down and said, "I know you must be tired, so

I'll try not to take too much of your time. There are just a few questions I have to ask everyone."

"I guess even with an accidental death, you need to find out how it happened."

Resting her elbows on the desk and folding her hands, Perez said, "Unfortunately, Mrs. Fitzwilliam's death doesn't appear to be an accident." She spoke slowly, as if she were taking care with her words. "You see, there's some evidence that isn't clear. A large amount of money is missing from a case she keeps in her room. And, as you've probably heard, the handyman Rob Covelo left last night unexpectedly."

"Sounds like you think he's the thief. You're also assuming he killed Kassandra?"

The comment seemed to catch Perez off guard. "Nothing's determined yet. We just have to find him."

She picked up her pen. "I need to know a few things about the family and the guests. The questions may seem unrelated to you. But please bear with me. How well do you know the Fitzwilliams?" she said.

Who knows anybody else well? David wanted to say, but resigning himself to the ordeal, he said, "Gerald was my first boss when I came into the Foreign Service. We served together in three overseas posts and another time in Washington. I haven't seen him since he retired three years ago, but we've kept in touch."

Perez wrote a few words on her pad. "And Mrs. Fitzwilliam?" she said.

"I seldom spent much time with her outside of official functions."

"Would you say she and Mr. Fitzwilliam were happy together?"

David found the question annoying. Did he know anybody he could say was obviously "happy"?

"Well, they made a good team. Most of the socializing in our business is official, to some extent, especially overseas. We don't spend a lot of time interacting casually."

His explanation was rewarded with a look of suspicion. "You mean you never just hang out with each other?"

The thought of "hanging out" with the Fitzwilliams was amusing. "Gerald was a bit senior in grade to me. We know each other very well as colleagues, but, honestly, I can't tell you how he and his wife got along privately."

"Are you familiar with Mrs. Fitzwilliam's collection of statues?"

"I noticed those displayed in the living room." He glanced around the room, expecting to find a few pieces here and was surprised not to see a single one. Had Gerald really managed to preserve a sanctuary in this room from Kassandra's collection?

"What can you tell me about the other guests, Mr. Markam? You all know each other?"

David said nothing until he overcame an urge to get up and leave. His wounded arm had begun to ache, and he didn't feel like talking about the past or any of these people.

"I doubt I can add much to the information you

have. I met Theo Greg years ago in India. He was a photojournalist at the time. I saw him once or twice in the course of our mutual migrations, but that was a long time ago."

"Mrs. Greg was with him?"

"Never met her before." Again, Perez looked as if she suspected him of telling less than he might.

"How about Colonel Laird?"

"He's an area specialist for the Middle East. He and Gerald have worked together a few times. I've run across him in Washington occasionally. Blaine-Poole, I can't tell you anything about."

Perez's gaze focused more sharply. "Does that mean you don't know him or you don't know anything about him?"

"Both. From what Gerald says, he buys and sells antiquities. Presumably, he's a foreign national."

She looked doubtful. "The State Department keeps track of people who do that kind of traveling, don't they?"

"Somebody does. I just haven't come across him myself."

Looking over her notes, Perez said, "How long have you known Melanie Fitzwilliam?"

David felt a sliver of alarm at the mention of Melanie. Until he'd had a chance to talk to her, he didn't want to say much. "Since she was about ten or eleven, I guess. Before her mother died."

He moved his shoulders to relieve the ache spreading across his back. "I don't understand why you're asking me questions like this. What, exactly, are you looking for?"

Perez held his gaze. "This must seem like a hassle to you, Mr. Markam. I mean, you didn't even get here until this morning, and I'm sure you don't believe any of those people would kill—."

"I don't have any illusions about what people will do with sufficient motivation."

Perez glanced at his wounded arm. After a pause, she said, "You know, I really *am* sorry to add more stress to your life. I respect what you've been through, and I respect the ambassador. We all do. He and Mrs. Fitzwilliam are important people in St. Judith. And I know them personally. That's why I'm trying to handle this investigation carefully. I don't want to make things worse for him. But I've got a suspicious death here. Probably a murder."

"Is Gerald a suspect?"

She lowered her eyes. "I think he's hiding something. That's all I can say right now."

Remembering Gerald's desperation and the anger against Kassandra he'd expressed earlier, David's sense of alarm grew stronger. "You've got to see the position I'm in."

"I do understand. I'm not asking you to betray any confidences. It's these other people—the guests—I really need your help with," Perez said quickly. "You've got a lot of resources I don't have access to. If you could give me a little help—say, with the British guy and his overseas activities, for example, this whole process might be easier."

David looked away from the expectation in her face. He did *not* want to be sucked into this mire. Neither could he walk away when his mentor needed him.

He glanced up at a picture of Gerald riding in a ceremonial procession on the back of an Indian elephant. He was waving cheerfully with one hand. But the other hand had a white-knuckled hold on the side of the wooden *howdah*.

"I'll do what I can," he said.

Chapter Eight

Of the hundreds of dinner parties he had endured in seventeen years of public service, David decided this meal probably did not rank among the worst. Mrs. Sawyer had done what she could to minimize the discomfort by setting up a buffet on the sideboard in the breakfast room instead of using the dining room.

They had gotten through the eating with subdued general conversation, and after the housekeeper came to remove the plates, Gerald stood up wearily. "I want to say just a few words to all of you," he began. "First, Kassandra's death has left us all in shock, and your concern and support have been comforting to me. I appreciate that very much. I also want to apologize for the inconvenience this will be for you. Detective Perez has asked you to stay for some time longer. I hope we'll know soon how long that might be.

"Theo has very generously agreed to finish

photographing Kass's collection. A complete record will be useful when we decide what to do with it. The book publication will *not* go forward, of course."

"That's too bad. It was her big dream," Theo said with surprising clarity, considering the amount of wine he'd consumed.

Gerald looked uncomfortable. "It just doesn't seem feasible—" he began.

"I'll be carrying on as well," Blaine-Poole said, leaning back in his chair and crossing his arms. "You'll want an appraisal of the collection to go on with."

Listening to the conversation, David felt himself drifting into a limbo space. Between countries, lost in time zones, nothing seemed real. He wondered at the ease with which life flowed on after a death. Kassandra had been living among them just hours ago. Yet, not one of these people behaved as if her death had changed anything of significance in their lives. He had a fleeting sense of seeing Gerald and the rest of them from a great distance, as if they were in a play, and he, watching from the second balcony.

As soon as Gerald sat down, the dinner was clearly over. There would be no lingering over coffee, no slogging through conversation nobody wanted. Melanie rose, went to her father, and embraced him. "Père, you should get some rest," she said, smoothing his hair. "Ken and Michael are going to take me out for a drink. I have to be away from this house for a while. You won't feel neglected if we go, will you?"

Gerald caressed her cheek and looked at her with

tenderness. "It will be good for you to go out. I'm not up to much socializing tonight."

When he and Gerald were alone, David sighed with relief. He pushed away the last of the key lime pie Mrs. Sawyer had pressed on him. Feeling stuffed and exhausted, he helped himself to water from the pitcher on the sideboard. His body was still on Washington, D.C. time, and it was nearly midnight there. He would have liked to go out for a walk to get some fresh air, but glancing at Gerald, who was sipping herbal tea, he sat down across the table from him. There were dark smudges under his eyes, and a kind of pasty gray had replaced his usual ruddy coloring. "Are you all right?" David said.

"I think I am. It still seems impossible to me that Kass is gone. I just don't understand how it happened. How could she have gotten close enough to the edge of that bluff to fall off?"

David was unsure how to respond. Hadn't Perez told him Kassandra's death was not an accident? Was he refusing to accept reality? "A person out there alone, in the dark," he began.

"She wouldn't have been in total darkness. The path leading to her meditation room is lighted at night. Kass had a solar-powered collector installed on top of the building when it was constructed. It powers the lights in the garden, too. She was very proud of it."

"Maybe she went away from the path."

"I can't see why. That's what worries me the most. She would never have gone so near the edge; she suffers from vertigo. She thought the bluffs were dangerous, even in the daylight. Everybody knows how treacherous the dry, loose sand is at the edge. That's why she wanted to install fencing along the headland, from her meditation room to Christine's cottage."

"Even with lights, going out there alone so late at night seems like a risky thing for a woman to do. Didn't she feel at all uneasy about it?"

"I'm sure she wasn't afraid of intruders or any such thing. We're really quite private here." He shook his head. "Maybe I should have tried to stop her. But you know how she was when she made up her mind to do something." He paused and his eyes grew sad. "Kass never lacked courage."

The door from the kitchen opened, and Mrs. Sawyer looked in at them.

Her manner had changed since Kassandra's death. It was clear that the woman was shocked and grieving. She was, in fact, the only one who had openly shed tears. Now, she had taken on an air of calm capability.

"Excuse me, Mr. Fitzwilliam, Dr. Moreland is here to see you."

Gerald seemed to inflate. "Christine. Oh, yes. Ask her to come in."

He rose from his chair and greeted the tall, slender woman who came into the room. "I'm so sorry, Gerald," she murmured. She took his hands, then leaned closer and brushed his cheek with her lips. Her gray eyes were soft with compassion. "I just came to see if there's anything I can do."

Gerald bowed his head, looking as if he were resisting tears. David had stood up when she came in, and she reached across the table to him. "I'm Christine Moreland. You must be David. I'm sorry I don't know your last name. It's fortunate that you're here."

"A pleasure." David took her hand. She must be the woman he had seen standing on the far side of the garden that morning. Up close, she was even more attractive. But the serenity she radiated was as powerful as her beauty. She was like warmth flowing over chilled skin.

Gerald recovered himself. "My dear Christine, I do appreciate your coming. Won't you sit down? Let me get you a cup of tea."

Christine hesitated, then smiled. "Well, all right; I'll have a cup of chamomile. I can get it," she said when Gerald hurried to the sideboard.

"It's no trouble," he insisted.

Mrs. Sawyer, who had been hovering in the doorway, moved to the table and began to clear the remaining dessert dishes, her long work-reddened fingers grasping the delicate porcelain with care. She paused as she was leaving. "I hate to bother you with more trouble, sir, but somebody ought to call all those people Mrs. Fitzwilliam invited to the reception and tell them not to come."

Gerald put the teacup on the table and sat down heavily on a chair. "Lord, I forgot completely. Forty people are invited here for a reception tomorrow evening!" His elbows on the table, he buried his face in his hands.

Christine grasped his forearm gently. "I can do that for you, Gerald. Really. It won't be a bother."

He began to protest, but she waved away his concern. "I know some of the people on the guest list. I'll call those and ask them to call others. They will be more comfortable hearing the news from someone outside of the family."

Gerald looked at her for a long moment. "You're absolutely right," he said finally. "I suppose Melanie and I ought to do it, but I'm not quite up to dealing with condolences just now. I would be most grateful. If you're sure you don't mind."

David watched them, uncertain how to interpret what he was seeing. He glanced at Mrs. Sawyer's stony face. Picking up his plate, he said, "The pie was superb. Can I help you with these dishes?"

She seized his plate and turned to the door. "No, sir. I'll clear the rest of it later."

Gerald stood up. "I'd better see if I can find the list of guests for you, Christine. It must be in Kass's desk upstairs." He hurried out the door to the hallway.

Christine sipped her tea and looked at David with concern in her eyes. "I'm so glad you're here," she said. "Gerald will need support from a friend during this time. Of course, it can't be easy for you, either. He told me about your experience in Turkey. It must have been truly terrible."

David realized she was offering sympathy but did not expect any explanations. "Not something I'd want to do again."

"I treated a number of people with post-traumatic stress when I was in practice in San Francisco. So many diverse reactions, all difficult to work through."

"You're not in practice anymore?"

She blushed slightly and then folded her hands. "I gave up my practice a few years ago. I suppose you could call it burnout. I reached a point where I simply had to do something else."

"I know that feeling intimately," David said.

Christine gave him a small, wry smile. "The stresses in your work must take quite a toll, especially in some parts of the world." When he did not respond, she said, "I work with meditation groups now—guided imagery and other methods. If you think it might help, I could teach you one or two strategies to deal with the pain from your wound or any anxiety you may be having."

David leaned back in his chair feeling a familiar resistance. "I had a few therapy sessions in Washington. They gave me a hefty supply of painkillers for good measure, so all I'm looking for now is a little rest."

Although she nodded sympathetically, he could see a spark of amusement in her eyes. "Well, I'll leave the invitation open. I get up early, and I'm usually free until about ten."

"I appreciate your concern. Thank you," he said, trying to keep his tone friendly. He liked her openness, her intelligence, and did not want to cut off any possibility of seeing her again. But he didn't want to be her patient.

The hall door opened and Gerald bustled back into the room with a sheaf of papers in his hand. "I've found the list. I hope this won't take up an inordinate amount of your time," he said, handing it to Christine. "Some of these people are bound to keep you on the phone wanting to know details."

"I'll simply say there has been an accident and that Kassandra has died. I'll tell them you will let everyone know when the funeral arrangements have been made. If they ask for details, I can say she seems to have fallen from the bluffs while she was out walking last night."

Gerald considered what she had said. "That sounds good. I don't suppose people knew about her meditation ritual."

"There's no reason for them to know now," Christine said firmly. "Curiosity doesn't obligate us to violate our own privacy."

After Christine had gone, David said, "If she ever decides to change careers again, you ought to get her an application for a job with the State Department. She would make a great diplomat."

For a moment, Gerald seemed not to have heard. "Yes, I've had the same thought," he said finally. "She's the most attractive woman I've ever known. Thoughtful, gracious—just a beautiful human being all around."

Listening to him, David began to understand why Detective Perez thought Gerald was holding something back when she interviewed him. What was really going on here? Deciding on directness, he said, "Do you have feelings for her?"

"What?" Gerald started as if he had been jerked out of a daydream. "What do you mean?"

"I worked with you a long time, Mr. Ambassador. I've seen you charming women and women charming you. I never saw you look at any of them the way you looked at Christine Moreland tonight."

Gerald drew back in apparent shock. "David! How can you say such a thing with Kass just—just—?"

Realizing his own emotions might be coloring his perception of Gerald's, David said, "I shouldn't have said that. It was crass." He tried to find a neutral conversation path, but he had begun to feel the irresistible enervation of jet lag. "It's been a long day."

"You look exhausted, my friend," Gerald said. I can't possibly tell you how sorry I am that I brought you into this chaos."

"We've been through hard times together before. We'll make it this time. What would you like for me to do?"

"Rest! I really want you to get some rest. That's why I asked you to come. Unfortunately, doing it now won't be easy, at least until we get rid of the guests."

"Can I help you with any of the arrangements? What plans do you have?"

"Hardly any," Gerald said. "I don't have the brainpower to think about anything tonight. Let's leave it all for now. Tomorrow, if you feel up to it, you might look over Kass's collection. Even though circumstances have changed, something will have to be done with it. Your opinion would be a great help to me. I am, as she often said, lacking in aesthetic refinement. I don't even know where to begin, with that or anything else, at the moment."

"Isn't Blaine-Poole supposed to be evaluating the collection? He must have more expertise than I do. Distinguishing one period of South Asian art from another is about the limit of my knowledge."

Gerald grimaced. "I think Kass hired him for that. His status has always been vague to me. I really have no idea what he was contracted to do beyond acquiring new and ever more costly pieces for her."

He tapped his fingers on the table as if enumerating talking points. "I don't know if Kass paid him and Theo Greg for their work or what commitments she made to the museum, the printer, any of them. And speaking of money, where's the cash she had in her valise? What happened to it? I just don't know."

"You can handle those things when you're feeling better. As for the collection, I doubt anybody can be very precise about the dollar value of antiquities, so his guess may be good enough for the purpose. Since he's here, you might as well make use of him."

"I don't care what kind of expertise Blaine-Poole has. I don't trust him," Gerald insisted. Then he paused and then said, "I suppose the concern I expressed this morning is no longer an issue. But there's still a lot of rough water to navigate, David." There was appeal for understanding in his eyes.

David stood up. He didn't want to think about how bad Gerald's troubles might get before this was all over.

"I'll talk to Blaine-Poole in the morning and take a look at the collection. I would like to see what's in it."

They went out into the hallway. Pointing toward the stairs, Gerald said, "Most of the pieces are in Kass's bedroom. I suppose Blaine-Poole will be busy doing whatever he does with them. That might present a good opportunity to see how he goes about it. Here, let me show you the rest of it."

From experience, David recognized Gerald's "laying out the plan" mode. He took a deep breath and tried to focus his attention.

In the living room, they stopped in front of one of the massive wood-and-glass cabinets built into the long wall across the room from the fireplace. "Kass put out these pieces to display for the reception tomorrow," Gerald said. "Theo's still got his gear set up. He's been photographing the collection in here." He indicated a table, portable reflectors, floodlights, and a camera tripod between two of the cabinets.

Glancing at the bronze statues in the cabinet on the right, David said, "Is something missing from this one? That center shelf is empty."

Gerald peered into the cabinet. "That's the space Kass reserved for her new acquisition. Last year, when Blaine-Poole brought her that stone elephant god, she had a cocktail reception to show it off. She planned an even bigger event for this year, since she was trying to impress the museum board with the quality of her collection. Rather pathetic, really."

Sighing, he rested his hand on David's shoulder.

"What would I ever do without you, my friend?"

The question was a familiar one, and David knew the gratitude was sincere. In an odd way, he felt as if they were preparing to handle another diplomatic crisis together. But for the first time, he was not certain that Gerald entirely trusted him.

Chapter Nine

David sat on the side of his bed. He'd been dreaming of a woman, of Christine Moreland, running on a long, empty beach, a blue chiffon garment streaming behind her. He had caught her and embraced her. Then, in a ´ caprice of fantasy, it was his wife's laughing mouth he kissed.

Another dream. Different from the anger-filled nightmares he'd had the first months after Layne left, or even the occasional confusing one in the following years that trailed empty longing in its wake. These strange, joyful dreams brought a new kind of misery.

He stood up and stretched, pushing away the dregs of emotion. The throbbing in his arm that kept him awake during the night had become a dull, tight ache. Today, he could probably do without the sling.

In front of the dresser mirror, he eased his arm out of his pajama sleeve, unable to resist an examination of the wound. Trying to be philosophical about it hadn't worked so far. It still irritated him to think of having that puckered gouge in his upper arm the rest of his life.

He pulled on sweat clothes and went downstairs. The small exercise room across from Gerald's study was furnished with a treadmill, a recumbent bicycle, and a variety of weights. David began with the treadmill, reveling in the pleasure of stretching his legs again. In ten minutes, he was aware that he was working too hard. Still, he kept at it, trying to feel less alien in his own skin.

After a shower, he was on his way downstairs again when he heard the sound of drawers closing in a room farther down the hallway. The door to Kassandra's bedroom stood open, and he looked inside. Holly Greg, in a robe and slippers, was crouched in front of the small white desk at the far end of the room, thumbing through file folders in the bottom drawer.

She flushed when she saw him. "I'm looking for Theo's pictures. They belong to him," she said, as if he had challenged her.

"Gerald can probably help you find them. Do you need them right away?"

Rifling through the remaining folders, she said, "I don't want to leave here without them."

David took a few more steps into the room. "Are you planning to leave soon? I thought Theo was going to finish photographing the collection."

Holly closed the drawer and stood up, her face angry red. "Why should he take any more pictures? That book's never going to be finished. Didn't you hear Gerald say that?"

She came toward him, holding the front of her robe tightly closed in a protective gesture. "You have to excuse me. I need to get dressed," she said, avoiding his eyes as she passed.

When she had gone, he went to the desk and tried the drawers, glancing through their contents. All were unlocked except the middle one. He suspected Holly was searching for something other than pictures, but he had no idea what that might be. Later, he'd get the key from Gerald and find out what Kassandra kept in the locked drawer.

Before leaving, he spent a few minutes looking at the collection of antiquities. As interesting, even beautiful, as some of the bronze figures were, he couldn't imagine sleeping in this room. A display wall so massive would inspire awe in a museum. In a bedroom—which, in his opinion, ought to have warmth and privacy—it was unnerving. How could Kassandra lie in that opulent bed, aware that all of those eyes were observing her throughout the night?

He shook off the fanciful image, feeling more baffled by Kassandra than ever. Had the woman he knew as Gerald's wife never existed? The fanatical collector she had become was a stranger. Like most fanatics, she had apparently inspired strong emotion. In one person, strong enough to kill.

Seeing the platform ladder at the far end of the wall, he decided to come back and have a closer look at

Kassandra's obsession after he had something to eat.

The breakfast room was empty when he got downstairs. He helped himself to coffee and began to browse through the newspapers stacked on the sideboard, pleased that he didn't have to make conversation with anyone.

When Mrs. Sawyer came in, looking puffy-eyed and subdued, he asked for an English muffin, but she urged him to try one of her omelets. He agreed, and she left as if she were anxious to get away.

He wondered where the others were. Theo Greg was likely still in bed, recovering from his drunken night. Presumably, his wife was keeping him company. Unless she had gone back to Kassandra's room to do more searching. Ken Laird and Blaine-Poole might be jogging. That left Melanie, probably still sleeping. And Gerald. Where was Gerald? It felt strange not to know Gerald's habits any more. For so many years, they'd have been in a meeting together at this hour.

A movement outside the windows caught his attention. He recognized Detective Perez's sturdy, athletic form walking with purpose toward the headland. Probably reexamining the area where Kassandra's body was found, he thought. He rose, curious to find out. In the kitchen, Mrs. Sawyer held an omelet on a spatula, suspended between pan and plate. She looked annoyed when he asked her to hold it for a few minutes. In truth, he found it hard to like the woman, but he couldn't blame her for banging the door of the warming oven as he went outside.

The breeze off the ocean was stronger when he left the shelter of the garden hedges. Perez stood near the edge of the bluff, her hands on her hips, hair whipping around her head. She turned quickly when she heard his footsteps. Her expression suggested that she expected to see him.

"Good morning! Is there any news?" he said when he stopped beside her.

"It's nice to see you again, Mr. Markam. Did you get any rest last night?"

"Some."

Shading her eyes with her hand, she said, "Did you get a chance to talk to any of your contacts in Washington?"

"The people I know aren't generally in their offices on Sunday. I'll try first thing tomorrow morning."

"Good."

"So, do you have any news to tell me? I assumed the arrangement we made would work both ways."

"I guess that's fair. Though I didn't make any promises. What do you want to know?"

She was obviously going to make him fish for answers. "I'll tell you one thing I've been wondering about. When you examined Kassandra's body after it came up in the litter, what did the other deputy point out to you?"

Looking smug, she said, "He used to be a Navy corpsman. He noticed an unusual bruise on the back of her neck."

"So that's why you don't think it was an accident.

She must have been unconscious or even dead before she was thrown off the bluff. Gerald swears Kassandra would never have gone near the edge willingly." He stepped a few inches closer to the rim of the bluff and slid his foot through the loose sand. "Do you know what kind of weapon might have made the bruise?"

"Whoa! I didn't say anything about weapons. The M.E. hasn't given us a report yet."

"I guess you're still looking for the handyman."

"Not anymore." Her dark eyes held a gleam of triumph, and he knew this was the news she had been holding back. "We found Rob Covelo."

"You arrested him?"

"We didn't have to. The Santa Rosa P.D. got him on possession of a controlled substance early Saturday morning."

"How early? Was he in jail when Kassandra was killed?"

"They picked him up just before 1:00 a.m. Santa Rosa's at least two and a half hours from here if you take 101, longer if he went down the coast. He couldn't have left any later than 10:30. And we know Mrs. Fitzwilliam was alive after that time. So, unless he beamed down there in a transporter, . . . But that's not the whole story. He only had about ten bucks on him."

Perez waited, and David knew she expected him to make the connection between what she said and a further implication.

"So you don't think he stole the money from Kassandra's room?"

"That question's still open. He just didn't have it when he was arrested."

"You aren't surprised about this, are you?"

"Let's just say I knew we'd turn him up in a day or two. He's not smart enough to evade us for long."

"You know him, then?"

"This is a small town. Covelo is one of those guys who has come across our radar a couple of times—for one thing or another."

David moved a little closer to her, turning his back to the sea wind. "The odds are against his taking the money," he persisted. "Whoever did that had to have access to the house and know it was there."

"Maybe one of the guests makes a more palatable option," she said casually.

"You didn't find any money when you searched their rooms, did you? Why would the Gregs or Blaine-Poole want to steal from Kassandra? Or kill her?"

The detective reached down to smack away a streak of dirt from her immaculate trousers. "So you're saying I shouldn't spend my time considering those folks as suspects?"

At the moment, David was prepared to believe they were all guilty. "I don't know enough to speculate. I just think somebody would have noticed if the handyman came into the house."

Perez held his gaze. "I wouldn't take any bets on that. Everybody knew Mrs. Fitzwilliam's routine. Mrs. Sawyer couldn't be in the kitchen twenty-four/seven to see who came and went."

"How could Covelo know there was cash in the valise in the bedroom? And if he did steal it while Kassandra was outside, why did he need to kill her? None of that makes sense. Unless somebody else put him up to it."

"Now that's a possibility! What do you think about Ellie Victor—the maid?"

The question seemed absurd. "The maid? Why?"

Perez turned away, obviously not intending to answer.

"Has she come across your radar too? Is she a local?"

"Mrs. Sawyer says she came up from Petaluma. We get a lot of short-term citizens up here."

"Has anyone told you she disliked Kassandra? Enough to kill her?"

Her look made it clear she thought he was naïve. "Liking or disliking doesn't make any difference if you're after money. Ellie went into Mrs. Fitzwilliam's room every day. And Ellie's the only one who spent time with Covelo. They could have planned it together. She takes the cash and stashes it somewhere. There are plenty of places around here to hide things." She gestured toward the garden.

"Maybe, but with that kind of access, the girl didn't need to kill Kassandra to get the money. Unless Kassandra saw her take it and confronted her. What did Ellie say she was doing that night?"

"Watching TV all evening after she finished cleaning up the dinner dishes. She claims she heard somebody in the kitchen around midnight and assumed it was Mrs. Fitzwilliam, since that was her usual time to come in."

"Is that true? Could she have heard somebody in the kitchen if she had her TV on?"

"She was probably wasted and just made up that part. We found empty wine bottles in her room, and Mrs. Sawyer says she hits the booze in a big way. Incidentally, all the people sleeping upstairs say they didn't hear anything outside their rooms. What do you think? Could you hear any sounds last night?"

David considered the question. With the window open a few inches he heard gusts of wind and surf pounding faintly. Between pain and jet lag, he'd been awake often. He tried to remember impressions he'd had. Only a door closing softly once or twice in the hallway. He couldn't be sure of the times.

"Not really," he said. "People could easily have come and gone without my knowing. The bedrooms all have their own baths, so there wasn't a lot of traffic in the halls."

"Yeah. So there we are. We keep coming back to the same point, don't we?"

"You're right. Somebody had to have a reason to kill her."

"Like her husband," she said with satisfaction, as if he had admitted Gerald's guilt and she was simply reinforcing the conclusion.

He stared at her, wondering if she could see how much her suspicion alarmed him. "Gerald didn't do it," he said finally.

"Then why is he being so vague about Friday night? Something's going on with him. I know that."

When he said nothing, Perez shrugged and checked her watch. "Look, I've got to talk to Christine Moreland again. She wasn't very helpful when we interviewed her the first time."

"You can hardly blame her if you suggested she might be a killer. That has a way of putting people off."

"Maybe you ought to give me some lessons in diplomacy."

When he grinned at her, she said, "I didn't accuse Christine Moreland of anything. I was just hoping to get some insight from her. She used to be a psychologist, and she understands people pretty well."

"She's probably used to keeping confidences, too."

Perez gave him a searching look, and he saw humor in her eyes when she turned to go. "You'll call me after you talk to your people in Washington, won't you?" she said.

He started back to the house. It disturbed him that she had apparently decided Gerald was guilty. Perez didn't seem to be a person who made unsupported assumptions. She had obviously sensed, as he had, that there was something important Gerald did not want to talk about.

Following a new path toward the south side of the garden, he came upon an area he hadn't realized was there. Sheltered by a long hedge were lush rows of vegetables and berries, even a few fruit trees. Seeing a thin, weathered man weeding a bed of tomato plants, he stopped to watch. The man looked at him curiously, and murmured, "*Buenos dias.*"

David managed to dredge up enough of the Castilian Spanish he knew from school to admire the man's work and follow most of his rapid explanation of the garden's layout.

A few yards farther along the path, he rounded another hedge and nearly collided with a second man who was trimming the ground cover between flagstones in a secluded alcove. He remembered seeing the gardeners standing next to Christine Moreland on the far side of the police tape yesterday. It was hard to believe that Kassandra had died less than two days ago. Here, in this inviting little sanctuary with flowering vines and a rustic wooden bench, she had left much better evidence of her taste for beauty than she had in all of the exotic treasurers she collected.

Mrs. Sawyer had apparently been watching for him because she was taking a plate from the oven when he walked into the kitchen.

"It smells wonderful. Thank you for keeping it warm. I really didn't mean to inconvenience you," he said, hoping to head off whatever resentment she'd stored up. In his experience, the cook was not a person you wanted to alienate in any house, and in this case, he would need her cooperation as well.

"Am I still the only one up?" he said, reaching to take the plate from her.

She drew it back. "I'll serve you in the breakfast room."

"Why not have a cup of coffee with me? I really don't feel like eating by myself."

Mrs. Sawyer glanced around the kitchen as if looking for an excuse. "Well, I don't know. I mean, I used to sit with Mrs. Fitzwilliam sometimes if she was alone, but you being a guest and all that."

"Please," David said, holding the door open for her. "We could both use some company, don't you think?"

She put his plate on the table and filled his coffee cup from the urn before drawing some for herself. Rattling the cup slightly in the saucer, she sat down across the table from him and folded her hands in her lap as if to compose herself.

David tasted the eggs, stuffed with sautéed spinach, onions, and pungent feta cheese. "Delicious. Just the way I like it," he said with his mouth full.

Mrs. Sawyer grimaced to disclaim the praise, but he knew her cook's pride was touched.

"I don't see how you manage, especially at a time like this."

"All I do is my job," she said repressively.

She tasted her coffee, and stared out the window with an air of discomfort, but David knew her need to talk was building.

"You certainly do it well. The house is beautifully kept."

"I do what I can with the help I have. When I first came here, we had another full-time maid and a crew of people to come in once a month for heavy cleaning."

"I saw a couple of gardeners outside. They do all the work on the grounds?"

"That's Ezequiel and his helper. They keep up that

big garden by themselves. Used to be twice as many gardeners, but Mrs. F had to let the others go last year. She kept saying she'd get us more help." She sighed. "I guess things are just a lot more expensive than they used to be."

David nodded sympathetically. "It must be a tremendous job."

She shook her head. "I try to help them with picking vegetables and things, but all I've got is two hands. And that Ezequiel don't like anybody to touch his garden."

David laughed. "You know, with his vegetables and your expertise, this omelet is as fine as any gourmet chef could make."

Mrs. Sawyer did not hide her pleasure this time. "Mrs. F always said I should've been a chef."

"Well, she was certainly right. She must have been grateful to you for all of your work," David said gently. He sipped his coffee and waited.

"Mrs. F was nicer to me than anybody has ever been," she said after a pause. "She taught me how to make foreign dishes. Kabobs and curries, lots of different recipes I never heard of. She never acted like a boss. She used to talk to me about all her plans. I don't care too much for the statues and old pots and things she was collecting, but she would get so excited about them; I couldn't help but get excited too."

She pointed toward the ceiling. She told me some of the ones in her bedroom are priceless, so I take care of those myself."

"That can't be easy."

"It's a big job all right. I have to climb up on that library ladder and stand on the platform to dust them."

"You don't have anyone to help you with that?"

"Rob Covelo cleans the statues up higher than I can reach. I let Ellie dust some of the bronze ones, but I still have to stand over her to make sure she don't break anything."

Reluctant to upset her even more with the news he'd heard from Perez, he said, "If Covelo doesn't come back, you'll have only Ellie to help you."

"Then we'll really be in a mess! That girl's more trouble than she's worth. Hungover half the time."

David took a blueberry muffin from the basket on the table. "I've heard Ellie's got a drinking problem. The deputies found empty bottles in her room when they searched the house?"

Mrs. Sawyer leaned forward, encouraged. "Would you believe, *three*? All in one night!" She held up three fingers.

"And that wasn't the first time! A couple of days ago, I saw her putting bottles into the recycle bin, and I checked them after she'd gone to see if she'd been drinking Mr. Fitzwilliam's good wine. You wouldn't believe it. She had that expensive stuff from Napa Valley that Mr. Greg ordered for himself. I thought there'd be a blowup when he found out."

David smiled, imagining Theo's reaction to losing his wine. "What did he say?"

Her eyes widened. "He didn't find out. Mr. Fitzwilliam said not to tell him. He'd replace it. He called the store in town where he shops, but they didn't have it. They had to special order it from Napa. You know he's like that. He always wants everybody to get along."

"Where is Theo's wine stored?"

"In the wine cellar, down those stairs near the back door. I keep the cellar locked, but the key stays in the kitchen in case Mr. Fitzwilliam wants to go down there. I thought Ellie was probably sneaking some wine out. But I never thought she'd take Mr. Greg's expensive stuff. She knows it's his. You'd think Mr. Fitzwilliam would've fired her, but no, not him."

"Gerald does like to see everybody happy," David said.

"Being too generous can be a fault sometimes. Just look at poor Mrs. F. She was too nice to the wrong kind of people, and look what it got her." Tears welled in her eyes, and David felt sympathy for her.

He also wondered just who the "wrong kind of people" were.

Chapter Ten

After Mrs. Sawyer had gone, David sat in the breakfast room alone, sorting through what she had told him. Her devotion to Kassandra and Gerald appeared to be genuine, and her frustration with the maid wasn't out of the ordinary. In every diplomatic social gathering he'd ever attended, people complained about servants. But the problems Ellie had weren't the usual.

Perez might be right. This could have been no more than a sordid little crime. Maybe Ellie stole Kassandra's money and killed her—by accident or in panic. If so, why didn't the girl leave the house afterward? Would she really go back to her room and guzzle three bottles of wine, thinking no one would suspect her? The more he considered it, the less certain he was of anything.

To understand Kassandra's death, he had to know more about her life than the housekeeper could tell him. Carrying his dishes into the kitchen, he was surprised to find it deserted. He went down the hall, hoping Gerald was in his study and willing to talk. It was time for him to stop ducking the issues. The study was empty, too.

Standing in the central hallway, David thought about Christine Moreland, who used to be a psychologist. Possibly Gerald was visiting her. But maybe he wasn't. Either way, she seemed to be the only person around with an objective point of view. And besides, he wanted to see her again.

He took the long way around the garden, crossed the stretch of open headland, and then found the path again, leading into a grove of pines. He came upon Christine Moreland's house unprepared.

Here, protected by the trees from ocean wind, was a white country cottage. Geraniums along the picket fence glowed in the morning light, and a gnarled wisteria vine above the door still held a few pale blooms. The place felt familiar, like something in a storybook. But he also saw that the shelter was partly an illusion. On the side of the house, where no trees grew, the windows must look full-face to the sea.

Pushing the gate open, he walked down the cobbled path, avoiding the bushes of yellow roses that grew on either side. When he reached the arbor, a long branch of the wisteria brushed his arm, leaving its dust on the sleeve of his shirt. The scent brought memory of his dream surging back. He felt awkward, a little embarrassed at the intimacy his fantasy had conjured up, and nervous at the prospect of being alone with Christine.

He mastered himself quickly. This interaction would be hard enough to control without having to struggle with his emotions. It irritated him that he felt ill at ease. Psychotherapists always affected him that way, in spite of his own training and experience in assessing human vulnerability. Ignoring the doorbell button at the side, he knocked with authority on the door.

Christine opened it almost immediately. She seemed surprised, but the clear gray eyes were cordial.

"David! I didn't expect to see you so soon."

So soon? She had been sure he would come. "I wonder if you have a few minutes to talk—if my timing isn't too bad," he said.

She held a notepad in her left hand and reading glasses in her right. She glanced at the notepad. For an instant, he thought she might say, "You'll have to make an appointment," but she stepped back and motioned for him to enter.

David took his time looking at the small living room, trying to gather impressions of Christine while he decided what he wanted to say. There were two bamboo chairs and a couch upholstered in a pale beige fabric that matched the sweep of drapery covering the whole wall. The only color came from four blue and green pillows stacked at one edge of a silky Flokati rug. It was a simple space that made him feel at peace.

"Please sit down," she said. She went to the other side of the room and put her notepad and glasses on a teakwood desk. She seemed about to sit at the desk but changed her mind.

"Would you like some tea? I'm afraid that's all I have. I don't drink coffee."

When he declined, she sat in the wicker chair next to the one he had chosen. She crossed her legs, her long cotton skirt draping gracefully, and leaned toward him. "I see you're not using your arm sling today. I hope that means your pain level is better," she said.

"It was nice of you to offer help with that, but I didn't come to talk about myself," he said and cursed himself for his bluntness.

Starting over, he said, "I talked with Detective Perez a while ago, so I know I'm not the first interruption you've had this morning. In fact, I'm here for more or less the same reason."

"For my opinions about the people who're staying in the house?"

"Yes. She asked for mine, too. There's not much I could tell her. How about you?"

"She asked me if I had noticed any unusual behavior. I told her I hadn't seen them more than two or three times. I don't know any of them well enough to say what might be usual or unusual for them."

David was sure Perez would not have been satisfied with that answer. "She seems to think highly of your insight into people's behavior."

"I admire her, too. She has such a pragmatic intelligence, and she's an expert in martial arts—I'm often in awe of what she can do." She shook her head. "This is such a strange situation. I don't think any of us knows how to behave or what to say. I hope Gerald's doing all right. I haven't had a chance to talk to him today."

"Neither have I. I don't even know where he is. By the way, when Perez came to see you, did she ask you any questions about Gerald?"

Christine raised her eyebrows. "What kind of questions?"

"How he and Kassandra got along and so forth."

"Yes, she did ask questions like that. It's very stressful to have to talk about friends' private lives."

Suspecting that Perez's second interview with Christine had met with as much resistance as the first one, he said, "Did you get the impression Perez thinks Gerald killed Kassandra?"

Her face grew pale with alarm. "No. She said nothing like that. Did she say it to you?"

"She's apparently considering it. For some reason, Gerald refuses to explain where he was Friday night or what he was doing. He's always been stubborn. I knew that the first day I met him. But this seems to defy reason."

"No matter what he was doing, it's impossible to think he would be capable of killing anyone."

"I agree. I don't know why he's acting as if the problem will just go away. That's not like him. I was hoping you'd help me understand what's going on. Can you tell me something about Kassandra? I didn't really see her outside of the superficial social interactions we had. You may not have known her well, either, but you've got the advantage of objectivity. What kind of a person was she?"

Christine took some time before she spoke. He watched her tense face, unsure of the emotion she was struggling with. "Actually, I've known Kassandra for a long time—even before she married Gerald," she said.

Disconcerted, David said, "I'm sorry. I didn't realize you were close to her yourself."

Christine's expression softened. "We shared a flat in San Francisco for nearly two years. It was such a long time ago. Kassandra had a job at the Asian Art Museum, and I had just started graduate school. We became good friends."

"Did something happen to change that?" David said, aware that it might be an insensitive thing to say.

Christine seemed saddened by the question. She raised her shoulders in a slight shrug. "Her life went in a very different direction when she married Gerald."

"But you kept in touch?" Before she could speak, he held up his hand. "Wait. No need to answer that. Kassandra had a reputation for keeping in touch with more people than anyone else on the planet."

"That's true. We exchanged birthday cards every year, but not much more. She always knew what was going on in my life. I'm not sure how, but she did. It was rather flattering."

"When she came back to California, she had changed? In what way?" he said.

She laughed lightly. "Well, she was a great deal more sophisticated than I was, for one thing."

David grinned. "Diplomatic life tends to coat us in a

shiny veneer."

"And then there was the collecting. That was a part of her personality I'd never seen before."

"The obsession, you mean?"

"That's rather a judgmental word. And not particularly accurate," she said stiffly. "Even Sigmund Freud collected antiquities."

Having read about Freud's rather neurotic relationship with antiquities, David thought the analogy was less than persuasive. Obsession, apparently, was a relative concept.

When he did not respond, Christine said, "I know Kassandra's behavior upset Gerald. But really, I wouldn't say she acted compulsively. It seemed to me that the hunt was what fascinated her. A great deal of her self-esteem came from that, too."

She hesitated, and David waited, hoping she'd expand on her analysis. Finally, she said, "Kassandra was very kind to me when I was going through a difficult transition."

"The burnout you mentioned yesterday?"

She nodded. "It was a dark part of my life." She hesitated as if deciding how much she wanted to tell him. "I was truly desperate when she called me from Washington, D.C., to ask if I'd be willing to take the cottage. The house was being renovated for their retirement, and she wanted someone on site to keep an eye on things. It seemed like a godsend at the time."

Longing to know much more, but sensing that Christine's discomfort was growing, he said, "Before I go, I want to ask one other question. No matter how I try, I can't imagine this meditation Kassandra did. Can you tell me about it?"

Christine seemed to relax. "She was in one of my groups when I first set up my program here. That group used guided imagery in different forms. She stopped coming to the meetings after a few weeks, so I don't know what kind of practice she did on her own."

David leaned back in his chair. "I guess I'm not very enlightened, but I have a hard time understanding all of this. Didn't this 'ritual' she did every night seem odd to you?"

Christine looked as if she had never considered that idea. After a few moments, she said, "The sensations one feels in that room make it almost impossible *not* to go into a contemplative state. The pool itself is like—well, almost like a womb of bubbling water. Underneath the floor, the waves come in with the regularity of breath. But now and then one crashes into the sea cave below with such violence that you feel like—" She flushed, apparently embarrassed.

"It sounds like you've experienced it yourself."

"Only once! I found it overwhelming. Kassandra and I talked about holding group meditation sessions for women in the pool, but that never materialized. I think she was the only one who used it—except when they had guests."

David knew he should leave, but he liked sitting with her. Her calmness seemed to spread itself over everything around her.

"Those meditation practices you mentioned, which one did you have in mind when you offered to teach me some techniques?"

She looked concerned. "So you *are* having pain. And flashbacks of the attack?"

Disappointed, David felt himself begin to tense. He hadn't intended for things to go in this direction. But he heard himself saying, "I do have some pain from time to time."

Christine drew a deep breath. Almost imperceptibly, she changed, slipping back into the professional persona he had been aware of when he first arrived. Her posture straightened, even her voice took on a rounder tone as she said, "You've never tried meditation? Not even in India?"

"I did try meditating—along with several other things—when I was in the Peace Corps. Part of my misspent youth. I found it tedious and not worth the time."

Smiling, she said, "I think I can offer you a different experience." She looked at the clock on the wall above her desk. "I still have a few minutes before I have to leave for an appointment. Why not let me show you a simple technique?"

Discarding the caution he had intended to use, he agreed, and she led him down a short hallway, into a cool, softly lighted room. Four wicker chairs were arranged at the corners of a muted blue Persian rug.

"Beautiful carpet," he observed.

"It was a gift from Kassandra," she said.

"I almost bought one like it the last time I was in Tehran. That was right before the 'unfortunate events' in Iran. A lost opportunity."

She made no comment, but sat in one of the chairs and invited him to choose one for himself. Taking the seat directly across from hers, he stretched out his legs and tried to relax.

"Here's what I'd like you to do," she began. When she had explained the technique, she said, "We'll add a bit of ambiance." She pushed a button on a CD player resting on the low table next to her chair. Haunting flute music, the sound of waves lapping gently against a pier, the occasional cry of seagulls, and the low, visceral hoot of a foghorn filled the room, irresistibly soothing, evocative. He sat for a while letting the images flow, undisturbed.

"Are you comfortable, David?"

Still wary, but wanting to hold on to the soothing sensations, he adjusted his position and began to count as she had told him to do.

She went on speaking in a low, unhurried voice. "When I listen to this music, I can feel the fog drifting past, carrying me along . . . ."

A moist breeze enveloped him, filled with the smell of ocean.

"The fog is drifting away and I am relaxed now. I am floating in a calm sea . . . ."

Her voice came to him from far away. He was lying in clear water, sunlight shining down through layers of apple green and yellow leaves. His body was warm and fluid, he wanted to go on floating, floating forever, but the voice urged him up through the drifting colors, toward the light.

"You can open your eyes slowly now, if you're ready," Christine said.

It was too soon to lose the infinite peace. Surely she could let him float just a few seconds longer. Becoming aware of a kind of hollow silence, he opened his eyes.

"How do you feel?" she said, a hint of amusement in her voice.

David sat up straight. His chest felt empty, as if all emotion and sensation had drained from him. "Sorry. I must have dozed off for a couple of seconds."

Christine rose and turned a wall switch. The room brightened.

David looked at his watch. Twenty minutes had vanished. "You hypnotized me!"

"Not really. You must have needed some deep rest. I can show you other techniques like this. Unless you still think meditation is tedious."

He stared at her, stunned.

She returned his gaze with compassion. "Many people find the first experience unsettling. I hope you'll be willing to try it again," she said, still kindly, but with an edge of professional neutrality in her voice.

He thanked her and got out of the cottage with as much dignity as he could manage. To give himself time to recover his equilibrium, he took one of the longest paths that snaked through the garden. As he walked, questions rocketed around his mind: What had he told her during those twenty minutes? What had she said to him? How could he have given this woman such complete control over him?

At the same time, he was aware of feelings almost as disturbing. Christine fascinated him. She was as complex and interesting as he'd imagined she might be. He already knew he would be going back to that cottage. The memory of the profound peace was irresistible. He wanted it again. Even more, he wanted to be with her.

Chapter Eleven

Leaving the garden, David walked out onto the headland. He felt the fresh, sun-warmed breeze on his face. His head was clearer. The session with Christine—hypnotism, enchantment, whatever it was—had lifted the fog of jet lag. Even his sense of balance was better.

He gazed with pleasure at the vast expanse of the Pacific. Standing on these jagged cliffs that had heaved themselves up from the core, he thought there was a larger sky, a keenness in the light that he had never seen before.

Musing about the differences between this place and the ones he was used to, he suddenly felt an intense longing to be surrounded by the soft light of the Mediterranean Sea. Not even the horror of those last days in Istanbul had changed the love he had for that light. He stared at the broad, bright ocean before him, aware of an unnerving sensation of being lost. In a minute, he would wake in his flat in Izmir. Instead of going to the Consulate today, he would walk over to the Kordon, choose a table outside his favorite café, and watch the boats on the Aegean.

As quickly as the sensation had come, it left him. Only a flat sense of futility remained. He would not be going back overseas for a while. If he stayed with the Foreign Service, he'd be looking for an apartment in Washington, D.C., next month. And he would still be alone.

Nearing Kassandra's "meditation room," he heard the low hum of a motor coming from the wooden building. After Christine's description of the pool, he wanted to see it for himself. Climbing the three stairs, he decided on discretion and knocked. A female voice said, "The door's open."

He stepped inside, expecting the room to be dim. Instead, sunlight streamed through floor-to-ceiling windows facing the ocean. Through a cloud of steam, drifting from the pool to the rafters, he could see Ellie, the young maid, lying in the frothy water of the tub. Sensing a risky situation, he turned to leave.

"You don't have to go. There's lots of room in here," she said lazily.

Curiosity made him stop and glance at her again. She had raised herself into a sitting position, and he could see that she was, in fact, wearing a bathing suit, one that did more to enhance her attributes than hide them, but the vital areas were covered.

"Nice view, huh?" She motioned toward the window

with the wine glass she held.

David walked to the window, staying as far from the pool as he could. "I've never seen anything quite like it," he said.

The building was anchored at the edge of the bluff. It gave him the feeling of being suspended in midair above the ocean. Suddenly, a wave slammed into the sea cave below with a boom that vibrated through his feet up to his gut, staggering in its intensity. He understood Christine's struggle to describe this place.

It was hard to imagine Kassandra lying, as Ellie was doing now, enveloped in soothing warmth while the ocean thundered beneath her. This was a side of the woman's personality he had never imagined. She had sought out the most savage point of the headland and erected her special refuge at the mouth of the fury. He shivered. It was somehow perverse but the noise and wildness of the place excited him.

Sitting down on the bench along the wall, he brushed away the moisture collecting on his face and looked again at Ellie.

She was watching him. "Why don't you come in here with me?" she said. "These bubbles will make you feel really good."

"I don't think so."

"I've been wondering about you. They said you got shot in Turkey. I thought you must be Turkish."

"Well, I'm not," David said.

She closed her eyes. With her hair pulled up into a tight little knot, its corn silk tendrils curling around her face, she looked like a pouting baby doll. He wondered what she'd do if he took her up on her offer. No doubt, he'd be the one to regret it.

The girl seemed insecure and, from what he'd heard, manipulative, but that was a long way from being a killer. Under these circumstances, he didn't really expect to learn anything useful about her or her relationship with Kassandra, but he tried again. "I guess you like this place," he said casually. "I hear you spend a lot of time here."

Ellie reached for the wine bottle behind her shoulder and filled her glass. "Mrs. F let me come in here anytime I wanted. But I'll like it even more if you get in here with me."

"No, thanks, Ellie. I don't like hot tubs."

"Why not? I could make you feel better than you ever felt before."

"I wouldn't want to interfere with your relaxation. I've heard how much work you have to do. Too bad Mrs. Fitzwilliam didn't hire more people to help you."

"She kept promising to do it. But she didn't. Anyway, I don't care anymore. I won't be here much longer."

So Ellie intended to leave. Maybe this was her plan all along. If she stole money from Kassandra and stayed around pretending innocence until the hunt died down, she might get away with it. Killing Kassandra in the process wouldn't necessarily change things. That was a plausible possibility.

Two quick thuds on the wooden steps outside startled

them. The door swung open and Melanie, her face pinched with anger, stood in the doorway.

"I *knew* you were in here," she said to Ellie. She glanced at David and registered surprise, but strode to the edge of the pool. "Mrs. Sawyer is looking for you. You know damned well you're supposed to be working."

Ellie raised her arms over her head nonchalantly. "Since when are you the boss around here?"

"Get your ass into that kitchen now!" Melanie said through gritted teeth. She rolled her eyes in derision and turned to David. "I need to talk to you." She whirled out of the room, slamming the door.

David stood up. Ellie would be in an even more belligerent mood now, and he needed to get away from the noise and tension of this place.

"Looks like Miss Snippy Pants has you on her leash, too, just like everybody else," Ellie taunted. "Don't worry about her, just come see me. I've got Rob's apartment now."

David wrenched the door open and swung down the steps, repelled by the girl and the feelings she aroused in him.

He expected Melanie to be going back to the house. Instead, she was walking rapidly along the path that led into the garden hedges. When he caught up with her, he said, "I don't think that girl is cut out to be a maid."

"She wasn't cut out to be anything but the slut she is." Her voice was hoarse with indignation. "And she's about to be fired as soon as I can find someone to replace her."

"She seems pretty insecure."

Melanie stopped and turned on him. "If she appeals to you, I'm sure you can have her. Just buy the little pig a bottle of booze. With that half-witted handyman gone, she's probably up for grabs."

"Do you suppose she knows what happened to Kassandra?" he said.

"I don't spend my time thinking about what servants know or don't know. We'll all be better off when that little pig is away from this place—forever."

"She just told me she's planning to leave. Do you think she and Covelo stole the cash Kassandra had in her room?"

Melanie threw up her hands melodramatically. "If they had a chance to, I'm sure they did. It was unbelievable the way she hired these people. Practically off the street."

"The girl told Detective Perez she was alone watching TV the night Kassandra was killed."

"Ha! She's lying. She wasn't alone in that room. I'm sure somebody was in there with her. I listened at her door around 11:00. All I could hear was the TV, but even a lush couldn't drink all three bottles of Theo's wine by herself."

"Why did you listen at her door?"

She tossed her head. "I was curious."

"How do you know Covelo was with her? Maybe it was somebody else."

Melanie seemed to consider the question, then started walking again. "If you mean Ken or Michael, forget it.

They're not that hard up. Besides, Ken loves me."

"Does Blaine-Poole love you, too?"

"Maybe not, but he has better taste." She went on doggedly, "Who else could have been in there with her? Père has found solace somewhere, but he's too much of a snob to fool around with the help. You know that." She chuckled spitefully. "Maybe old Theo lusted after the little bitch. God knows, I'd lust after somebody if I was married to Holly."

David caught her arm. "Wait a minute. What's that you're saying about your father? You think he's having an affair?"

A shadow, perhaps of pain, crossed Melanie's eyes, but her expression was fixed in a mocking grimace. "Come on, David. Père and Kassandra had separate bedrooms for years. It was only a matter of time before he would go looking for someone. To console him, he might say."

"Did Kassandra think your father was having an affair?" he said, feeling a growing frustration with Gerald for not telling him what was really going on here.

Melanie ran her fingers through her heavy hair, pushing it back as if she were clearing her mind of unwanted thoughts. "Actually, I wondered about that myself. Kassandra's specialty was finding out things she didn't have any business knowing. That, and making all kinds of promises she never intended to keep. Père's not really heartbroken about her death. It's guilt that's eating at him."

"Guilt over what?"

Melanie flung her arms wide. "Who knows? Maybe he told Kassandra his secrets and she jumped off the cliff in despair." She laughed bitterly.

"Melanie! You're making up this stuff about your father."

She looked away and then said slowly, "I used to think Père was so full of integrity, so invincible. And when Kassandra cut him apart with those nasty little jabs, that mocking she thought made her look so clever, I couldn't stand it. 'You're a great man,' I'd think. 'Why don't you stand up to her, walk away from her?' But he never would. He just never would."

"It's hard for kids to understand how human their parents are," he said, wishing he had something better to say.

She glared at him, fury distorting her features. "I knew he was human! I just wanted him to care more about me than he cared about prestige, about advancing his career. That's why he put me in a cage in Switzerland. My job was to be expensively educated in Leysin while he climbed the diplomatic ladder. It was the same with Phillip, that bastard I was married to. All they ever wanted from me was a well-polished asset."

"Melanie, that's not true! You can't believe that about your father!"

She began to tremble. "Don't tell me how hard he worked to pay for the privileges he gave me, David. My stepmother reminded me a thousand times."

He grasped her hand. "Melanie! Listen to me. Gerald loves you deeply. His face beams every time he mentions your name."

"Then why did he leave me alone? Why did I have to live with that pack of materialistic jackals in a boarding school instead of in my own home like a real person? And why did he marry that . . . that—?"

She tried to jerk her hand away, but he held on to her. In spite of the tears in her beautiful eyes, he knew sympathy was not what she wanted. "So your father exiled you to Switzerland, did he? I think your memory's a little hazy. I was there in Delhi that summer after your mother died."

"Why are you bringing that up?"

"Your father did everything he could for you. He left a position he loved in Saudi Arabia and transferred to Delhi so you could live with him and enroll at the American School. Then, a week before fall classes started, *you* insisted on going back to Switzerland."

"Stop trying to make me feel guilty! You don't understand what it was like."

"There's no nice way to say this, Melanie. You were a real brat back then. A foul-mouthed one, at that!"

She turned to stare at him in shock.

"Remember that time I caught you flirting with the Marine guards at the Embassy? You thought I couldn't understand those names you called me in French, didn't you?

"And let's not forget the night Gerald and I had to drive three hours to Agra to get you when you and that bunch of Indian teenagers were arrested for drinking beer in the Taj Mahal!"

Melanie tried again to wrench free. "When did you turn into such a prig, David Markam? Let go of me!"

He dropped her hand. "I'm just giving you a little perspective, Melanie Fitzwilliam. Your father needs *your* help now. Can't you see that?"

"I didn't realize what a terrible opinion you had of me," she said, rubbing her wrist. She looked up at him through the long fringes of her eyelashes. "I wonder how you'd feel if you knew me as well as you think you do."

At that moment, Ken Laird come around the corner of a hedge. Melanie ran to him, and he gathered her in his arms. "I needed you," David heard her say.

Laird looked at him as if he expected an explanation, but David shook his head. He'd had enough of Melanie for a while. He started back to the house. As he passed them on the other side of the hedge, he heard Melanie saying angrily, "Tomorrow isn't soon enough. I'm going to hire somebody to replace that stupid bitch today! She's the last piece of filth Kassandra left behind."

"The police probably won't let her leave here. Not until they finish the investigation," Laird said.

"Well, they can object all they want. She's going to be off of this property as soon as I can make it happen."

David reached the terrace, more worried than ever. Melanie had grown from a tormented teenager into a troubled woman, impulsive, apparently even violent. Was she as reckless as she appeared to be? The thought was more than disturbing. Maybe Gerald was refusing to talk about Kassandra's death because he was afraid of what his daughter might have done.

Chapter Twelve

Gerald was standing in the central hallway when David went downstairs the next morning. There were still dark circles under his eyes, but his face had more color.

"Well, we're in for it again," he said when he saw David. "Detective Perez just called. She wants us to come to town for another interview."

"Does that include me?"

"What? Oh, no. Just Melanie and me and the out-of-town bunch. Such a nuisance. But I suppose it's necessary," he added, turning toward the breakfast room.

"Presumably. It must be hard on you, though. I was hoping we could have some time to talk today."

Gerald avoided his eyes. "I must apologize for abandoning you yesterday. I had to go into town to buy some things Mrs. Sawyer needed. When I started back here, I realized I couldn't face anyone. I hope you understand. I parked on the edge of the road and sat there looking at the ocean."

David put a hand on Gerald's shoulder. "I'm sure you needed the respite. You looked pretty done in last night. How are you feeling now?"

"Oh, better, I suppose. But I have to make two trips to town today. First, this business with the sheriff. Then, I need to see Kassandra's lawyer this afternoon. Would you like to drive in with me after lunch? I'll probably be tied up with the legal stuff for a while, but it would give us a chance to talk on the way there. You could have a look around the town. There's even an old house that might interest you," he added with a grin that almost brought back the impish humor David had seen in his eyes so often.

"Sounds good. While you're all away this morning, I'm going to call a few people in Washington. If I'm lucky, I might get some information on that subject we talked about yesterday," David said.

Gerald thanked him, but he was clearly too distracted to think about Kassandra's collection or any of the other demands on his attention.

While they ate breakfast, Gerald brought up a treaty negotiation he'd been part of in the early days of his career. "I want to include this phase of the talks in my memoir," he said, launching into details. David listened, knowing that Gerald was occupying his mind with the safe territory of the past to stay away from the fearful ground of the present. He had done the same thing the evening before, and it was obvious this morning that whatever he was keeping at bay worried him deeply. Breaking through that wall of resistance without alienating him would be a challenge.

He decided not to mention his conversation with Melanie. The wild things she'd said about her father's affair probably came out of her own fear and frustration. But it also might be true. Regardless, this wasn't the time to bring it up.

"Looks like the roadrunners are back," Gerald said, interrupting himself in mid-sentence.

David glanced out the window at Laird and Blaine-Poole coming across the terrace. It struck him as interesting that the men found each other's company tolerable. From what he'd seen the past two days, they were clearly rivals for Melanie's attention. Laird's feelings were apparent every time he looked at her. But her flirting with Blaine-Poole suggested that he was making a play for her, too. David smiled to himself. No doubt Melanie enjoyed this competition.

Laying his fork down, Gerald said, "I have to get ready to go into town. Forgive me for abandoning you just when the locusts are landing."

After he had gone, David glanced at the nearly full plate he had left. As each day passed since Kassandra's death, Gerald was eating less. Still another sign of how badly worried he must be. In the past, when a crisis came up, even when he had been so stressed he couldn't sleep, Gerald had never lost his appetite. If anything, he usually gained a pound or two.

David poured a glass of water and picked up a newspaper. He was just sitting down when the door opened with a bang. Theo lumbered in and raised his hand in a careless greeting. He flopped into a chair that creaked under his weight. "Still here, Markam? You part of the sheriff's roundup this morning?"

"My name's not on the list."

Theo looked resentful. "So you're excused, huh? You get to hang out here while the rest of us sit on our butts waiting for some jerk to ask us the same stupid questions."

"I'll be using the time to make a few phone calls to Washington," David said.

He saw alarm in Theo's eyes. Then, the door opened, and Holly came in. Glancing at David, she sat down across from her husband. "I gave Mrs. Sawyer our order for breakfast. She had better boil the water for my tea this time. I'm not in any mood for lukewarm, insipid tea."

Theo picked up a section of newspaper. He began to read, holding the paper in front of his face as a shield against his wife.

Undeterred, Holly said, "I think we should have refused to go to the sheriff's office. They can't make us talk to them. We do still have some rights. They can't even make us stay here if we don't want to. We should drive back to the Bay Area this afternoon. What can they do to us?"

"I'll be damned if I leave before I get the shots I want of that cypress. I'm going out there this afternoon,"

Theo said, still holding up his paper barrier.

Amused, David left them and went up to his room. The muscle stiffness provoked by his workout yesterday was causing him more pain than he had anticipated. He stretched out on the bed to wait until everyone had gone before he started making calls to Washington.

The sound of car engines roused him, and he realized he had dozed. Sprinting downstairs, he reached a living room window in time to see the cars pass the front of the house. Gerald was driving his car alone. Holly and Theo followed, and Melanie came last in her red Jaguar, chauffeuring Laird and Blaine-Poole. They had the harassed look of people keeping an appointment they dreaded.

It was a little surprising, he thought, that these people who were used to having their own way hadn't refused Perez's instructions to come into town for the interviews. But she was a very persuasive woman, and her purpose was clear. Getting the suspects into an environment that she controlled gave her a good psychological advantage.

When they had gone, he turned back to the chilly, cavernous living room. Like other opulent rooms he'd been in, this one was an evening place. Kassandra's ancient statuary, the brocade-covered chairs, the rich Persian carpets looked warm and exotic in the glow of lamp and firelight.

In the morning sunshine, the dominant impression was clutter. He wondered if Gerald would bother redecorating. When he had asked him yesterday whether he wanted to keep the house, he had simply looked overwhelmed.

David went to the study and closed the door. It was time to call in the reinforcements. He jotted down a list of contacts in the State Department who were most likely to help and looked at his watch. Ten o'clock. That meant it was 1:00 on the East Coast. On a Monday afternoon, he might be able to catch his friend Mary Beltran before she left her office for afternoon meetings. She had access to any information they had on Theo and could find out whether there was a dossier on Blaine-Poole.

Disappointed that she didn't answer her phone, he left a message asking her to call him. His luck was better at Interpol. An individual he had worked with on several occasions agreed to do a record check and call him back as soon as there was something to report. As he had expected, his call to Immigration and Customs ended in frustration. Looking at his list, he decided the other possibilities could wait until later.

Saving the best for last, he smiled as he dialed "Antique" Chaney in Cultural Affairs. Chaney, a friend who shared his interest in the ruins of ancient civilizations, would be eager to help in the hunt for Blaine-Poole's trail. David had to tell him about Kassandra's death so he would understand the situation, but he asked him not to spread the word at the State Department.

He outlined Gerald's concerns about Blaine-Poole and the pieces in Kassandra's collection. Chaney said, "I don't have much time right now, but I'll see what I can do in the next day or two. You know, a lot of government agencies—U.S. and international—try to keep track of the movement of antiquities, especially important ones. And a few private organizations are trying to do their bit. There's IFAR—International Foundation for Art Research—in New York that maintains an archive on stolen pieces, but you're talking about some heavy research here, David. I think Gerald's best bet is to hire professionals to evaluate the collection and let them dispose of it."

"I agree with you wholeheartedly," David said, "but I also know Gerald's stubbornness when he thinks a principle's at stake. He's got a copy of the"—he picked up the booklet—"*UNESCO Convention on the Means of Prohibiting and Preventing the Illicit Import and Export and Transfer of Ownership of Cultural Property* on his desk. I think he's made up his mind to repatriate all of the pieces in the collection—the whole lot."

"It will be a monumental task," Chaney said, groaning.

"I know. And if any of Kassandra's pieces turn out to be looted artifacts—which I think is likely—that will be an even bigger can of worms."

"You should try to talk him out of that if possible," Chaney said. Before hanging up, he added, "I just thought of something; I know a guy who works at the Smithsonian. I'll give him a call to see if he's heard about this Blaine-Poole. He claims to know the black market in antiquities like an insider."

Probably *is* an insider, David thought, giving way to the cynicism that overtook him often these days.

On the way upstairs, he stopped to help himself to tea in the breakfast room. Kassandra's absence was already making room for small changes. Instead of fragile porcelain cups, there were now decent-sized china mugs on the sideboard. He heard the faint whir of a mixer and the sound of Mrs. Sawyer's voice from the kitchen. He'd looked in earlier, and she and Ellie were making pies.

Ellie, when she saw him, turned away petulantly. Now that she was more or less sober, she might be embarrassed about the little scene in the meditation room. Or she might resent him for turning her down. Either way, he had probably missed the chance to find out what part she had played in Kassandra's plans.

He carried his mug upstairs, turned on the lights in Kassandra's bedroom, and surveyed the wall of niches. He had only a broad knowledge of classical Indian history—the dynasties and empires, but he'd spent enough time in museums to recognize major differences between periods and styles.

After an hour of climbing up and down the ladder to study the pieces, he had a general grasp of Kassandra's collection. Aside from two or three small pots, she apparently favored a fairly narrow range of Hindu gods and goddesses. The majority of the pieces were male— stone heads or small figures of Brahma, Vishnu, or Krishna, and a variety of bronze statues, including two Shiva Nataraj. Only a few of the goddesses—Parvati,

Durga, and, of course, Kali—were represented. The large center niche was occupied by a robust stone statue of the elephant-headed Ganesh.

He thought the pieces were mainly medieval, a few from the earlier Gupta Empire, and three beautiful bronze statues from the South Indian Chola Period. Having seen similar pieces displayed in museums from South Asia to New York, he knew it was not a unique collection. Even so, it reflected a sophisticated aesthetic sense and represented a great deal of money. It would make an enviable collection for a small museum. And a huge headache for Gerald, no matter what he decided to do with it.

The only piece that really puzzled him was a small stone carving he found in a niche at the far end of the wall. When he first noticed it behind a bronze statue of the frightful goddess Kali, he thought it was a rock. Picking it up, he saw that it was a crude stone carving of a copulating couple—a young, voluptuous woman astride a very old man.

Studying the carving, he rubbed his fingernail along a crease in its base and dislodged a few crumbs of soil. Artificial aging in soil or water, he knew, was a common practice of dealers who produced fakes for the antiquities market. What was something so crude doing here?

Hoping to find an inventory of the collection to answer these questions, he picked up the small bunch of keys on top of Kassandra's desk and opened the center drawer.

A ringed binder, over two inches thick, took up half

of the space. As soon as he turned the first page, he realized this was Kassandra's famous address book—the wellspring of her notorious reputation for keeping in touch with everyone. Going through it would take hours. Under the binder were three ledgers and, to the side, a carefully arranged box of paper and writing supplies. No clutter here, not even a stray rubber band or pencil stub.

Quickly, he leafed through one of the ledgers. As he anticipated, Kassandra had been methodical in keeping the household accounts. There were neat columns of utilities and other household expenses, food, wine, and liquor. One item seemed odd. A column headed "Ellie" listed varieties of wine, prices, and quantities.

Was Kassandra buying wine for the girl? Why would Ellie have taken Theo's wine if she were allowed to help herself to the contents of the wine cellar? But she wasn't. Mrs. Sawyer made it clear that she had to keep Ellie from sneaking wine out of there.

Trying to remember how Kassandra treated servants overseas, he thought she had a reputation for generosity. But he also recalled, one time at a reception, hearing Kassandra laugh about having to get rid of a servant she had caught stealing.

Had she indulged Ellie's drinking because domestic help was hard to get? Or was there another reason for keeping the girl in the house? Maybe this column of figures was the slow feed of rope with which Ellie might find herself hanged. At some point he'd have to talk to the girl again—if he could manage to find her clothed and more or less sober.

The second ledger was a record of maintenance for the house and grounds. Attached to a back page were estimates of enormous amounts of money for installing fencing along the edge of the headland. Gerald mentioned that Kassandra intended to have the work done. But the estimates were several months old. The delay, along with what Mrs. Sawyer said about cuts in staff, must mean that Kassandra's resources really were stretched.

Was she forced to choose between adding to her collection and keeping up her estate? Considering that she already had the cash in her room to pay Blaine-Poole, it was obvious which had been more important to her.

He thumbed through lists of charitable contributions in the last ledger. Following these records was a single unlabeled page of two columns. One, titled "Loans," listed three sets of numbers and dates but no clue to their meaning. The other, headed "P-Overseas," was followed by a range of dates. He put the ledgers away. What he really wanted to find was paperwork on her collection.

The top drawers and the lower one that Holly had opened held files of auction announcements and museum catalogs. Finally, in the lower left drawer, he found a leather portfolio holding a packet of typed pages titled *The Kassandra Fitzwilliam Collection*. It had not been in that drawer when he'd looked there the last time. He moved to the sofa, switched on a lamp at one end, and settled down to explore Kassandra's obsession.

Almost immediately, he was disappointed. The list was dated three years earlier. She had certainly acquired pieces since then. More than fifty items were listed, each described with a general term such as "bronze Shiva," its historical period, and the place of origin. But nowhere had she written a seller's name, the provenance, or the price paid for it.

A more up-to-date, detailed list had to exist. As methodical as Kassandra was about keeping records, she must have reams of information on these pieces somewhere. She planned to publish a book on the collection with Theo's photographs. Where were the notes or the written text?

And where were Theo's photographs? If Holly was searching for them as she claimed, who had them? David shoved the portfolio back into the drawer and sat musing. Why had the mention of phone calls to Washington put fear in Theo's eyes?

Chapter Thirteen

A vacuum cleaner roared to life in the hallway. David glanced at his watch. It was after twelve. Mrs. Sawyer must be trying to get cleaning done before the crowd came back from town. The woman was a dynamo.

He'd made notes of what he knew so far about the household, and he read through them, hoping for a flash of enlightenment. None came. Talking to each person alone seemed the only option now. It would probably be best to tackle Theo first. The earlier he got to him, the better chance he would have of finding him coherent.

The vacuum cleaner stopped suddenly, and a car horn sounded outside. On his way downstairs, he heard Theo shouting for a drink. Mrs. Sawyer, who was putting her machine away into a hall closet, rolled her eyes when David passed. "Time for the next feeding," she said softly.

He nodded sympathetically and went with her to the

living room. Holly was already enthroned on one of the couches in front of the fireplace, a large leather purse like a peddler's pack at her side. She had picked up a magazine and was ostensibly absorbed in its pages, her legs crossed and her foot, in its green sandal, swinging impatiently. Theo stood at the sideboard pouring vodka into two tall glasses.

"Orange juice," he bellowed at Mrs. Sawyer. "And some food. Nuts or cheese. Anything of substance. The law saw fit to sustain us on vile coffee and that powered chalk they pass off as cream. Criminal exploitation. Asking us the same questions over and over again. Total idiots. Dammed lucky you didn't have to go," he added, waving the empty ice bucket at David.

Mrs. Sawyer took the bucket and retreated to the kitchen.

"I'd rather have a Bloody Mary," Holly said.

"Bring tomato juice too," Theo shouted at the wall. He turned, bottle in hand, his eyes registering surprise. "Oh, Mrs. Sawyer, where did you go?" he crooned in a mocking falsetto.

Disgusted, David went to the kitchen, intending to help the housekeeper if he could. There, he was met by the warm, spicy fragrance of baked pies cooling on the counter. Ellie, dressed in jeans and a T-shirt, stood on the other side of the counter with her back to him, chopping vegetables.

Mrs. Sawyer was pouring juice into two pitchers. When she saw David, she gave vent to her indignation. "Typical of those two! Drinks before lunch, wine with the meal, and then they start up again with cocktails before dinner. I hope Mr. Fitzwilliam won't ever have to entertain those people again." She put the pitchers on a tray and began to release ice into the bucket from the dispenser in the refrigerator door. Her words were momentarily drowned out by the crash and crunch of the ice.

"I don't blame Mrs. F," she was saying when the noise ended. Distracted, she handed the bucket to David, wiped her hands on a towel, and then, flushing with embarrassment, took the bucket back from him. "I'm sorry. I shouldn't be spouting off like this. It's just that they don't seem to care that Mrs. F. has just died." She hugged the ice bucket to her bosom and looked as if she might cry, but she pulled herself together and turned to the maid. "Ellie, are those vegetables ready? Ellie!"

"Almost," the girl said without turning around. Mrs. Sawyer seized the tray of juice pitchers, refusing David's offer to carry it. She paused at the door. "None of them ever realized what a kind, generous woman Mrs. F was. People were always taking advantage of her." She whirled out the door.

Ellie turned around and looked directly at David. "If you believe that bullshit, you're crazy."

David returned her gaze. The girl's hostility toward Kassandra couldn't be much plainer. Perez's speculation was beginning to seem more plausible.

Mrs. Sawyer swished into the room, and at almost the same moment, Gerald came in the back door. He was obviously tired, his face pale and haggard.

"Hello, Mrs. Sawyer," he said. "I hope you haven't gone to more trouble than usual. Melanie, Ken, and Michael have decided to stay in town for lunch."

Mrs. Sawyer was obviously not pleased, but she thanked him for letting her know.

"They should have told you earlier; I'm sorry." Gerald sighed. "I could really use something to drink. How about you, David?"

"You probably don't want to have it in your living room. It's occupied territory right now."

Gerald frowned. "Why don't we go into the breakfast room? Mrs. Sawyer, is there anything to drink in there?"

"I opened a bottle of Chablis, sir, and put it on ice."

"What a saint you are," Gerald said.

In the breakfast room, he poured two glasses of the wine. Handing one to David, he sat down at the table and rubbed his eyes.

"I hope you weren't too bored here by yourself. This is certainly not what I planned when I asked you to fly all the way across the country."

David tasted the wine and leaned against the wall. "I made some phone calls this morning. Chaney, a friend of mine in Cultural Affairs, is working on information about your guests. I started inquiries at Interpol and a couple of other agencies, too. We should have some responses by the end of the day."

Gerald looked at him bleakly and took a large gulp of wine. "If the police decide that I killed Kass, a few looted antiquities won't matter much."

"Have they accused you of doing that?"

"Let me put it this way: If I had a guilty conscience, I'd be highly interested in the departure times for planes out of the country right now—preferably those going to countries with which we have no extradition agreements."

He drained his glass and slumped in the chair. "I'm so sick of it all, David. When I retired, I expected to be free. I'm more trapped now than I ever was."

On the drive into town after lunch, Gerald looked less tired and depressed. David hated to put him under more stress, but he didn't want to lose the opportunity for some straight talk with him.

"I've been thinking about what you said earlier," he began. "Did Perez actually accuse you of killing Kassandra?"

Gerald waved away his concern. "You know I'm prone to exaggeration, David. I was tired and hungry. Don't let what I said worry you."

Trying a different approach, David said, "Did she question you about anyone in particular?"

"No, I don't think so. She wanted to know how everyone got along with Kassandra. There were quite a few questions relating to the servants."

"Perez told me she thinks your maid Ellie had a hand in the robbery, and maybe Kassandra's death, too. Did she make that suggestion to you?"

"I thought it was rather unlikely."

"You're saying Kassandra never had trouble with servants?"

Looking sheepish, Gerald shook his head. "I really don't know. She always managed everything. I was used to leaving those concerns to her. I barely even noticed the household staff. I tried to explain the situation to Detective Perez, but she seemed to have difficulty understanding me."

David remembered Melanie's comment that her father was "too much of a snob to fool around with the help." He'd never thought of Gerald as arrogant. Nor had he ever known him to be so obviously disingenuous.

Abandoning the effort to break through his resistance, David fell back on the kind of innocuous conversation that had become second nature in their professional lives. "I'm still wondering how you ended up retiring here instead of on the East Coast," he said.

Gerald seemed relieved. "Kass grew up in this area. Settling down in a small town was always her dream." His expression grew nostalgic. "St. Judith wasn't so bad at first. We traveled around to several of these small gold rush and lumber towns when we first moved out west. Some of them are quite charming."

The scruffy fast food stands and empty lots David saw on either side of the narrow highway seemed anything but charming. He was about to say so when they crossed a bridge. In a change as abrupt as traveling through a time portal, they were on a wide street bordered by the storefronts of an old western town. Or at least, the illusion of one. False-front facades were painted French blue or white. Signboards that might once have read, *General Store* or *Saloon* advertised *Antiques* and *Frozen Yogurt*. The town had a look of determination to endure that David found appealing.

Even so, he could not imagine Gerald being happy in this place. He belonged in rushing cities, at the heart of crises. "The lifestyle changes when you got here must have been hard for you," he said.

"Well, Kass was never happy in Washington."

"I can't imagine *your* being happy anywhere else."

Looking as if he had just become of aware of the fact himself, Gerald said, "It's true. As soon as I moved away from Washington, I felt like I'd been exiled from the real world."

He parked the car outside a gingerbread cottage with an attorney's name on its door. Sighing deeply, he said, "I know I'm behaving irrationally, David. Please bear with me. I'll answer your questions as soon as I can. There's no point in pretending. Coming out here to retire was an absurd mistake. I've been miserable. Kass just got more and more frantic. And now that she's gone, all I feel is regret that I didn't know how to handle it better."

"I'm sorry it turned out so badly," David said.

Assuming the expression of his public persona as he got out of the car, Gerald said, "By the way, I forgot to tell you, I got two condolence calls from the State Department this afternoon. I don't know how they found out about Kass."

"I had to tell a couple of people, but I asked them not to pass the information on. My guess is that Perez called State even earlier than I did to see what she could find out about us. She's certainly efficient."

"Oh, she's a fine young woman. I know she's doing all she can to make the investigation less onerous for us."

Pausing on his way into the lawyer's office, Gerald said, "You mentioned talking to Theo. I think he's working somewhere beyond those trees near the coastline. And there's Milstone House." He pointed to the Victorian mansion dominating a grass-covered knoll at the far end of the street. "It's a museum now. Kass was going to display her collection there." He frowned. "That place badly needs a new roof."

David stood looking at the mansion. He was frustrated and baffled by Gerald's behavior. The Gerald Fitzwilliam he knew had run a diplomatic mission with competence and élan, had made decisions that affected international policy every day. He had always faced head-on whatever came at him. Why was he acting as if he did not dare to confront what was happening in his life now?

Chapter Fourteen

David wanted to see the museum, but he decided to look for Theo Greg first. With luck, he might find him more coherent than he was earlier. Leaving the sidewalk, he took a path that led to the stand of pines out on the headland. A few puffs of cloud drifted across the sky, and a warm salt breeze blew against his face as he walked.

Near the trees, he saw that he'd have to go down to the beach and back up to get across a narrow gully. Since he was wearing the arm sling to ease the soreness from yesterday's workout, continuing this way was probably not wise, but he felt the need to do it.

At the edge of the bluff, the easy dirt path became a steep, rutted trail. Again, he knew he should turn back and didn't. Halfway down he lost his footing. His left elbow took the impact, sending burning pain through the nerves and muscles around his wound as he slid over rocks and tufts of sea grass.

"Really stupid move," he said aloud when he stopped. Pulling himself up, he adjusted the sling. Now, he really needed the damned thing.

He looked at what he had expected to be a beach. Incoming waves flattened over a shallow swash zone, reversing at the edge as if they were reluctant to associate with the stench of trash and decaying seaweed that littered the strip of shale. He made his way among the debris until he reached a flight of crude wooden stairs built against the side of the bluff.

He climbed up to a broad, flat headland, barren except for a mound of boulders and a few stunted bushes. The coastline jutted out before rounding into another bay, and on that finger of land stood a single, massive cypress tree. Some yards from the tree, Theo Greg was hunched over a tripod and camera.

Walking across the rocky ground, David thought about the day fifteen years ago when he'd first encountered Theo. In Delhi that week, it had been hard to find a party where Theo, still basking in his Pulitzer fame, wasn't the featured attraction. The beefy, sunburned hero would saunter in, wearing a sweat-streaked bush shirt and smelling of Scotch. And women would look at him the way they gazed into the shop windows at a gold souk.

David could still taste the envy he knew was stifled under his contempt for Theo. The fame hadn't mattered. It was Theo's mistress he had coveted. He could still recall every detail of that first time he saw

Eva Dusant.

The party hosted by the UPI bureau chief was like most of the others in Delhi, crowded, noisy, and predictable. But when Eva walked in, the room went silent. She drifted among them, wearing a sari made of gauzy fabric, her pointed breasts bare under the tight silk blouse, her silvery hair cascading straight down her back to her buttocks. Eva had ignited his senses like the sudden, overwhelming scent of *raat rani*—night jasmine—in the summer darkness.

It was a profound mystery to him why Eva loved Theo Greg enough to fly halfway around the world to spend an occasional week with him, year after year, even though she must always have known he'd never divorce his wife.

The memory was so vivid that David felt a little dizzy as he approached the smooth boulders on which Holly Greg sat. She was reading a paperback novel, her head tilted in the unconsciously supercilious angle imposed by reading through bifocals.

She seemed as absorbed in the book as her husband was in his camera, but she had an air of anxious martyrdom about her, as if the reading were only a diversion while she did the primary task of waiting.

David studied her face as he got closer, wondering if she ever found out about Theo's affair with Eva.

"Hello, Holly."

Holly looked up, apparently startled. She flattened her open book against her chest like a fan and frowned. "Have you heard anything from the sheriff? When are they going to let us leave here?"

He sat on the boulder next to hers. "They haven't told me anything. Did you find the pictures you were looking for?"

"No. Gerald doesn't know where they are either." She went back to her reading.

Ignoring the dismissal, David said, "I was surprised that you and Theo are living in California now. Quite a change from New York City."

Holly put her book down. "You've been there?"

"As often as I can when I'm posted in Washington. I have a friend who lives in the Upper West Side. We go to the museums, Yankees games." While he talked, David kept an eye on Theo. He saw him glance over his shoulder.

"Oh, it's you, Markam. Exploring the neighborhood, huh?"

David strolled to his side. In the bright sunlight, the toll taken by Theo Greg's years of hard living was even more obvious. "It's been a long time since I last saw you behind a camera," he said. "A riot outside the embassy in Delhi, wasn't it?"

Theo half turned, apparently torn between reluctance to be interrupted and eagerness to talk. "That summer in Delhi was a good time. I went on to Bangladesh after that. Covered that monster flood. Then, I think it was Beirut—some war, somewhere." Straightening up, he wiped perspiration from his forehead and looked out to sea. "*Ubi Sant*, huh? Where are the wars worth recording these days, Markam? No more fire and conviction. Cartoon missile tiffs and wretched little truck drivers spattering each other's guts on the sidewalk. No real wars anymore."

David drew in a breath and released it slowly. "I doubt that peace is in danger of becoming the status quo anytime soon."

Theo expelled a congested wheeze that passed for a sigh. "Maybe not, but we're evolving toward an abysmal dullness. Obsessive affluence and cautious baby-begetting—that's all that matters these days. What's the point of rising to greet the morning of a twilight world, Markam?"

David fixed his eyes on the stiff limbs of the distant cypress. He pitied the undergraduates forced to endure whole semesters of Theo's maudlin philosophizing. The energy that drove the man fifteen years ago had stagnated and grown toxic. He wondered how likely it was that this frustration could spawn murder, with the right provocation.

"Have you kept in touch with Gerald and Kassandra all these years?" he said conversationally.

Theo bent over his camera again. "More a case of Kassandra keeping in touch with me. She's one of those who writes to everybody." He glanced at David. "Well, you know what I mean. I can't really believe she's gone. Holly's crushed," he added, turning to his work.

David looked at Holly, who was still reading her book. Though the boulder she perched on was a few yards behind them, it seemed likely that she could hear what they were saying. She looked bored and annoyed, but hardly inconsolable.

"I didn't realize Holly knew Kassandra very well."

"She met the Fitzwilliams after Gerald retired. Kassandra called us when they came through San Francisco on the way up here." Theo's voice was distracted.

Nothing David knew about Gerald or Kassandra could explain their cultivating a social relationship with Theo Greg. "Holly must get bored listening to all the stories about the good old days overseas," he persisted.

"Just look at that cypress over there," Theo said loudly. "Who knows how many decades it's stood there? 'Majestic Venerability,' I'm calling this study." He strode toward the gnarled, windblown tree, motioning to David. "Come on, I want you to see this bark close up."

David went with him, well aware that Theo was getting him out of Holly's earshot. When they reached the tree, Theo touched the bark reverently. "Just look at it! See how that branch curves up like a long-necked bird. And the bark is laid on in ragged shingles, like feathers. It's a seabird in wood. Battered, but unbowed!"

"An albatross?" David suggested, running his fingers over the coarse, gray bark.

Theo stood wheezing, staring out to sea, and then he moved closer. David could smell the coffee on his breath and the rancid tang of alcohol in his sweat. "Holly never knew about the kind of life I lived overseas, Markam. And I don't see any point in enlightening her now. Aren't you supposed to be a diplomat? You should know what discretion is."

David stepped away. "You don't want me to mention Eva, then."

Theo's fleshy lips hardened in a scowl. "Don't see it's any of your business. Besides, it was all such a long time ago. Why rake up all that muck?"

"If you don't want her to know about your mistress, why did you bring Holly up here where somebody might let it slip inadvertently?"

Theo stared at him blankly for an instant and then turned away. "The situation is a lot more complicated than you realize." He plodded back toward his camera.

David looked at the sparkle of afternoon sunlight on the ocean, debating whether or not to press Theo further. Was the man really afraid his wife might hear about an affair that must have ended years ago? It was ludicrous.

But secrets did strange things to people. If Theo felt the need to hide his relationship with Eva, his fear could be used as leverage by somebody—like Kassandra—to force him to do something. It still seemed implausible. Why would she need to do that? Theo appeared eager enough to photograph her collection.

He strolled back, noting the watchful look in Theo's eyes, and sat on the boulder near Holly again. On the ground between them was a large canvas tote bag. He could see a metal thermos protruding from it, along with a couple of plastic food containers and several more paperback books.

David tried to read the titles of the books, hoping to find an opening for conversation. One of them was a novel by Virginia Woolf. Another was a Dorothy Sayers mystery. The Virginia Woolf surprised him, and he felt less sure where to begin.

Holly grasped the handles of her bag, pulled it closer, and rummaged through it. Taking out a tissue, she blew her nose delicately and looked at his wounded arm. "How long were you in the hospital?"

"A few days. Overkill, if you ask me. Hospitals are like jails." He hoped she might counter with her experience.

"I've never been in a hospital." She opened her book and David realized more small talk would antagonize her. He slid a few inches closer.

"I've been wanting to ask you one or two things about Kassandra."

"Why? Haven't we had enough third degree from that detective?"

"I'm sure those interviews were stressful for you. Theo said they were frustrating."

Holly pushed her bag away. "Well, of course, it's frustrating when you tell them what you saw and they act like you're making it up."

"Sounds pretty arbitrary. I don't blame you for being annoyed. What did you see?"

She stared at him as if she were gauging his sincerity.

David said, "Gerald told me it was a stormy night. You weren't outside, were you?"

"Of course not. I got out of bed to open the window. While I was doing that, I saw a shadow moving on the lighted path. I thought it was a woman. The wind was swaying the bushes, so it was hard to see more than a black shape."

"Who did you think it was?"

"At first, I thought it might be Melanie. Though I doubt the little princess ever has insomnia. Then, I realized it was probably Kassandra coming back from that ridiculous meditation room of hers."

"That's important. What time was it?"

"I read for a while after I got Theo into bed. It must have been nearly midnight."

David felt a flicker of compassion for this unhappy woman. She must have to look after her bear of a husband as if he were a child. "The sheriff's investigators probably wanted you to be more definite about what you saw."

"I said I could see the whole terrace and part of the garden from my window, but the shadow wasn't clear enough to tell who it was. They seemed to think I didn't see anything."

Nodding reassuringly, David said, "Do you think everybody in the house knew what Kassandra's routine was?"

She looked at him as if he were an annoying bug. "How could we *not* know it? You should have heard the fuss she made last week when she caught that girl—the maid—using her precious hot tub the day before. She complained about it for two hours."

So Ellie was lying to him, David thought. Kassandra did *not* allow her to use the hot tub as she claimed. "Why was she so upset?" he said.

Holly clearly did not want to be bothered explaining. "Well, it was obvious to all of us that the girl did it out of spite, but you'd have thought she used Kassandra's bed instead of her silly hot tub. The woman had no sense of proportion!"

Chapter Fifteen

Gerald's car was gone when David got back to Main Street. Annoyed, he went into the lawyer's office to find out what had happened. A middle-aged woman came into the tiny reception area from an adjoining room. She glanced at the scrap of paper she was holding. "Are you Mr. Markam?"

David nodded. "I'm looking for Gerald Fitzwilliam."

"He asked me to tell you he had to go over to the bank. He's coming right back, but I'm afraid it will be another hour or so before he finishes here. You're welcome to wait. Can I get you something to drink?" She stared at his arm, and he knew she was on the verge of asking what had happened to him.

"Thank you, but I'd like to have a look at the museum," he said.

He left and walked down the street. The three-storied Joshua Milstone House was a gabled Victorian of the grand home variety. Its dark blue paint was new in contrast to the deteriorating shake roof. Climbing the drive that circled up from the street, David imagined carriages rattling up the cobbles to deposit visitors at the front steps.

In spite of the constant ocean breeze, he was sweating and his arm was throbbing by the time he reached the top. He hoped that what he could learn here about Kassandra and her collection would be worth the trouble.

The large porch looked freshly restored. New boards that matched the original wide floor planks had been used, which probably reflected a generous renovation budget. And maybe Kassandra's guiding hand.

Opening one side of the double front door, he stepped into a narrow foyer and was enveloped by close, chilly air. The walls were paneled in rich mahogany rectangles all the way to the beams of the lofty ceiling. To the right of the door was a gleaming Queen Anne desk displaying a stack of Milstone House brochures and a discreetly labeled box for "much appreciated" donations.

A small, elderly woman rose from her chair behind the desk. David liked her immediately. She must be nearly ninety, he thought, but she still met the world with vigor and a straight back. Her blue eyes were cordial behind thick glasses.

"Welcome to Milstone House," she said and composed herself to recite. "The house was built in 1889 by Joshua Milstone for his bride, Mildred, and it was deeded to the town by their heirs in 1976, in honor of the bicentennial." She paused for breath and held out a brochure—green ink on buff-colored paper, with a grainy picture of Joshua himself. "The tour is self-guided. You just follow the route as it is marked here, but I'll be happy to answer any questions."

David took the brochure and glanced through it. "These Victorians are real treasures," he said. "You can certainly tell lumber was abundant around here." He ran his fingers along the dark paneling. "Are you involved in the restoration?"

The guide's wrinkled cheeks warmed to a powdery rose. "Yes, I'm a trustee. We've been lucky to have a great deal of support in the community. Of course, it's a monumental project."

She abandoned her official-guide voice along with her shyness and looked at him with sympathy. "I see you're injured. A fall from a ladder, perhaps?"

"Something a little different."

"It's not often we have men on our tours who really take the time to appreciate the house. Even if they come in to do research, they just go straight to the exhibit they want."

This was obviously his cue to explain his interest. "I do like old houses. In fact, I'm staying in one that's almost this old. I'm visiting with Gerald Fitzwilliam."

"Oh, then you know what's happened!" Confusion followed her initial surprise. "We were all so shocked when we heard," she said. "I can't imagine how we'll manage without Kassandra. How is Gerald?" she added, genuine concern in her eyes as she peered up at him.

David wondered what she would think if he told her Gerald seemed more relieved than grieving. "He's coping as best he can. And his daughter is with him," he said, matching her reliance on platitudes.

She nodded slowly, avoiding his eyes. "I'm Marjorie Bailey," she said. "We really are terribly sorry about Kassandra."

David told her his name, and they waited while a group of people came down the stairs and filed past them, wearing slightly dazed expressions. Marjorie left the greeting duties to the docent who was leading them and touched David's arm gently. "I'd like to show you the rest of the house. Considering the circumstances, I think you deserve a little special treatment."

They climbed the carved staircase and began a desultory tour of the predictable Victorian rooms. Fringed spreads covered the sagging mattresses of narrow beds, bowfront dressers displayed mustache cups, straight razors, implements for curling hair, a wreath made of human hair, a cradle and christening gown in one room, three petite adult dresses in another, yellowed and puckered with time.

Although the stairs were challenging for her, Marjorie seemed determined to give him a thorough tour. On the third floor, which smelled faintly of fresh paint, David spotted a pair of armchairs at the end of the hall. He knew better than to suggest that she might need a rest, so he pleaded his own need. They sat down, and he shifted his shoulders in his jacket, wishing he could take it off. Marjorie had perched on the edge of the other chair, but she stood up and reached for his sleeve. "Let me help you take off your jacket, Mr. Markam. It's too hot up here to be formal."

Feeling comfortable with her now, he said, "Did you know Kassandra before she married Gerald? I understand she grew up in this area."

"So I have heard. I don't recall knowing her family. I believe she attended the Art Academy in San Francisco and worked for one of the museums afterward—the Asian Art Museum, was it? That's how she met Ambassador Fitzwilliam, you see."

"Through the Art in Embassies program, yes. She supervised the exhibit her museum sent to New Delhi that year. Gerald and I were both working at the Embassy when she came."

"My, what fascinating lives you all lead!"

It was always difficult to find a reasonable response to that statement, so he steered the conversation in another direction. "Kassandra was involved with development for your museum, wasn't she?"

"Yes, indeed. She did just about everything," Marjorie said, thoughtfully. Her voice had lost both the forced brightness of her guide persona and the carefully modulated "in the presence of grief" tone. She sounded like a good observer who probably understood Kassandra for what she was.

"She has been chairperson of the committee for the past two years, and she knew enough about business to give us some good advice. When it came to fundraising, well, let's say we were a bunch of amateurs until

Kassandra took us in hand." She laughed in self-deprecation, but David didn't miss the rueful tone under the praise. Kassandra's loss had apparently left mixed feelings among the museum's volunteers.

"I hope this doesn't sound tactless, but why do you think she wanted Milstone House to be the home for her antiquities collection? I . . . It just isn't the kind of place I'd have expected her to choose."

Marjorie gazed at him for a long moment, and he was sure he'd made the blunder he'd wanted to avoid.

"I don't mean the house isn't worthy of—"

"No, of course you don't mean that," she said, fluttering a fragile hand. It's just that I don't quite know how to answer you. I doubt that Kassandra had any real interest in Milstone House itself. It may have been a matter of expediency. The museum was here. I suppose it's easier to convert an existing building than to build a new one."

"When did you expect to receive the collection?"

"That's another thing I can't really tell you. We all knew about Kassandra's legacy. She told us when she took over the committee that she intended to donate her collection to the museum and fund an endowment for its preservation and display. None of us knew when that might happen." She shook her head sadly. "I just feel so terrible about it all now."

"About what?"

"You see, we wouldn't want to hurt the ambassador's feelings for anything in the world. He has always been such a gentleman and such an asset to our little town.

But we simply must do what is best for the museum. I hope he will understand."

"I don't quite follow you."

"It isn't that we aren't grateful. Heaven knows, a collection like that might certainly draw visitors to St. Judith. But it simply won't work for *us*."

She lowered her voice, her distress evident in her face. "I'm afraid it has been an ongoing struggle. You see, we have no formal Collections Policy, so it was hard to find specific reasons for refusing the gift. Frankly, some of our members are offended by certain pieces in the collection." She glanced at him and was apparently satisfied that he understood her meaning.

"We knew how much it meant to her, and we tried to tell her in subtle ways that displaying her collection would overshadow—eliminate really—the focus of the museum as it is. The one we're proud of and have worked hard to maintain. The legacy of money would have been more than welcome, it's true, but what she wanted was just impossible."

David looked at the paneled hallway. "You would have to make some expensive changes to the building if the collection were displayed here."

"That's the whole point! Those statues and things would need special display cases, and they have to be kept at a certain temperature. Not to mention the insurance and the extra security we would need. Even if she left a huge amount to pay for those changes, we wouldn't see them as 'improvements.' To us, they would be the end of Milstone House."

She sighed. "We'll have to draft some kind of letter, I suppose. There's no easy way to handle this. And, as I said, we respect the ambassador so much. We do feel truly sorry about it, but we simply can't accept the collection here."

She held his gaze and he realized what she wanted from him. "Would you like for me to mention this to him?"

"Oh, yes!" She let out a relieved breath. "I was hoping you would understand. If you could just prepare him in some personal way."

David knew exactly how Gerald would react to the news. He said gently, "I don't think you need to worry about hurting his feelings. The collection was Kassandra's interest, not his."

She pressed her fingertips to her eyelids. "I can't tell you how glad I am to hear that. He is such a dear man. We will think of some other way to honor Kassandra's memory. There hasn't been time to discuss it, really, but I'm sure we can."

As they made their way down the stairs, David said, "By the way, did your committee ever have an inventory of the collection?"

Marjorie frowned. "I don't think so. We have seen the things she had on display in her living room. And last year, she invited us all to see that huge stone Ganesh statue. Possibly, she intended to show us the whole collection at this year's party. We expected a dramatic announcement of some kind." She shook her head again. "It was just so impossible."

As he left, David felt more baffled than ever by Kassandra's motives. Why couldn't she see how inappropriate her collection was for this little town? Was it the humiliation of being rejected by the museum in San Francisco that had driven her to such a misguided decision?

His sense of absurdity grew as he went down the driveway to the sidewalk. Why was Kassandra so relentless, such a juggernaut in her determination to force her dream on these people? He thought of the visit he'd made to Puri, in Eastern India, to see the massive Jagannath temple chariot roll inexorably down the hill. Unstoppable. But Kassandra had not been truly unstoppable. Someone had found a way.

Chapter Sixteen

Lost in his memories of India, David stepped into the street between two parked cars. His toe hit a crack in the pavement and he stumbled, slapping his palm on the hood of a silver sports car to keep from falling. Earsplitting beeps and sirens blared from the car. Startled, he backed into the street. A horn sounded behind him, and he spun around. Detective Perez waved to him from the driver's seat of her SUV. She leaned out her window and shouted, "Citizens are not allowed to stand in the middle of the street, Mr. Markam."

"This car alarm ought to be against the law," he yelled back.

"You'll have to take up noise control laws with the town council."

"This is barbaric!" David insisted. "In Turkey they'd give that guy a ticket."

The detective's grin disappeared. "You're in America

now, Mr. Markam."

He recoiled at the rebuke. Looking back at Milstone House, he felt a powerful urge to disappear into the past, to fly back to the distant places where he was comfortable, away from this infuriating country in whose service he had almost lost his life.

The sports car owner ran out from a store. As soon as he had turned off the alarm and gone away, Perez said in a more relaxed voice, "Where's Mr. Fitzwilliam? I was on my way out to the house. I need to talk to him again."

David walked over to her vehicle, curious but not quite ready to forgive her.

"He's still in the lawyer's office. I'm waiting for him. How about letting me buy you a cup of coffee?"

After hesitating, she jerked her thumb toward the passenger seat. "Hop in. I'll give you a lift."

He got in beside her, and they were silent while she wheeled the vehicle—a bit recklessly, he thought—through narrow streets of shops and small cottages. She zipped into a parking space, and they went into a storefront café called Judith Joe's. It was an inviting place, with only three or four customers at wooden tables and booths. Fans in the high ceiling circulated the acrid fragrance of roasted coffee, and blues music played lazily from a speaker.

On the other side of the long counter, a young woman stood before the factory of espresso machines, frothing a pitcher of milk. She raised her hand when she saw them and called out, "Double nonfat latte to go."

Perez waved back. "I'll drink it here today. What do you want?" she said to David.

He scanned the menu board, surprised at the sophisticated variety it offered. "It may be gauche to have cappuccino after noon, but that's what I want."

"We don't do gauche here," Perez said.

David paid for the drinks, deciding to save retaliation for a better time.

When they slid into a booth, she rested her forearms on the table. Opening her palms as if she were offering him a pair of bowls, she curled each hand into a fist, one finger at a time, and uncurled them the same way. The graceful movement seemed so natural that he doubted she was even aware of doing it.

In the muted light of the café, with her mass of honey-colored hair pulled into a braid, her face had a kind of severe beauty. "What's your first name?" he said.

"Why?"

"Now that we're having a drink together, maybe we're almost on a first-name basis."

"I'm still on duty, Mr. Markam. After we finish this case, if we happen to have a drink again, I might let you call me Dita."

"Spanish name?"

She nodded.

"Interesting. It's an Urdu name, too. I think it means 'joyous'."

"They're probably related. Mine means something like 'joys of war'."

"Seems fitting."

She grinned. "I found out some things about you today, too. From the State Department."

"I trust they were complimentary."

"They said you're who you say you are."

"I'm glad to hear that. Did they tell you anything else?"

"One person said you'd be a good one to have around if we were doing any negotiating."

"Who told you that?"

She tilted her head. "Well, let me see; I don't remember his name, but he seemed to know you well."

He nodded. It wouldn't take him long to find out who had talked to her.

The barista came toward them with their drinks, and he seized the diversion. When she put the cups on the table, he said, "They couldn't do a better job than this in Rome."

Looking pleased, she raised her eyebrows at Perez. The detective took a gulp of coffee.

"I should have taken you to the office," she said when the woman had gone.

"This is better. And the coffee really is good. I'm impressed."

"We aren't total hicks out here, you know."

David smiled and tasted the rich, fragrant coffee again. He was trying to think of a line of conversation that would prolong the friendlier mood, but Perez put her cup down and leaned closer.

"How about sharing some of the information *you* got

from the State Department."

"My timing wasn't as good as yours. I'm waiting for callbacks. I did, however, put some people onto Blaine-Poole's trail. As soon as I hear from a colleague of mine, I'll know more about Theo Greg and Ken Laird."

Perez seemed satisfied. "I sent a deputy down to Santa Rosa to talk to Covelo this morning. We wanted to bring him back up here, but we don't have enough to hold him."

"Did Covelo say anything useful in the interview?"

"Total washout. Didn't see it, didn't do it, knows nothing."

"I assume the deputy questioned him about the missing money. How about his relationship with the maid, Ellie?"

"Same story. Never touched a cent, never had sex with Ellie. Which I don't believe."

"Neither do I. Melanie told me Covelo was in the habit of spending time in the girl's room at night. She thought he was in there with Ellie the night Kassandra was killed. But she said that was around eleven. Covelo had already gone by then."

"See? That's what we're up against. It's like juggling frozen peas."

"What are you going to do now?"

"We basically started over," she said briskly. "The interviews this morning didn't give us much, but we've got to break through the resistance somehow. Have you talked to Mr. Fitzwilliam about any of it yet?"

The coffee taste in David's mouth grew bitter. "I've

tried. I know you think he's hiding something. That's why you're going back to the house to talk to him, right?"

Perez drained the last of her coffee and smacked the cup down. "Not entirely. I teach a Tai Chi class out at the Fitzwilliams' house. In fact"—she glanced at her watch—"I've got to be there at five. Mr. Fitzwilliam is in the class, and he asked me not to cancel it. He said he needs the exercise, and it isn't fair to the rest of the people to cancel." She looked at David. "He's a nice man. I like him. I absolutely don't want to believe he's guilty of homicide."

"So why do you still have questions to ask him?"

Perez shifted impatiently. "Let's talk about the guests. Do they seem to be stressed? Have you noticed them doing or saying anything that might be out of character?"

"Everybody in that house is probably acting out of character right now, including me. Which one do you have in mind?"

"I'm not singling any person out, but like I told you on Saturday, I need to know what's going on. All I want are your impressions," she urged. "We have to work this case through the psychology of the people. The physical evidence isn't enough."

David laid his good arm across the back of the booth and drummed his fingers. "Okay, let's see. Theo Greg and his wife are both very unhappy about having to stay here. Neither of them had much to say. Though I did see her searching through the desk in Kassandra's bedroom. She claimed to be looking for Theo's pictures."

Perez pulled out a small notebook and wrote a few words. "What do you think about Mrs. Greg? Does she seem reliable to you?"

"I have no idea. Why?"

"She claims she saw somebody who might have been Melanie Fitzwilliam outside the night Mrs. Fitzwilliam died. Is that something you'd believe?"

"Again, I don't know. She told me the same thing. It could be true. More likely, it's spite. I understand Melanie's been pretty nasty to the Gregs."

"Why is that? Have you talked to her about them?"

He thought about the encounters he'd had with Melanie, but he was not ready to share his concerns with Perez. "I think she's a little too used to having her own way."

"My interview with her this morning didn't go very well. She's a pretty volatile person."

"She's always been high-strung. Her mother died when Melanie was fifteen. Gerald tried to get help for her, but it was a difficult time for both of them."

"Yeah, that happens." An expression crossed Perez's face that made David certain she'd had tragedies of her own.

"It's hard to say what matters and what doesn't right now," she went on. "We need volume at this point. Gather what we can and sift it with care."

"Christine Moreland told me a little about Kassandra's background. Probably things you already know," David said.

"I wouldn't bet on that." Perez's dark eyes were hard. "I just got some information on Christine yesterday that surprised me."

"Something you're planning to tell me?" he said evenly.

"I guess so. It's a matter of public record. I found out why she isn't a psychologist any more. Apparently, she had an inappropriate relationship with a client, and some big mouth reported her to the licensing board." Perez looked disgusted. "Bunch of self-righteous hypocrites."

David was silent, trying to sort through simultaneous feelings of pity for Christine and chagrin at the naiveté of his assumptions about her.

"I know fraternizing is taboo for therapists and teachers—cops, too," Perez said. "But I can also tell you what it's like to have some jealous co-worker talk behind your back and nearly wreck your career. Christine has helped a lot of people up here. It's just not fair."

"I agree with you," David said. "But from what I've seen of her, she may be happier with the work she's doing now than what she did before."

Perez didn't seem convinced. "What's the British guy—Michael Blaine-Poole—been doing? You said you put somebody on his trail."

"I haven't had a chance to talk to him alone yet. I've made inquiries at Interpol and a friend of mine in the State Department has some contacts that may be helpful."

"Maybe you could have a little chat with him today,"

she urged.

"Yes, I'm going to talk to him, but don't get your hopes up. He's apparently very good at what he does."

Perez grinned. "So are we.

Chapter Seventeen

When they reached the house, David helped Gerald unload the three plastic file boxes and a large briefcase he had brought from the lawyer's office. "I had to lug all of this stuff home with me, but I don't have the least interest in looking at a single piece of paper right now," Gerald said as they carried them into his study.

He flopped into a chair and leaned his head back. "I've got to get dressed for the Tai Chi class. My God, I wish I were a couple of decades younger."

"Let me get you a glass of sherry," David said. "Or maybe some orange juice."

"Mrs. Sawyer will have some juice for me," Gerald said wearily. "Detective Perez might ban me from the class if I show up with sherry breath. Did I tell you she's our instructor?"

"She told me. I had coffee with her this afternoon. If you like, we can go through these boxes later. I still haven't found a recent inventory of Kassandra's collection."

Hauling himself out of the chair, Gerald said, "I welcome any help you can give me. But it will have to be tomorrow. I'll be lucky if I can make it through dinner tonight."

David went upstairs and stretched out on his bed. His muscles ached, and he was more tired than he remembered being in a long time. A faint strain of flute and sitar music coming in through his open window woke him. He pushed the curtain aside and looked out. Sunset was still two hours away, but the dozen people moving in unison on the terrace below cast long shadows.

Dressed in a black workout suit, Perez led the group through a graceful routine of Tai Chi with practiced skill. The movements she was teaching were slow and almost trance-like, the muscles holding their strength. David realized how accomplished she was at martial arts. Each of her arm swings and sweeping kicks was precise, its power held in check by the discipline of Tai Chi. Released with speed and force, those same movements could certainly inflict injury.

In the back row, Gerald was performing the routine surprisingly well, apparently unconcerned about being the only man in the group of women. Next to him, Christine was more flexible and balanced, her long limbs giving her movements an appealing elegance.

The group gathered in a circle to end the practice and then dispersed. Gerald began talking enthusiastically to Christine. He looked reinvigorated, as if he'd gotten his wish to be years younger. Though they didn't touch, their body language suggested a comfortable, familiar connection. Watching them, David wondered with mixed feelings if Gerald might already have chosen the next Mrs. Gerald Fitzwilliam.

On his way downstairs, he heard the sound of the library ladder creaking in Kassandra's bedroom. Blaine-Poole was standing on the platform in front of the wall of niches.

"Hey, Markam. What're you up to?" he called down to him.

David had planned to ask him a similar question. Instead, he said, "I wanted to have a look at the last piece you bought for Kassandra. Is it in one of these niches?"

"Still in the traveling case. Kassandra never put them out straightaway. She was going to make a big do about unveiling it."

"Would you mind letting me see it?"

As he had hoped, Blaine-Poole was eager to show off his find. In his bedroom down the hall, he opened the door of his armoire and brought out a dark wooden box, about fifteen inches square. He carried it to the pedestal table in front of the window.

"This looks like a Malabar box," David said, touching the brass ornamentation.

"From Southwest India, yeah. I had it made to transport small pieces. Steel lining, waterproof, and padded well." He rubbed his finger across a scratch in the polished wood. "I might step up to an all-metal one soon." Taking a leather case from his pocket, he selected a key and fitted it into the lock.

"You carry this on the plane with you?"

"Never let it out of my sight. This piece is irreplaceable." He raised the lid slightly and paused, a pitchman's gleam in his eyes. "Know anything about antiquities, Markam?"

"I was hoping you'd enlighten me."

"The question is, after you've seen it, will you know what you're looking at?"

"I doubt it," David said, rejecting the challenge.

Blaine-Poole seemed disappointed, but he opened the box, exposing a silk-wrapped bundle, resting in a bed of foam rubber. He began to unwrap it, still with the air of a showman building an audience to the big moment. "You probably couldn't place this piece, even if you were in the trade. I've been buying antiquities for more than a decade, and I've never seen its equal."

Unsure of what he expected, David was not prepared for the exquisite piece of statuary Blaine-Poole brought out. It was the stone head, approximately life size, of a man, but not one of the stylized faces he had seen so often in Hindu and Buddhist sculpture. This was the image of an individual human being, whose fleshy, sensuous lips, wide straight nose and large, poignantly expressive eyes made him stunningly real.

"I've never seen anything like it either," he said when Blaine-Poole handed it to him. It was heavier than he'd imagined. He turned it carefully, feeling the cool, smooth stone. Never, until this moment, had he understood the compulsion—the need—that drove a collector like Kassandra. It brought a humbling sense of new insight, perhaps of sympathy for her. "This must be a rare piece. How old is it?"

"It's Gupta period. Sixth century." Blaine-Poole was apparently satisfied with the impression he'd made.

David couldn't disguise his admiration. "How did you get it out of India?"

"Contacts, naturally. Experience. You name it and I've likely got it past someone's Customs checks."

"I'm amazed," David said, reluctantly. He had spent enough of his career dealing with government ministries to appreciate the skill and sheer force of personality this feat represented.

He handed the sculpture back. "How much did you pay for it?"

Blaine-Poole laughed and began to rewrap the head with deliberate care.

"Gerald mentioned that Kassandra had the cash to pay you. He thought it was at least $100,000."

"A bit more than that," Blaine-Poole said easily.

"Did she get around to paying you?"

"Where have I heard that question before? You and the lady copper make a matched set, don't you?"

"You have the papers to authenticate provenance, the import and export licenses?" David persisted.

Blaine-Poole's face took on a sheen of absolute confidence. "Documents, museum and Customs seals. We did our 'due diligence.' Kassandra knew what she was about."

David had seen that expression on the faces of other men who made their livings by outguessing and manipulating. Whatever he did, legal or otherwise, would be handled with professional precision. Blaine-Poole would take risks frequently, but he probably didn't often make mistakes.

When they went back to Kassandra's room, Blaine-Poole climbed up to the platform and went on with his work. David strolled along the display wall, looking at the pieces. At the far end, he saw that the small stone carving he had been curious about was no longer there.

"What happened to the little carving that was here this morning?" he said.

Blaine-Poole bent over the rail to look.

"It was in this niche, behind this bronze Kali," David said. He began to describe it, and Blaine-Poole snickered.

"That one with the young lovely shagging the old git, you mean? Never saw it after Kassandra took it."

"But you bought it for her? Where did it come from?"

Turning back to his examination of the Ganesh statue, Blaine-Poole said, "You've been to Khajuraho, haven't you, Markam?"

David looked at him doubtfully. The small piece had been a primitive work, the pose explicit but considerably more modest than the carvings he had seen on the infamous tenth century temples of Madhya Pradesh in central India. "That piece was actually found at

Khajuraho? It looked like some kind of fanciful souvenir they'd sell in the shops around there."

"Kassandra reckoned it was genuine," Blaine-Poole said.

"That temple complex was made a UNESCO World Heritage site not long ago. How do you go about getting an artifact away from there these days?" David persisted.

When Blaine-Poole appeared not to hear him, he said, "Why did Kassandra want the piece?"

"Bit of fun for Gerald, I expect. She saw one like it in a catalog and asked me to bring it back for his birthday. I actually picked it up in New York. Couldn't manage it before I left India."

"She surely didn't intend for it to be part of her collection. Did you put it here behind this Kali statue?"

"Didn't know it was there. She made off with it the day I arrived."

He came down the ladder and stretched his shoulders. "Believe I've given this lot its due for the day. See you down below."

David considered trying to get him to talk more about his dealings with Kassandra, but he really didn't feel like continuing this sparing match with Blaine-Poole. He looked at the niche again. Why would somebody in this household put that crude little carving there? Gerald, if Kassandra had given it to him as a joke, might have put it back into the collection to avoid embarrassment. But who took it away again?

Ellie the maid seemed most likely. The girl had been

in all of their rooms cleaning and making beds every day. She might have thought it was valuable and wouldn't be missed because it was so small.

Finally, he shook his head and went to change his clothes. Like Gerald, he had to summon the will to get through dinner.

The interviews that morning had added another layer of tension to the atmosphere in the house. Blaine-Poole and the Gregs complained and ridiculed Perez and her staff. In spite of their sardonic humor and Gerald's attempts to steer the conversation to other topics, David could sense each one's wariness in the others' company.

Melanie had not appeared for the meal, and when David asked about her, Gerald said, "She's in her room. I don't know what's wrong with her." From his tone, David assumed there had been a disagreement between them. Asking what had caused it was not likely to solicit anything more than platitudes.

After dinner, the Gregs went to their room, and Gerald asked David to help him make a start with the papers he had retrieved from Kassandra's safe deposit boxes. They worked at sorting the material until Gerald complained of a headache. "Sufficient unto this day is the bad news thereof," he said. "Let's give it a rest."

David stayed on to finish looking through a file of newspaper and magazine clippings. The longer he read, the more impressed he was by Kassandra's information gathering. She'd apparently been as obsessive about this activity as she was about her collection.

Considering the volume of material, it was frustrating

that none of it mentioned any of the guests or Melanie. Kassandra must have held each of them in her power in some way. He could feel the pervasiveness of that hold.

As he left the study, he met Ken Laird coming down the stairs with a dinner tray.

"How's Melanie?" David said.

Ken frowned and shook his head. "I don't know what's going on. She's in one of her crazy moods. First, she's furious with everybody. Next minute, she's crying. She's been like that ever since we got back from town. She won't tell me what's bothering her." He deposited the tray on a console table near the door to the kitchen.

"I think she and Gerald had an argument. He wouldn't say anything about it either," David said.

"I just want to get her away from this house. I've only got a few more days of leave before I have to get back to Washington. I'm hoping she'll go with me."

"Sounds like a good idea. Though you'll still have your hands full if she doesn't deal with whatever it is that's got her so upset."

Laird said, "Look, I'm going out to get a beer at that little pub down the road. It's called the Last Chance— how apt is that? You want to come?"

"Is Blaine-Poole going?"

"Yeah, he's the one who suggested it."

"I'll pass," David said. "I've had all of his company I can take today."

In his room, he pulled the armchair closer to the window and sat down. Listening to the ocean, he tried to sort through what he knew. Melanie's behavior worried him deeply. Her refusal to come down for dinner might have been one of her usual bids for attention. Or she might be trying to hide something she'd done. Perez certainly seemed to believe that.

Holly's furtiveness when he'd found her in Kassandra's room still bothered him, too. He doubted she was really looking for pictures. What if she were searching for evidence of something Kassandra knew about Theo? Probably not a recent transgression. What could Theo have done in the past that would make him vulnerable now? Maybe one of the notations in the *Loans* column in Kassandra's ledger was an account of money she had lent or paid to Theo. But for what?

Blaine-Poole, he did not even want to think about. Finding real information about him required more than conversation. Tomorrow, he would get up early to call Mary Beltran in Washington. She was bound to have something useful.

In the realm of resources, he thought he might visit Christine again. Aside from the pleasure of talking to her, he wanted to ask her what she knew about the maid Ellie. The girl was another enigma in this house of shifting shapes.

Chapter Eighteen

David was in Gerald's study at five the next morning. He dialed Mary Beltran's direct number, looking forward to hearing her voice. They had worked together both in India and Washington, and she had helped him through those first chaotic months after Layne left him. They'd become close friends, but never more. She was the sister he would have liked to have.

"M. Beltran."

"Hi, M. How's the weather in the center of the world?"

"Well, if it hain't me ol' pal David. Baskin' in the California sun, are ya?"

She was cockney today. Must be *My Fair Lady*. Mary was noted for her misquotations of lines from musicals when she was in a good mood.

"Hasn't been a lot of basking going on here. You heard about Kassandra Fitzwilliam?" David said.

"Yes, we did. I didn't know her very well. Is the ambassador doing okay?"

"As well as can be expected, to quote a cliché. It's stressful for him."

"How about you? Weren't terrorism and PTSD enough? Now, you've got a grieving friend on top of that. Not to mention jet lag and culture shock."

"Aside from being clumsy and baffled by what's going on here, I'm fine. This is a small town. The culture shock hasn't hit too hard yet."

"Just you wayt, 'Enry Markam."

David laughed. "So, you got the message I left for you yesterday?"

"How did the Fitzwilliams get mixed up with this agent—this Michael Blaine-Poole? God, those Brits with their hyphenated names!"

"Kassandra planned to donate her collection of antiquities to a museum and publish a book about it. Blaine-Poole was buying pieces for her, so she hired him to value the collection. I'm still trying to find out how she contacted him initially."

"The ambassador suspects the Brit's involved in something not so savory?"

"To put it mildly. I guess you haven't had a chance to find anything on him."

"Never underestimate the efficiency of a dedicated woman. But you're going to be disappointed, old chap. I'll send you what I have on him and a few details on the others you mentioned. How do you want it to travel? I could overnight it to you."

"Believe it or not, Gerald has a fax machine. Just a minute. I'll find the number."

"'Done!' said the queen to the bloke!" She paused and then said in a serious tone, "Speaking of females. I don't want to add to your woes, David, but I think you'll want to know this. We got a note about Layne the other day. She's applied for permission to do research in India again. It looks like it's going to be approved this time."

David was silent, waiting for an unwelcome frisson of hope to pass. It wasn't surprising that Layne wanted to go back to India. Each time her previous requests were turned down, she'd kept trying. Her research there had always meant more to her than anything else in the world. It just irked him that he still cared about what she did.

"She's still using the name Layne Darius Singh, but I'm pretty sure she's on her own now," Mary said.

"Thanks, M. I appreciate . . . everything."

"Any time, guv. When are you coming back here?"

"A week or so, I guess. I'll call you when I get to town."

The notes arrived within a few minutes, and he sat down at Gerald's desk to read them. As Mary had predicted, the results on Blaine-Poole were slim but not entirely disappointing. His dossier was leaded with conjecture. He had a residence in Switzerland. Not unexpected, given the Swiss laws that made the country a good safe harbor for stolen or doubtful art and antiquities. The other notes were mainly about foreign business agents he dealt with and a couple of dealers in

New York. Mary noted that one of those New York dealers had a sizable file of his own and was a person of interest in a current investigation.

David's grudging admiration for Blaine-Poole's skill was even greater. The web of contacts he must have to maintain—from antiquities dealers to wealthy collectors, Customs people to museum officials—was formidable.

Ken Laird's file was predictable. He had been in college during the Vietnam War and was progressing along an apparently normal course of assignments for a Military Intelligence officer. Armed Forces Staff College, language school, tours of duty in Saudi Arabia and the UAE, two in Washington. A pretty blameless life.

He put the notes on Laird aside and moved on to Theo Greg's history. The information there was as ancient as the man himself. Following a couple of entries about his photojournalistic exploits during the Vietnam War, there was a mention of that wartime photograph that had won him fame.

Other minor incidents were noted. Theo had continued to be a pain in the butt throughout his career as a photojournalist. He repeatedly came to the State Department's reluctant attention by slipping into restricted areas of countries the U.S. had touchy relations with or by getting into fights with foreign nationals in bars.

Skimming the rest of the notes, David wondered why Theo's mistress Eva was not mentioned. The State Department might have a separate dossier on her. In spite of Theo's years as a troublemaker, nothing in his file would make him vulnerable to blackmail.

Somehow, he had the feeling the famous photograph was what really mattered. Before his moment of glory, Theo had been a run-of-the-mill photojournalist, working for a wire service in New York. Everything, even his current job as an associate professor at a small California college, must have been built on that one accidental miracle.

Still mulling over what he had learned, David put on the windbreaker he'd brought with him and went through the darkened kitchen, out into the flattened stillness of early dawn.

A mist drifted just above the ground. He swung his arms while he walked to counter the chill of the moist air. As his muscles loosened, the ache in his left arm settled into a bearable state, and he quickened his pace.

Reaching Kassandra's meditation room, he heard the sound of the motor. Ellie in the pool again? Surely, not at this hour. Mrs. Sawyer seemed to be the only early riser. It would certainly not be her.

On the headland, he pulled in gulps of sea air, feeling better than he had in weeks. Just before Christine Moreland's cottage came into view, he turned and went along the access road, then cut back into the garden. He made the loop four times, calculating that he'd covered at least two miles.

Instead of going back to the house, he slowed to a walk and took the path toward the ocean. As he passed the meditation room again, he could see steam drifting from the air vents in the roof. It occurred to him that someone must have left the jets running all night.

He knocked on the door to be sure of not intruding but heard only the monotonous hum of the motor blending with bird chatter and the intermittent crash of the ocean into the cave below. He opened the door slowly. A blast of hot steam rushed into his face, laden with chlorine and a stench like sewage. He wiped away the moisture clouding his eyes.

"Is anybody here?" he called, walking cautiously into the room. The pale light from the towering window suffused the drifting steam with a ghostly essence; the chlorine stung his eyes. Between the crash of each wave into the sea cave below, the only sound was the energetic bubbling of the tub. But the stench was sickening.

David felt along the wall and found the switches for the lights and the pool jets. Bright light and a moment of complete silence came simultaneously. Then another wave slammed into the sea cave. In the instant of its boom, he saw the grayish shape floating in the dark water of the pool.

Struggling out of his jacket, he knelt at the edge and grasped the woman's body with his right hand. He pulled her up, lost his grip, and had to force himself to dig his fingers into the bloated flesh of her underarm and shoulder to haul her far enough out of the water to be more than certain that she was dead.

He released the body gently, and it bobbed just under the water's surface. Picking up a towel from the tile, he stood up and wiped his hands. Horror, pity, a terrible stab of panic fled through his mind. The silence in the room had a tinny quality in between each nerve-jarring crash of waves. He went outside and stood inhaling deeply to overcome nausea.

After a while, he went back to look at the girl's body, floating face down, the curly blond hair strung out like brownish seaweed in the murky water. In the brief glimpse he'd had of her shoulders, he hadn't seen any marks, but he thought there had been a darkened area—perhaps a bruise—on the vulnerable nape of her neck.

The skin had felt soft and pliable when he lifted her, and the smooth, young skin was still faintly pink. He wished he hadn't seen that face, swollen and blank as if manufactured in a rubber mask factory. Impossible to believe she was the girl who laughed and taunted him in this pool.

As the steam cleared through the open door, he surveyed the litter of what appeared to be Ellie's evening of solitary indulgence. Three thick slices of cheddar cheese, a few damp crackers, and a nearly bare stem of red grapes lay on a china plate next to a soggy paperback romance novel. Moisture drops had formed on the grapes and the darkening surface of the cheese, making them look like plastic food.

An empty wine bottle lay on its side near a large crystal glass. David nudged the bottle with his fingernail so he could see the label. It was a Cabernet Sauvignon from a vineyard in Napa Valley. The same brand Theo drank. But according to Mrs. Sawyer, the cellar door had been locked and she herself had kept the key after

Kassandra's death.

How did the girl get the wine? From Theo, in payment for some special favor? Unlikely. He doubted that Theo Greg was still capable of participating in the sort of favor Ellie might have bestowed. It was even harder to imagine him giving up any of his special vintage willingly.

Mrs. Sawyer said the wine wasn't sold in town. Ellie was hardly likely to be special ordering expensive wine on a maid's salary. So where did it come from?

Turning to leave, he noticed an apricot-colored towel on the bench. The same color as the ones in Kassandra's bathroom. The girl must have brought it here. He held the towel to his nose and inhaled a light, lilac scent, old-fashioned and probably expensive. That would not be Kassandra's. Gerald said she never wore perfume.

David looked back at the pool, remembering the scorn on the girl's face as she held up her wine glass to him. She had been drunk then, or close to it. Was that how she died? Had she passed out and slipped under the water? Or had she chosen the wrong person to taunt?

He retrieved his jacket from the floor where he had dropped it and set out for the house.

Chapter Nineteen

David sat on the same wrought iron bench where Gerald had been after Kassandra's death. The air around him had the moist, poignant newness of early morning. A capricious breeze, carrying the scent of some sweet vine from the garden, touched his skin. It would be a glorious day. Incongruous, as nature often was, with the grim activities that were in progress a few feet away from where he sat.

Detective Perez had arrived less than fifteen minutes after his call. She, her deputies, and their armada of vehicles and equipment were busy at their trade. When Perez had secured the crime scene with quietly terse orders, she listened to David's brief account of finding Ellie Victor's body and then asked him to wait.

For a while, he sat thinking, trying to understand why both the girl and Kassandra had died in this beautiful place. Gradually, a sense of horror overcame him, as if he were caught in some formless tunnel. His mind filled with the sound of boots running in the hallway. The stab of alarm. The door bursting open. The sharp *Ak, ak, ak* of the AK-47. Voices yelling, words flitting at the edges of meaning; a sting of pain in his left arm. The crack and crash of Bill Ralston's body hitting the table. Boots running. Distant gunfire. Silence. A trickle of blood oozing from the hole in Ralston's temple—

"I brought you some tea, Mr. Markam."

Startled, David looked up to see Mrs. Sawyer standing beside the bench.

"That deputy told me I couldn't come inside the tape, and I said I was going to give this to you no matter what he said."

He blinked to clear his eyes. His throat was so dry that his voice cracked when he thanked her.

"I just can't believe all these terrible things are happening," she said once he had the mug in his hand.

He sipped the strong brown liquid, sweetened with honey.

Mrs. Sawyer jiggled the round tray nervously. "They told us we all had to stay in the house until Detective Perez said we could come out. Mr. Fitzwilliam tried to argue with them, but I just made the tea and brought it. I guess I'm going to get into trouble, but I don't care. You had to have something hot to drink."

David looked at her with a new sense of respect and gratitude. He reached for her hand and squeezed it. "You are a wonderful lady."

Instead of leaving, she moved closer and said in a low, urgent voice, "Mr. Markam, I know this is an awful time for you, but there's something I need to talk to you about."

At that moment, Detective Perez came out of the wooden building, notebook in hand. Mrs. Sawyer jerked back guiltily and hurried away toward the house.

The detective watched her go. Then, she bent to look at a small twist of white tissue that lay in the sand beside the path. She examined it briefly but left it where it lay and pointed it out to one of the deputies.

Sitting down on the other end of the bench, she lifted her face to the sun and closed her eyes. A gust of breeze ruffled the tendrils of her hair that had escaped the long braid. The gesture was a reassuring one. David thought she would not have done it if she felt any serious doubt about him. Still, he wondered if finding Ellie's body had changed his status.

"What do you think happened here, Mr. Markam?" she said, turning to look at him.

He sipped his tea and thought about what he knew. "I can't tell you much more than you can see for yourself. I don't know anything about the girl. Once, I did see her in the pool—the day after Kassandra died."

Perez scowled, and the lines around her mouth deepened in a way that reminded David of wizened women, in black scarves, he had seen trudging along a dusty village street in southern Spain. "Tell me again how you found her," she said.

He went through his explanation again, clearing his

throat several times as he recited the details.

When he finished, she sighed. "This is a rotten experience for you. I wish I didn't have to put you through more questions."

"It isn't a good time for anybody," he said wearily.

"There's no phone out here in this building. Where did you call us from?"

"The kitchen."

"Was Mrs. Sawyer there? How did she react?"

"She was upset, of course," David said, remembering the woman standing next to the stove, a pair of tongs suspended in air, shock and fear in her face. Her distress had seemed genuine, in fact a little unexpected, considering her habitual irritation with the girl. "I think she said something like, 'Oh, my God, she's done it. I told her she would drink herself to death.'"

He swallowed the last of the tea, wishing he had more.

"Did you stay in the kitchen with her after you called us?"

"No, I went upstairs and knocked on Gerald's door. I told him what had happened, and he said he'd get dressed and come down. Then, I came back out here to wait for you."

"Didn't Mr. Fitzwilliam seem surprised when you told him?"

David felt his mind overload. What was he doing sitting here assessing people's mental states when he could barely fathom his own? "I don't think I can even speculate. He was just dazed," he said, his voice betraying his exasperation.

"Only a little longer," Perez said, soothingly. She lifted her hand as if to touch his arm, but drew it back, flushing slightly. "Did you think Mrs. Sawyer was right about the way the girl died?"

David sat up straighter, flexing his shoulders and neck, impatient now to finish. "She knew the girl better than I did."

"You say you examined the body?" The question sounded innocuous, but David saw speculation in the dark eyes.

"Not really. As I said, I pulled her head and shoulders out of the water just far enough to see that she was dead—had been dead a while."

Perez made some notes and then, without looking at him, said, "What about the first time you saw the girl in this building? Did she appear to be drunk then?"

"Probably. You told me yourself that she had a drinking problem."

"Could somebody have drowned her, held her under the water?"

David moved his aching shoulders again. He turned to look straight at her. "I once saw the result of a forced drowning. This wasn't like that. I'd guess the girl was strong. She would have put up a fight. There would be signs of a struggle."

Perez's eyes narrowed. "What if he'd pulled her under the water by her ankles?"

David held her gaze, disliking the callousness in her voice. He shook his head.

"Element of surprise," she said, ignoring his distaste. "Nose and mouth fill up with water. They're gone like that!" She snapped her fingers and waited for his reaction.

Reluctantly, he considered the suggestion. An image formed in his mind of the execution Perez described being carried out. Any of them could have managed that, even wheezing old Theo, if he had been desperate enough. Or one of the women. He had a disturbing memory of Melanie's face when she confronted the girl in the pool.

"I don't know anyone who had a reason to kill this girl," he said sternly. At the moment, all he wanted was to get away, but Perez was determined.

"What if Ellie knew something about Kassandra's killer? You know what they say about a little knowledge."

David stood up, disgusted. "I've got to stop now. I need to take a shower and eat something."

Perez relented and they walked to the house together. He expected her to come in, but at the kitchen door, she said, "Thank you, Mr. Markam. I do appreciate what you've done to help me, and I'm sorry you've had to deal with all of this. I won't bother you again for a while."

After he had showered and dressed, David went to the kitchen. Pots and pans were piled in the sink and the place felt deserted. Mrs. Sawyer was absent from her post. He assumed she was in the living room where Perez had gathered the others.

In the breakfast room, he helped himself to a strawberry scone and scrambled eggs from the buffet dishes on the sideboard, amazed at the housekeeper's fortitude. He sat down at the table, littered with the remains of other breakfasts, and tried to eat. After a few bites, he pushed the plate away, picked up a section of the San Francisco newspaper lying on the table, and read two or three articles without much interest. He knew he was distracting himself, hoping to dislodge the sliver of horror that had wedged itself under the surface of his consciousness.

On the way back upstairs, he heard Theo's voice bellowing from the living room: "We've got a damned serial killer running loose around here. We need protection, not harassment." Detective Perez's words were too low to hear, but her tone had an edge of irritation. Blessing her for sparing him from the general melee, David went into his room.

He shoved the armchair closer to the window, sat down, and closed his eyes. He had to pull himself together. It was Perez's job to find out which of those seven people downstairs was hard pressed enough by fear, greed, or some other passion to kill.

But he still felt a responsibility to Gerald. If Melanie was the killer, or even Gerald, himself . . . . No! He was not going to accept either possibility. Kassandra's death had to be related to the information she had collected.

Then, why was the girl killed? How could she have aroused such powerful feelings? Mrs. Sawyer was frustrated and would have been glad to see her fired.

Melanie was offended by her impertinence and probably jealous of the attention she got. Even Holly disliked her.

Possibly her taunting and blatant sexiness had resulted in violence from one of the men, but Melanie seemed sure that none of them were interested in her. Even if that were not true, who would need to murder her?

He thought about Perez's theory that Ellie had killed Kassandra during or after a robbery attempt. Didn't the girl's death negate that possibility? And where was the money?

Frustrated, he got up and went back downstairs, planning to call Chaney in Washington again to see if he had turned up anything on Blaine-Poole.

In the study, he found Perez sitting behind Gerald's desk. She gave him a slight grin to indicate a truce. "No need to worry, Mr. Markam, I'm not going to bother you again. In fact, I've almost finished here for now. Christine Moreland is the last one I need to talk to."

"You called her house?"

"I did. No answer. Mrs. Sawyer says she must be home because she didn't see her car leave. I was just about to send a deputy over there to find out." Giving him a speculative look, she said, "Maybe you could do that."

"What?"

"Go to see Christine Moreland. I think she likes you. Maybe you can charm her into telling you more than she's told us."

"Well, I was going to make a phone call, but I'll walk

over there first," David said. "I'm not promising to be charming, though."

Perez's grin widened. "Probably best not to mention what I told you yesterday about her past."

David nodded. "It's not any of my business."

"After you talk to her, please bring her back here. I still want to check on one or two things. If she can't or won't come, tell her I'll be over to see her as soon as I can. Right now, I've got to finish with these folks so they can get on with their day."

"It sounded like some of them were getting restless."

"Restless and really mad. Who can blame them?"

David found Mrs. Sawyer slicing tomatoes in the kitchen. "Have they finished questioning you?" he said conversationally. He hadn't intended to stop and talk, but she put her knife down and came around the counter, wiping her hands on a dishcloth.

"Can you wait a minute, Mr. Markam? I need to ask you about this." She struggled to get something out of the deep pocket of her apron.

Realizing how agitated she was, he said, "Has something else happened? You said earlier that you wanted to talk to me."

She held out her hand, and he saw the stone carving of the copulating couple he had puzzled over in Kassandra's bedroom. It was smeared with mud.

"Ezequiel found it this morning. He knows every inch of that garden. He said he saw the dirt disturbed around one of the flagstones in that little alcove with the bench. This thing was half buried under the stone."

"Have you ever seen it before?" David said.

Mrs. Sawyer blushed. "It must be one of those things Mrs. F keeps in her bedroom. I didn't think she had anything this ugly."

"It was there yesterday. I saw it in one of the niches. Why would someone take it outside and bury it?"

"I don't know," she said, frowning. "Ellie might have pulled a stunt like that as a joke. But she never touched those old things if she could help it. This one's pretty bad," she said with a grimace. "Would you take it, please, Mr. Markam?" She wrapped it in the dishtowel she was holding and handed it to him.

Stifling a sigh, David took the bundle from her and dropped it into his jacket pocket. "I'll ask Blaine-Poole about it later. He's the one who bought it. He might know what happened. Right now, I'm going to see if Christine Moreland's at home. Detective Perez wants to talk to her."

"She could be home. The detective says her phone didn't answer, but she told me one time she turns off the ringer when she's working."

As he crossed the terrace, David felt the sun's warmth on his face. The deadened chill that had taken hold of him began to loosen. He veered left from the terrace and took the path that led to the access road.

Christine Moreland was not likely to be at home. She could hardly have missed the commotion of emergency vehicles arriving and leaving. He wondered if Gerald had also tried to reach her.

Chapter Twenty

The tall eucalyptus trees growing along the access road shaded the blacktop, their branches rasping in the breeze from the ocean. When he walked into the shadows, David felt a chill settle over him. He began to walk faster through the drifted masses of dry leaves, determined not to let memory of the stench, the feel of the girl's dead flesh, fling him back into the terror of Istanbul once again.

A horn sounded behind him and he turned, unsure why he hadn't heard Christine Moreland's small car coming. He stepped off the road. Instead of passing, she stopped and lowered the window. "You're on your way to see me?"

David bent to look in at her. "We've had another tragedy. Detective Perez needs to talk to you," he said.

"The deputy at the gate told me about it, but I can't go over to the house right now. I have an appointment with someone in an hour and a couple of things to do first. Will you tell her I'll be there in a few minutes?"

"You may need to cancel your appointment."

"I'll reschedule if I can. It's probably too late now." She hesitated and said, "Who is it, David? The deputy wouldn't tell me."

"The girl, Ellie, has been killed. Perez says she was murdered. I thought it could have been an accident myself."

"You've seen her?"

"I found her drowned in Kassandra's hot tub."

"You poor man," she murmured. Turning away, she sat very still. After a few moments, she glanced at her watch. "I have to make this call." She seemed reluctant to leave him. "Why not come with me to my place? We can walk back to the house together."

The suggestion was unexpected. Now, he didn't have to make an excuse to talk with her. His pleasure dampened when he realized she must be concerned about his emotional state. He appreciated the sentiment, but it did not do his ego much good.

He folded himself into the cramped seat next to her. So close, he could smell a light citrus scent in her hair. She was dressed in a linen pantsuit and silk blouse. He wondered where she had been so early in the morning.

Parking the car in the graveled circle next to her cottage, Christine moved with long, quick strides to the gate. As he followed her, David marveled again at the sense of shelter the pine trees gave this little garden. He could hear the crash of surf far below, but here, there were only bird chirps, the breeze in the treetops. And the meow of a cat. Ellie's white Persian got up from where it was lying behind a bush. It came toward Christine as if it had been waiting for her.

"Shoo! Go away," Christine said. "This thing seems to have adopted me lately. I don't mind cats, but I'm allergic to their dander. We should find another home for it now."

She unlocked the door. The sense of shelter vanished when they stepped into the living room. The sweep of beige drapery was drawn back, and brilliant light flooded through the windows.

David glanced around the room. On his last visit, it had been immaculate, serene. Now, it looked like the aftermath of a night of indulgence. Sunlight glinted off a pair of crystal liqueur glasses and a bottle of crème de cassis on the round coffee table. An open box of expensive chocolates and crumpled napkins lay with the glasses.

"Oh!" Christine said softly. She let the strap of her purse slide off her shoulder onto a chair. Without looking at him, she went to the table, swept up the glasses, and carried them into the kitchen. Seizing a cloth, she hurried back, gathered the rest of the litter and wiped away the last trace. David saw her embarrassment and cooperated in the pretense that nothing curious was happening.

"Please have a seat," she said, glancing at him from the other side of the long wooden counter that separated the kitchen and the living room. "I'll just make the call in my bedroom and then we can go."

David stood at the window, contemplating the sparkling ocean, his curiosity churning.

In five minutes she was back. "Fortunately, I caught my client before she'd left her house. I've rescheduled, so I have some time now." She went to the window and grasped the drapery cord. "Let me close these curtains. The sun fades colors so badly." The room was suddenly dim.

"Come and sit down for a few minutes, if you don't mind. I'd like to hear what happened before we go over to the house."

David sat in the bamboo chair next to hers and told her about finding Ellie's body.

Christine listened with obvious distress. "What a sad way for a young life to end. Does Detective Perez really believe she was murdered?" she said when he finished.

"I think so. She and her cohorts are questioning everyone in the house. You must have left before the commotion started this morning."

"Yes." She paused and then said, "I had an early appointment in Mendocino with my . . . a doctor's appointment." She studied her hands folded in her lap.

Alarmed, David said, "Is something wrong? You're not ill, are you?"

She looked up quickly. "Oh, no. Everything's fine. But I am upset by what you've told me. More than I would have expected. It's like a bad dream and, at the same time, terribly real and frightening. How are you doing?" she added, her eyes full of professional concern.

David drew back, disarmed. "Hard to say what I feel beyond the shock of finding her. I didn't know the girl personally."

Christine looked away. "I suppose I didn't really know her myself. Though it took me a while to realize that."

"Why was that?"

Sighing, she said, "She was such a troubled young girl. A few weeks after she was hired, Kassandra came over and told me Ellie had a drinking problem. I thought I could help her."

"It seems strange that Kassandra would hire her or keep her on under those circumstances. Did she say why?"

"I almost never knew Kassandra's reasons for doing things. But I felt sympathy for Ellie. She talked to me about her life. An abusive family, many problems. I took her to an AA meeting and tried to help her find other ways to cope with the emotional damage she was medicating with alcohol."

"I guess it didn't work."

"It was worse than unsuccessful," she said, flushing. "I misjudged the situation badly. What I meant as kindness, she seemed to interpret as weakness or gullibility on my part."

Remembering the record of Ellie's wine consumption he'd seen in Kassandra's ledger, David said, "How did Kassandra deal with her?"

Christine considered the question. Finally, she said, "I think Ellie met her match with Kassandra. They were both adept at framing themselves as victims when they wanted something. The person withholding what they wanted became the persecutor. Do you know what I mean?"

Grimacing, David said, "I've sat across the negotiating table from people using that tactic more times than I can count. It's masterful manipulation, when it works."

"That's true." Her expression softened. "I really shouldn't be talking about her this way. Ellie was very young and insecure. I wish I'd felt a little more compassion." She shook her head. "I suppose we ought to go."

David was reluctant to lose the comfortable feeling growing between them. He was just beginning to catch a glimpse of the ways Kassandra dealt with people. "We don't need to hurry. Perez and her staff still had their hands full when I left.

"Do you remember the last time I was here—the day you hypnotized me?" he said, trying to lighten the mood. "You said Kassandra had been very generous to you."

"I don't know what I'd have done if she hadn't helped me," she said softly.

"Mrs. Sawyer says she was generous, too. I just wonder whether her gifts came with a price."

"I'm not sure what you mean."

"Take that book of hers, for example. Gerald told me Kassandra hadn't been able to get it published until you persuaded someone you know in San Francisco to do it.

Is that right?"

"I owed Kassandra quite a lot, and I knew how important it was to her."

"So, she didn't put any pressure on you to make that happen?"

"You're saying she forced me to arrange the publication?" A small, choked laugh escaped her. "That's a little farfetched, isn't it?"

"Was she capable of doing something that ruthless if she had to?" he persisted.

She made a gesture of impatience. "What do you want me to say, David?"

He discarded caution. "I've been counting on you to tell me the truth about Kassandra. The things Gerald can't—or won't—tell me. Who seemed to be especially angry at her?"

Christine looked as if she were struggling to put her thoughts in order. "I don't know. There was always tension—even hostility—in the house whenever I was around. The tension was especially high on Friday night. Kassandra encouraged the conflict, even if she didn't start it. That was one of the more unpleasant evenings I've spent there."

"Was Melanie an instigator in any of it?"

She looked at him sharply. "You're concerned about the hostility between Melanie and Kassandra. Is that what you're really getting at?"

"Melanie's already told me what she thought of her stepmother."

"I know. I know," she said, shaking her head. "I'm

sure Gerald is worried to death about her. I hate to see what her behavior is doing to him. Melanie actively despised Kassandra. And she was intensely jealous of Ellie. I would never say this to Gerald, but I've been afraid Melanie might be *capable* of murder."

David studied her. There was no denying the truth of what she said. Even so, he thought Christine's own feelings were driving her conclusions about Melanie. He said, "From what I've been able to see, several people had strong feelings about Kassandra. Gerald among them."

One slender hand went convulsively to the amber beads she wore. She clutched the strand, keeping her face averted. Then, she lowered her hand to her lap, as if responding to an inner censurer. "He didn't kill Kassandra. He couldn't have."

"Is that a professional assessment?"

When she didn't answer, he tried again. "He has certainly been behaving strangely."

"In what way?"

"As if he's anxious to keep something a secret."

"There must be many things he prefers to keep private in his life."

He held her gaze, and after a moment, she made a small gesture of capitulation. "All right. There's no point in going on like this. Gerald obviously hasn't told you about our relationship."

"You must know him well enough by now to be sure he hasn't."

Christine stood up. She went to her desk, leafed

through some folders distractedly, and sat down in the desk chair. "A few weeks ago, Gerald came to see me, late one evening. He made an excuse. He said, 'I want to let you know there will be cars parked along the access road tomorrow. Kassandra is hosting a meeting of her museum committee. I hope it won't be an inconvenience.'

"It was obvious he just needed someone to talk to. His life here is so different from what it used to be. I gave him a cup of tea and let him talk. But it wasn't professional. I enjoyed being with Gerald. I loved hearing about his exploits overseas. He's had an exciting life!

"I thought that one time would be all there was. But a few days later, he called to ask if he could come again. We slipped into a kind of routine. Kassandra spent an hour at her ritual every night, and Gerald came to talk to me. Not always. Perhaps three times a week. I was usually just reading. I suppose I was glad to have the company," she added wistfully.

"It appears he was here last night. From the look of things, we aren't talking about just a casual chat."

If she felt anger, she hid it well. "Nor are we sitting in judgment, I assume," she said evenly.

David shook his head in chagrin. "That did sound judgmental, didn't it? Melanie accused me the other day of becoming a prig. She also told me Gerald was looking for comfort outside of his marriage."

The lovely winter-gray eyes widened. "The evenings Gerald and I spent together were not an *affair*. It wasn't an affair at all."

"Maybe not from your point of view, but I'd guess they meant a great deal more to Gerald. You probably gave him more emotional satisfaction than he's ever had. In fact, I'd say he's very much in love with you."

When she didn't respond, he said, "Gerald hasn't had a lot of experience, you know. He and Kassandra were married less than two years after his first wife died, and all the years I've known him, he never—well, he always had to be extremely careful about what he did in his private life."

They were both silent for a while. Finally, Christine said, "What are you thinking?"

David grinned. "I was just trying to remember if I've ever seen Gerald drink crème de cassis. You must have a lot of influence on him." Truly, he thought Gerald would drink flat beer if this woman asked him to. "He was here the night Kassandra died?"

Christine nodded.

"Have you told Detective Perez that?"

"Why would I? If she finds out Gerald came here while his wife was occupied, what conclusion do you think she will draw?"

"Perez isn't a prig like me. You said yourself she's pragmatic. Under ordinary circumstances, I doubt that she gives much thought to other people's relationships. But this isn't an ordinary situation. You ought to tell her as soon as we get to the house. If nothing else, it will take the pressure off of Gerald. That cliché about the spouse being the prime suspect is true, you know."

Christine rose and picked up her purse. "She may think we're both guilty. The idea that we'd conspire to kill Kassandra so we could be together is ridiculous, but even broadminded people make assumptions like that when they don't understand."

Chapter Twenty-One

An hour later, David found Gerald sitting behind his desk, looking morose. "How did your session with Detective Perez go?" David said.

"She's always very polite, but persistent. The same questions keep coming back in different ways. I just don't know what else to tell her."

David could imagine Perez's frustration. She was doing her best to be sensitive and respectful, and Gerald must still be refusing to say anything that might implicate Melanie. He was also probably transparently embarrassed if anything about Christine Moreland came up.

David decided it would do no good to reason with him or try to change his mind. He sat down in one of the wing chairs. "Why don't we go through some of this stuff you brought from the lawyer's office? I'm here to help."

Gerald looked hopelessly at the piles of papers and folders on his desk. He picked up a legal-sized accordion folder.

"This is one of the items I found in Kass's safe deposit box. None of it means anything to me. Several newspaper clippings, names, and addresses. They're people I've never heard of." He handed the folder to David and sat in the chair next to his.

"This could be what I've been looking for," David said, pulling out the contents of one file pocket. "Did you find an inventory of her collection?"

"Didn't notice anything of that sort when I glanced through these folders, but it may be there."

"I don't understand why we haven't found a current list. The one in her desk upstairs is dated three years ago, and some of the pieces displayed in her bedroom aren't on it."

He scanned a clipping he'd taken from the file. It was an obituary for a Korean-American war correspondent killed during the Vietnam War.

"Did Kassandra know any Koreans?"

Gerald looked blank. "Maybe she did. She knew so many people. But I really can't say. No names come to mind."

Three small pages of notebook paper were attached to the clipping. David read Kassandra's thin, precise writing and said, "There are a couple of addresses here, one in Korea and the other in New York City; some sets of dates and numbers. It will take me a while to check on this." He had begun to put the papers back into the folder when a thought struck him. "I wonder—"

"What?" Gerald said hopefully.

"Give me some time to think this through. It may be nothing. I need to make another phone call to Washington," David said.

There was a rap on the door. Gerald rose and opened it. Mrs. Sawyer stood there looking slightly more calm than usual. "I've got lunch ready for you, Mr. Fitzwilliam. I set everything out on the buffet again. It needs to be eaten while it's nice and hot."

"I'll come with you now," Gerald said. He nodded to David, who had already started to dial the phone, and closed the door.

David's contact in the Department of Defense was out of the office, so he left a message. If his idea was right, some of the things that puzzled him about Kassandra might be clearer. A new idea struck him. He went upstairs to Kassandra's bedroom and opened the hulking address book. As he had hoped, there was a phone number for Eva Dusant, Theo's former mistress. Back in Gerald's office, he called, and Eva answered.

He introduced himself and, irrationally, was disappointed that she didn't remember having met him in New Delhi. When he told her the reason for his call, she said, "Wow! I haven't seen old Theo in a long time—years."

David wondered if any of his own former lovers would someday call him "old David." It was a depressing thought!

"Theo told me you knew Michael Blaine-Poole, the

antiquities buyer," he said quickly. "Does he still do any work for you?"

She seemed to lose interest. "The bottom's fallen out of South Asian art the last few years. Those pieces don't sell anymore, especially the expensive ones. How did you happen to run into Theo?"

"We're both guests at Gerald Fitzwilliam's house in California. Theo's photographing Kassandra Fitzwilliam's antiquities for a book."

"Fitzwilliam? That name's familiar. Wait. Wasn't he an ambassador or something? Amazing that Theo's still working."

"Unfortunately, Kassandra has died, quite suddenly. We're trying to help Gerald sort out her affairs."

"That's too bad." Her voice became wary. "Why're you asking about Michael Blaine-Poole?"

"He bought some antiquities for Kassandra. I was told that you recommended him."

"I wouldn't say 'recommended.' He brought a few pieces into the U.S. for me. Did you want to get in touch with him?"

"No. He's staying here."

"You've got *him* there, too? What fun that house party must be!"

Amused by the sarcasm in her voice, David said, "Were you satisfied that the pieces he got for you were genuine?"

"I never thought they were. Reproductions were all I ever handled. Too much risk with the real ones."

"I'm sure there is. I need to ask you just one more

question—entirely in confidence."

"What is it?" she said doubtfully.

"I know you and Theo used to be close. Did you ever have the impression there was anything in his life he wanted to keep secret?"

She laughed. "You mean aside from me?"

"Well, perhaps—"

"I can think of half a dozen things he'd be arrested for if anybody knew them. Ask him yourself. He'll tell you his life story if you give him enough wine and sympathy."

"Anything that would make him vulnerable to blackmail?"

"Blackmail?" she said incredulously. "This is Theo we're talking about, right? He never let anybody's opinions bother him. Wait! The last time we were together, he told me a long tale about something he did overseas—in Vietnam. I don't remember the details. But who cares about any of that now?"

When he'd hung up the phone, David sat staring at the photographs on Gerald's wall. Pictures from the past. Theo must have taken thousands of them when he was a photojournalist in Vietnam. Was it a picture that Theo Greg wanted to keep secret? Some compromising situation he had been in?

He remembered his odd nervousness when they talked in town. Theo really had seemed worried. But why? As Eva said, it wasn't likely he cared what people knew about his exploits, past or present.

Well, he'd have to track him down again. Finding

Theo full of wine wouldn't require much effort, but giving him sympathy probably would.

When they had finished lunch, he and Gerald took their glasses of iced tea out to one of the wrought iron tables on the terrace. They sat comfortably in silence, a light breeze warm on their arms.

After a while, Gerald stretched. "I don't know what I'd do without Mrs. Sawyer. Those chicken kabobs were as good as any I ever had in the Middle East."

"Delicious. I can only recall one better. Back when I was still eating red meat. Johansen, an AID guy I knew in Izmir, had a cook who made Turkish lamb kabobs. Truly fabulous! You know the Turks think they make the best kabobs in the world?"

"Unless you ask the Iranians or the Pakistanis," Gerald said.

"Well, Johansen's were better than I ever had anywhere. They were so good, they'd make the saliva squirt out of your mouth when you took the first bite!"

"I know just what you mean. My God, how I miss those days," Gerald said. They laughed, the past an easy presence between them.

"However, if I keep eating like this, I'm going to put the pounds I lost back on," Gerald added, patting his stomach.

"I thought you got a lot of exercise these days. You looked really good doing Tai Chi with Detective Perez."

"It's okay for balance and coordination, but I need to do more to work off this pot."

David hated to change the mood, but he knew

nostalgia couldn't keep the present at bay. "Speaking of Detective Perez, we need to talk about this situation, Gerald. What did she question you about this morning?"

Sighing, Gerald said, "She asked me for probably the fourth time if I'd noticed any change in Kass's behavior these past few weeks—if she'd seemed worried about anything. I repeated the same thing I'd said before: 'I think she was worried about money.' I guess Perez doesn't believe me. It's hard for anybody to understand how Kass could pay preposterous amounts for pieces of statuary if she was having financial difficulty." He paused and shook his head. "Now that I've talked to Kass's lawyer, the whole thing is even more baffling."

David put his glass on the table. "You said yesterday that her finances are in a mess."

With a dismissive wave of his hand, Gerald said, "Her will designated a million dollars as a bequest for the Milstone House Foundation, and she left even more to Melanie."

"The docent at the museum told me Kassandra was going to make an endowment to pay for the upkeep of her collection," David said.

"I know! The trustees are undoubtedly counting on that bequest. But that's the problem. She didn't have any money! Even if she had liquidated all of her stock holdings, she would not have had anything like the amount she bequeathed."

"Well, that may take care of everybody's problem. I promised the trustee I'd break the news to you gently. They really don't want the collection."

They both shook their heads incredulously.

"Did Kassandra have that much money when she made her will?" David said.

Gerald shrugged. "Apparently. Her lawyer says she did. But she must have spent it all on the antiquities, or bad investments or something."

"Didn't you know she was having financial trouble?"

"She has always been very secretive about her business affairs. I didn't think about it. My income takes care of our living expenses. Taxes and so forth. And she had a fairly regular income from her investments. She paid for the renovation of the house before we moved in. That was an astronomical amount. Then she took care of repairs to the house and anything else she wanted, I guess. And, of course, she used her own money to buy the antiquities."

"Had she paid Blaine-Poole for the last piece he brought?"

Gerald shrugged. "I have no idea. He says she didn't, and there's no record of a large cash withdrawal in the checkbook I found. But she must have had another account somewhere. I realize now that I didn't know very much about my wife."

He was silent for a moment, his brows knitted in concentration. "Well, I guess I did vaguely realize something was wrong. She had been putting off repairs like that fence out on the headland. But you see, she never told me anything definite. And lately, she began to be extremely confident, as if she were absolutely certain that everything would go her way."

"Are you sure she paid for the antiquities herself?"

"What do you mean? How else could she get them? I certainly never bought any of them." He stood up abruptly and strode to the edge of the terrace. He looked as if he would like to keep on going, but he turned back and shoved his hands into his pockets. "I certainly couldn't afford to subsidize the enterprise, even if I wanted to. It was absolute madness." He sat down again, tasted his tea, and put the glass on the table.

David searched for a better way to say what he had to, but no inspiration came. He cleared his throat. "The reason I asked is that I think Kassandra got the money for her antiquities from another source. I believe she was blackmailing at least one of the people you have staying here, maybe all of them."

He had expected Gerald to be indignant at the suggestion. Instead, he uttered a low groan and sat staring at the ground. Finally, he said, "Are you sure?"

"I don't have proof yet, but I wouldn't say this if there weren't some strong indicators."

"No, I know you wouldn't." Gerald sat slumped in his chair, gazing at the garden with distracted, unfocused eyes.

Without being quite sure how he knew it, David realized that he had misread Gerald's reaction completely. "You aren't surprised, are you?" he said.

Gerald's gaze turned to him and snapped into focus. "I saw Christine for a minute or two this morning after Perez left. I guess you know now that we were together the night Kass died."

It took David a moment to follow the leap in thought.

"I knew when I asked you to come that you'd find out things about Kass," Gerald went on. "I didn't count on your finding out how I feel about Christine."

"You were with her all night?"

"No, of course not! I never stayed more than an hour. On Friday, I was very tired, so I wasn't there that long. This must sound lame to you, but there was nothing immoral between us. Much as I hope we might have more in the future, I don't know whether Christine feels quite the same way I do."

"You didn't realize what Kassandra had in mind when she invited these people to stay here?"

Gerald flushed with chagrin. "I'm afraid my feelings for Christine made it easy for me to ignore what was really going on around me. The museum donation seemed harmless. Then, suddenly, I found myself in the middle of a firestorm. I read some articles in the paper about antiquities looters being arrested, and that same week, Kass's motley crew descended on the house, and she announced she was publishing the book on the collection. I saw how disastrous the consequences would be."

He threw out his arms in a gesture of overwhelming emotion. "Don't you see? When I heard Kass was dead, my first feeling was elation. Release. God help me, for a moment I was glad!"

Bewildered, David waited.

Gerald sat forward eagerly, making short chops with

his hands as he talked. "I didn't understand how I felt about Kass until two days ago. It just came over me suddenly that I had passed from indifference to the point of actively wanting to be rid of her.

"I *wanted* it to be true that Kass was doing something illegal. It didn't occur to me that she might be blackmailing anyone, but I *hoped* she was breaking the law, doing something so bad that she could be stopped. I'm ashamed to admit it. That's what I really hoped you could find out for me."

"Do you feel responsible for what she did?"

"Perhaps I do, in a sense. I should have paid more attention to her when we were overseas. Not only was she buying a lot of antiquities, she was also inordinately interested in people's personal lives. No one ever said anything to me directly, but I imagine it was fairly common knowledge that she occasionally used what she'd learned about people in ways that weren't, well, kosher. I suppose I should have tried to intervene. But those incidents seemed trivial. It wasn't until a few weeks ago that I started to sense the real power she might have over other people."

David longed to stop him, to stop listening. With all of his being, he hoped Gerald had not killed Kassandra. But here he was, defiantly lacing a straitjacket of guilt around himself.

"She started a kind of cat and mouse game with me," Gerald said reflectively, as if he were recalling details from a report. "Last Friday, it became even more obvious. She invited Christine to the house for dinner and kept making not very subtle insinuations. It was uncomfortable, to say the least. I suppose I might have realized what she was doing if I hadn't been so caught up in my own . . . concerns."

Even though he sympathized with Gerald's feelings, David doubted that he was telling him everything. Did he have a part in Kassandra's death? Or were his "concerns" a fear that Melanie might be a killer? David had no doubt that he would do almost anything to keep his child safe.

Gerald looked at him with a question in his eyes. Then, as if he did not want to hear an answer, he stood up. "Let's walk a bit. My knees are getting stiff," he said.

They set out toward the garden. When they had walked for a few minutes, David realized the conversation was not going any further. He said, "I think I'll go back to the house. Theo's probably up from his nap by now. I'd like to talk to him before he gets too far into his afternoon happy hour."

"I want to hear what he has to say, too," Gerald said. "Maybe we can find some clarity in this whole mess after all."

Chapter Twenty-Two

"I think he's in the living room," Gerald said.

They had come into the house by a side door opening into the passage that went past Gerald's study and led into the central hallway.

Theo still had his camera and light equipment set up by a table between the two large built-in cabinets in the living room. He was taking pictures of a bronze statue of Shiva meditating. For once, Holly was not with him.

He turned when he heard them and signaled them to wait. "I'll be finished here in a minute. Time for a break. How 'bout joining me for a drink?"

They exchanged glances. Theo had obviously taken a number of "breaks" already. This was the opportunity they needed. David made drinks for all three of them, and Theo lumbered over to his favorite sofa and plopped down.

Taking the chairs across the large round coffee table

from him, they raised their glasses in a toast, and David had an inclination to laugh. It was as if the three of them had encountered each other fortuitously, like strangers at a cocktail party.

"Did you get all the pictures you wanted of that cypress tree?" David said to start the conversation.

Theo launched into a self-congratulatory description of how well his tree pictures had progressed. "Considering the time I had to spend on the retakes for all those pieces of Kassandra's, it's a wonder I had time to think about anything else. You just wait until you see what I got with that tree. Talk about publishing a book! I might decide to do a whole book on trees. Maybe California trees, New Mexico trees, Colorado—work my way back to New York City. What an idea!"

David tried to calculate how drunk he was. The nap Mrs. Sawyer said he took every day might have mitigated the effects of the cocktails and wine he'd downed with lunch. But as he continued to speak, it was apparent that he had fortified himself further.

Gerald and David tried to keep a conversation going about old times they remembered from overseas posts. Theo participated sporadically, making frequent trips to the sideboard to pour himself glasses of straight Scotch.

Finally, he stumbled into his seat. "I s'pose you want me to tell you the story. Tha's what you want, innit?" He swished the whiskey in the glass and contemplated it, an expression of abject self-pity on his haggard features.

Gerald put his glass down and cleared his throat.

"Really, Theo, as I said—"

"It was so damn hot," Theo began, ignoring him. "You know what it was like in Nam, so humid sweat won't dry. No, tha's right! You two wouldn't know 'bout that, would you? You weren't there, were you?"

When neither took up his challenge, he nodded knowingly and tilted his head as if he were gazing at a distant horizon; his face assumed its air of martyred serenity.

"Another photographer and me were rottin' in a base camp. This other guy was workin' for one o' the wire services. He was a Korean—American, but Korean; you know what I mean. We heard a company was going out to secure a hill 'bove this artillery base."

"I believe South Korea had a battalion there fighting on our side," Gerald said.

Theo frowned at him. "No, he was one of ours. Amer'can, you know, but Korean." He took a swig of Scotch. "Yeah, well, this guy had been waitin' around to catch up with another company, but they were out in some hellhole we couldn't get to, so we just coolin' our heels. One day we heard 'bout this assault they were planning. So we got up there and talked our way onto one of the Chinooks.

"They dropped us in this clearing full of trees blown down by a bomb. I got to look for those pictures. Maybe put one in my tree book. So, anyway, big trees, piled up all 'round us like toothpicks." He swept his arm up in a wide arc, spilling a spot of whiskey on the couch. He rubbed the spots with two fingers and went on.

"At first it looked like we'd picked a bust. But then, when the last couple o' birds were comin' in, the bastards start firin' down on us from the ridge. Jesus! There we are, caught in this clearin' full of logs. We have to climb over, jump over, roll over these goddamned piles of tree trunks to get under cover.

"The noise was awful! Machine guns, choppers, screaming." His eyes brightened as he began to catch the excitement of the memory.

"Soon as my butt's covered, I start snappin' away! We're just shootin' pictures in any direction we can. The rest of the time, huggin' the dirt. I look up in the tree behind me and see this flash of metal. In a minute I realize it's a Claymore! One lucky shot and the bastards on the hill could set it off. It would'a shredded us!

"I told the Korean, 'Les get outta here.' We start to crawl away from the bomb. The noise keeps gettin' louder and louder! I'll never forget that noise. It'd drive you crazy all by itself."

He wiped his hand across his mouth, hunched forward in his enthusiasm, and took another gulp. "About an hour later, it gets quiet for a while, and the company commander tells us he sent for a Medevac bird for the wounded. He says, 'You two better get on it 'cause it might be your last ride outta here for hours.' He didn't have to convince us. The chopper comes in. They're gettin' the wounded aboard, and we make a run for it.

"Damn if the bastards on the hill don't start firin' on us again. We keep runnin' and jumpin' over those damned logs.

".Just before we made it to the bird, they got the Korean in the back. I grabbed him by the arm and tried to keep runnin'. Then a bullet caught me in the thigh." Theo rubbed his hand along the outside of his left thigh in what was apparently a habitual gesture.

"A medic runs over to help us, and we make it to the door of the chopper. They pulled us in, and somehow, they got us out of there. I was next to the door, hangin' on to a pole for dear life, and the Korean was lyin' up 'gainst the back wall of the plane. They get us out of range, and I look over and see he's dead." Theo stopped, his shoulders sagging. "He should'a waited for the other company."

"What about the picture?" David urged him.

Theo roused himself, blinking, and began again more slowly and clearly. "We got back to the base. When we landed, I saw this roll of exposed film on the floor, next to his body. Fell out of his hand or his pocket. I picked it up. I wasn't thinking. My leg hurt like hell. I just stuck the thing in my bag and forgot about it.

"Back in Saigon, I developed all the film I had. That's when I saw the picture!" His bloodshot eyes misted and his voice filled with awe. "One of those shots that happen like a miracle."

David had seen the photograph, as had millions around the world. It was one of a few that had become symbols of the Vietnam conflict, and it had made this man a minor legend in his field.

"That shot was pure chance! It wasn't like anybody

spent hours planning and setting it up. The firefight was happening right in front of us. We were aiming at the same things. That picture was an accident! A blood-sucking nemesis of an accident!" His voice cracked, and he sat with his head hanging.

The words "Oh, what a tangled web we weave" slid across David's mind, but Theo's revelation hadn't given him any satisfaction. He felt regret for the man whose work Theo had stolen. He even pitied Theo. Living with that burden had shaped the rest of his life. And when Kassandra came along, hungry for power, it served her purpose well.

"How did Kassandra find out about the picture?" he said.

Hunched in his misery, Theo did not appear to hear him.

David glanced at Gerald, who shook his head and shrugged.

"Damned witch divined it," Theo said suddenly. "Conjured it up with those bronze idols of hers."

"But you developed the film yourself. If you never told anyone else, how could she possibly have known?" David insisted.

"Divined it, like I said. Told me in Delhi she knew. Damned witch." A look of guilt or embarrassment crossed Theo's features. "Sorry, Gerald, but you know how she was." He looked at them in defiant appeal.

"You can't mean Kassandra's been blackmailing you since we were in New Delhi," Gerald said weakly.

Theo drained his glass and held it up for a moment.

"I need a refill," he mumbled, heaving his bulk out of the seat with a grunt. He lunged to the sideboard and held on with his left hand while he slopped whiskey into his glass. Still clinging to the furniture for balance, he raised his glass in a toast. "To tellers of secrets. May they burn in Hell! If there is a Hell to burn in." He swayed.

Frustrated with him, David said, "Even if Kassandra knew you didn't take the picture, what could she have gained by telling anyone about it?"

Theo lumbered toward them and eased his bulk carefully onto the couch. He leaned back in a dramatic pose. "What is honor but vanity? Tell the world Theo Greg's a fake." His lips trembled.

For an uneasy moment, it looked as though he might break down and cry.

"Let me get this straight," David said quickly. "Kassandra found out about the photograph when she was in India. Did she ask for money then?"

"Never said 'nother word for years. I thought all was forgotten. Ha!" He threw his head back and gazed into the shadowy ceiling beams.

David studied him. To be publicly exposed as a fraud and a thief, all of the work he had done since then devalued by the scandal. It would be devastating to any man. To one like Theo, unbearable. "How did she approach you? Did she write to you?"

Theo shook his head. "Comes to see us in San Francisco. Invites Holly and me here. Wants me to photograph her collection for the book! You 'member,

Gerald, year before last. Gets me out in the kitchen one night. Special bottle o' brandy she's savin' for me."

His voice rose to a grotesque falsetto. "Theo, I must have a really good record of my collection. I know you'll do a fabulous job with it. It will be your legacy." Dropping back to his own gravelly bass, he said, "Who's gonna pay for it? She says, 'We'll do it together, Theo.'" He scowled. "She pretends that's all she wants. But I know." He shook his finger portentously. "I'll never get away from her."

They sat in silence, stunned. In less than a minute, Theo began to snore softly.

"What a mess," Gerald said. "I can't excuse what he did, but my God, Kass made his life miserable. I feel responsible for that part. I should have done something."

"I think we have an explanation now for the clipping and the addresses in Korea and New York," David said. "Presumably, Kassandra knew or thought she knew the identity of the man who actually took the picture. I wonder if she got in touch with his family. More likely, she just kept the ammunition on hand to prove that her threat had substance."

Gerald shook his head. "If I were in Theo's shoes, I don't know what I'd have done."

Chapter Twenty-Three

On his way to get coffee, David glanced to the left toward Gerald's study. At the end of the hallway, the door that led outside stood ajar. He saw the shadow of someone who had just gone through it. Realizing that Holly must have overheard her husband's confession, he went after her.

When he rounded the corner of the house, he saw her nearly running across the lawn toward the garden. The breeze jerked at her long skirt and scarf, giving her the look of a tattered jade-green sail.

David sprinted after her, and as he came close, he could see that her shoulders were rigid with tension.

"Holly, wait! Let me talk to you a minute," he said.

She slowed, but kept walking.

He touched the back of her arm. "Please wait."

She stopped so quickly that he almost ran into her. She rounded on him with fury. "You just had to do it, didn't you? You goaded him until you got what you wanted. You ought to be ashamed of yourself. You came here pretending to be Theo's friend but you've been spying on all of us!"

Resisting an impulse to laugh at Holly's interpretation of his relationship with Theo, David said, "Theo's hurting himself by refusing to tell Detective Perez about Kassandra's blackmail. Perez is suspicious of you two because she knows you're hiding something."

Holly turned away and strode into the garden, her sandals smacking the hard walkway. David kept pace with her. When they reached the shade of the hedges and she slowed down, he said, "I'm sorry you had to hear what Theo told us. It must be upsetting to find out about it like that."

"Upsetting? Are you kidding? You think I didn't know what Kassandra was doing to him?"

"I meant what he told us about the past."

"That he took credit for the Korean's picture?" She looked away. "He's told me that story a dozen times."

David was even more surprised by this attitude from Holly than he had been by Theo's confession. "How did Kassandra find out?"

"The same way you did, I assume. She probably worked on him when he was drunk. It wouldn't take much to break him down. She was a witch all right, but not the kind he thinks."

"Could she really have done anything to damage his career after all this time?"

"She had proof. I'm sure she had."

"That's what you were looking for in Kassandra's room? Not the pictures or the notes for the book?"

"Of course, not. I got rid of the notes. Nobody would ever have published them anyway. I've always had the pictures. I knew she must have had something else, something she showed to Theo to scare him that much. Just a threat wouldn't have done it."

"Gerald found a clipping about a Korean-American along with a couple of addresses in her safe deposit box. The clipping was an obituary. I assume the addresses related to the man's family. Even so, nothing in that material proves who took the Vietnam picture. If Kassandra tried to make it public, Theo could just claim that she was mistaken."

Stopping, Holly said urgently, "You don't understand. She didn't say she was going to expose him, not one word about blackmail. She didn't even demand money directly. She just told him she wanted him to photograph her precious statues for a book and she was sure he would want to help her publish it.

"He kept making excuses for not doing it, and she kept after him, flattering him, telling him what a boost this book would be for his reputation. And hinting, always hinting; it drove me mad."

"How did she contact him initially? Didn't it seem odd that the Fitzwilliams would get in touch with Theo? They weren't friends."

"Kassandra claimed they were looking up all the people they'd known over the years. It was very friendly in the beginning. They came down to San Francisco. I think the excuse was to go to the symphony. She called Theo and invited us to dinner at the Oak Room in the St. Francis Hotel. We had to take a taxi. Parking is a pain around Union Square, but Theo was flattered, and she fooled me for a while, too, because she didn't start working on him then."

"You had no idea what she had in mind?"

"I didn't suspect anything. I never really liked her, but I just thought she was one of those silly women who somehow manage to get much more than they deserve from life."

David felt sympathy for Holly. He thought envy had probably been her life's mooring. "When did you find out what she really wanted?"

"Last year she invited us to come up here for a house party. She had a sort of reunion of journalists and other people who were in India when Theo was there. That was when she closed the trap. She gathered all of us in the living room and said, 'I'm so pleased to announce that Theo has agreed to photograph my collection.' What could he do then? He had to pretend to like the idea."

Recalling his conversation with Eva, David knew they'd both been wrong about Theo. He said, "I didn't think other people's opinions mattered to him."

"They were people in his profession!" Holly said impatiently. "All journalists. One teaches at the state university near us. I think one of them still works for AP. Every person there was part of Kassandra's web."

Hovering between amazement and laughter, David

said, "Kassandra couldn't have been blackmailing all of them!"

Holly almost smiled. "Why not? She might have been. I just know what it would have done to Theo if she'd started hinting about his picture in a group like that. A rumor is all it would take to humiliate him."

David was aware for the first time of how sophisticated Kassandra's network of manipulation had been. "Her weapon was the illusion of power she created. By gathering those people together, she let Theo and maybe her other victims know how easy it would be for her to expose them."

"Now you understand!" she said. "It shattered Theo when he realized what she was doing. Neither of us could sleep for weeks afterward."

"I had no idea she had put you through an ordeal like this," David said.

Holly looked gratified. "I tried to think of a way to get out of her clutches. Look what it's done to Theo," she continued, her voice rising. "His drinking, his wasted talent. He was trying so hard to finish those miserable pictures. The fall quarter at his college starts in September. He has to get back home to prepare his classes. Kassandra didn't care. She kept making him do retakes, even when the pictures were beautiful. She was the meanest human being I've ever known."

"What she did hurt you as much as it did Theo."

Her cheeks darkened, showing up the coarse, blotchy skin under her makeup and the ravages of a lifetime of discontent. She gave him a doubting look and then thrust her hand into her knitted bag. Pulling out a crumpled tissue, she held it to her mouth, as if to stem tears that might come. Her hand was trembling.

"You can't imagine how horrible it was. It wasn't just the threat hanging over us. It was living with that secret all these years. I've never been free of fear. Never!" She crossed her thin arms, hugging herself, and walked on, gazing miserably at the horizon. The little twist of tissue fluttered to the walkway, marring its immaculate surface.

David glanced at it, vaguely annoyed but unwilling to pick it up.

"Did you know about Theo's picture when Kassandra first contacted you two years ago?" he said.

"Of course I knew. Theo has never kept a secret from me in his life."

She looked at him sharply, and David thought it likely that she'd also known about Theo's long-term affair with Eva. Perhaps giving up his mistress had been the price Theo paid for Holly's willingness to keep the secret of the famous photograph.

"I suppose you think I don't know about that blond tramp he used to meet overseas, either," she said.

David couldn't react quite fast enough to keep her from seeing how disconcerted he was that she'd read his thoughts.

"Theo said you were in love with her, too," she went on. "Of course I knew about her. I knew everything. He is such a fool!"

Not bothering to correct Theo's lie about him, David

said, "How come you stayed with him if you knew about Eva?"

"Why shouldn't I? He was never going to marry her. When he couldn't keep up the crazy life he was living, I'd still be there. After a while, he couldn't get along without me," she went on. "That's why Kassandra had to have me in on the deal. All of our accounts are in my name. I write the checks."

"So Kassandra did demand some kind of payment from you?"

"She tried. I told her we couldn't afford to give her anything, but she still thought she could force Theo to pay for publishing her book. How many thousands of dollars would that have cost?"

Holly began walking again, slowly. "I made up my mind on Friday night that we were never coming back here. Never taking another one of her phone calls. Never giving her another moment of Theo's time and talent. It was up to me to stop her!"

She nodded several times, as if she were assuring herself of her determination. "I'm glad someone else did it, though. I'd hate to go to jail for something like that."

"Do you know who did it, Holly?"

"I told the police what I saw, but they didn't believe me."

"How about the night Ellie, the maid, died? Did you see who killed her?"

"I didn't see any killing either night, but I know Melanie was there. You can't mistake that mane of hair she's got."

"You went outside Monday night, didn't you?"

She looked up at him. "How do you know?"

"You were frustrated because Perez wouldn't believe you saw someone the night Kassandra died, so I'm thinking that when you saw that person again, you went outside to find out who it was. You've got a lot of courage."

Again, she looked pleased. "I had to get my shoes and my robe on, so by the time I got out here, she was gone."

"Then, you didn't actually see Melanie?"

"I'm sure it was her, and I think that detective believes me this time."

Chapter Twenty-Four

"Glad I caught up with you. I called you from the window but I suppose you couldn't hear me," Gerald said.

Flushed and agitated, he turned to Holly Greg. "Theo needs a little help, Holly. He . . . er, he's on the couch. I tried to get him to go upstairs."

Holly said nothing. Anger and humiliation in her eyes, she turned and stalked away.

David waited a moment before he said, "Theo's passed out?"

"He's snoring like a train. Would have left him there, but Detective Perez just called. She's coming to talk to us. To you and me anyway. I don't want her to see him passed out on the couch like some comatose bear."

"What does she want?"

"I'm trying not to let myself speculate." He rose up on his toes in a vain attempt to see over the hedges.

"This damned garden always feels like a maze to me."

"How much time do we have?" David said as they went along the path.

"She's already on her way here. We're supposed to meet her at the meditation room. She'll probably be there when we arrive." He was rubbing his left thumb against his forefinger rapidly, a habit David knew meant more than usual agitation.

"I tried to suggest meeting in the house instead, but she wants to talk to us about something in that appalling meditation building. I haven't been able to walk past it since the girl was found there. I'll tell you, I feel like having it bulldozed into the ocean."

"Is that what you're planning to do with it?"

Gerald threw him a sardonic look. "You obviously don't live in California. In this state, such an act would bring environmentalists and the coastal commissioners down on my head in droves."

David chuckled, and they walked on in silence until they came out of the garden near the meditation room.

Perez was waiting for them, her feet planted squarely and her expression grave.

Putting on his diplomat's smile, Gerald reached to shake hands with her, and David prepared to intervene if he became excessively gregarious, as he occasionally did when he was nervous.

Perez curtailed any tendency in that direction. "I'd like to go over one or two things about Ellie Victor's death again," she said curtly.

"I don't know what I can add. I told you all I know,"

Gerald began.

"We'll get through this as quickly as we can," Perez said. She detached the tape barrier, unlocked the door, and stood aside for them to enter.

David tensed, ready for the oppressiveness of the room, but it was warm and dry. It smelled strongly of chlorine and faintly of the stench he had encountered when he found the body. The waves came into the cave below in muted splashes.

"I've never liked this room," Gerald complained, his voice high and hollow in the domed space.

Perez looked far from relaxed herself. "We won't be long if you'll just help me out here."

They gathered around the empty pool. Where the water had been, the tile was covered with a crusty, whitish mineral deposit that would have to be scraped off by a professional pool cleaner, but David doubted that Gerald would bother with any maintenance now.

"You saw Ellie Victor in this pool one other time before the day you found her body. Right, Mr. Markam?" Perez said.

David acknowledged that he had, matching her businesslike tone. He sensed a change in her attitude toward him, and he wasn't sure why.

"You also saw her in other places around the estate?"

"In the kitchen the morning after I arrived. About ten, I'd guess. We had finished breakfast. And then a little later, she was sitting on the steps leading up to the apartment over the garage." He thought for a moment. "I must have seen her a couple more times. She was almost always in the kitchen with Mrs. Sawyer when I went through there."

"You had other conversations with her?"

"I'd hardly call them conversations. We exchanged a few words when she was here in the pool, before Melanie came in. Maybe a word or two in the house."

"When you talked to her here in the pool, was she wearing any clothing?"

He gave himself a moment to answer, wondering what she was getting at. "When I first came in, I thought she was naked. But then she sat up and I could see she had on a bathing suit."

Perez stepped away from the pool, frowning. Finally, she looked directly at him. "I'm sorry to have to put you through this—it's uncomfortable for all of us, but I need you to show me again exactly what you did when you came in and found the girl dead."

Gerald, who had sat down on the padded wall bench, raised his head. He looked thoroughly miserable.

Perez went around the pool and stood where she could watch both of them.

Moving closer to the pool, David said, "I couldn't see anything when I first came in. The room was full of steam. I heard the motor running. I felt along the wall until I found the switches to turn the light on and the motor off."

"Did you leave the door open?" Perez said.

"I don't remember. I must have. Or maybe one of the switches I pushed was an exhaust fan. The steam began to clear, and I saw the body. I tried to lift her."

"Why?"

He stared at her. "To see if she was still alive. It was a reflex."

"Can you show me how you did that?"

Reluctantly, David knelt on one knee by the pool. "I grabbed her arm with my right hand and pulled her up." He demonstrated the movement. "There wasn't any doubt she was dead."

"What did you do then?"

"I really don't remember too much. I looked around, trying to figure out what had happened."

Perez went back around the pool and stood near Gerald. "Did Ellie use this pool often, Mr. Fitzwilliam?"

Gerald started, as if he hadn't expected the questions to shift to him so quickly. His eyes widened. "Well, I . . . I don't think I know. This was Kassandra's place. I certainly never was in the pool myself. I can't even remember the last time I was in this building. Melanie came down here from time to time, I believe. Really, I can't say who else used it. Of course Kassandra's nightly meditation time was sacrosanct, as I told you before. Everyone respected that." He stood up and clasped his hands behind his back. His face was beginning to perspire.

"Do you ever go for walks in the garden in the evenings?" Perez said casually.

David kept his eyes on the ocean and sky he could see out the window, knowing Gerald would assume he had told Perez what he'd said about Christine.

"I've never enjoyed walking outside at night," Gerald

said. "Perhaps it comes from living too long in places where my movements were subject to security considerations."

"So you never went outside at night?"

"I may have strolled around the grounds on occasion. I wonder why you're asking."

Clearly not intending to satisfy that curiosity, Perez looked at David squarely as if she were calculating how much help or hindrance he might be if she confronted Gerald.

There was a knock on the door. Ken Laird opened it and walked in. "Do any of you know where Melanie's gone?" he said.

Perez looked annoyed. "She's not in the house? I need to talk to her as soon as we finish here."

Gerald moved closer to the door. "Is she out with Blaine-Poole again?"

Laird's eyes narrowed. "I didn't see her leave, but her car's gone."

Giving David an enigmatic look, Gerald said, "I hope you have finished with me, Detective Perez. We need to see what's going on. Ken, why don't you call the pub and ask if she's there?" He put a hand on Laird's shoulder, urging him out the door.

Perez made no attempt to stop him from leaving. When they had gone, she turned to David.

"Thank you for doing this. It helps me see things more clearly."

"You were more interested in Gerald's responses than in mine," he said.

She looked away. "It was all helpful." Scanning the room as if to fix impressions, she went down the stairs.

David followed her. "You told me the other day you thought Gerald was guilty. That's what this whole exercise today was for."

"No. I did not say that." She paused at the bottom of the stairs, then turned to go.

David stood his ground. "You implied it. When you and I talked about this investigation, you didn't tell me you were going to use me to get Gerald."

"And you didn't say you'd be trying to shelter your friends." She glanced back, not stopping.

He was beside her in three strides. "I'm not sheltering anybody. They aren't telling me much, either."

When they reached her SUV, she opened the door and put her foot on the step. Instead of getting in, she rested her arm on the frame of the open window and gave him a searching look.

"Maybe this whole idea of asking you to get involved was wrong. I'm sorry." The brown eyes were serious, and he knew she felt compassion for Gerald. But it wouldn't alter her intention.

When he didn't respond, she said, "I know these people have told you things; I can see it in your face. You're sure, or almost sure, that one of them is a killer, aren't you?"

"You don't expect me to answer that."

He saw a bitter frown before she bent her head. When she looked up again, he knew she'd chosen another line of approach. She shut the door of the vehicle and leaned against it, crossing her arms over her chest.

"The more I think about it, the more I think you're right about the ambassador," she said as if she were musing aloud. "He just doesn't seem like the kind who resorts to killing."

"I'm glad you think that. So do I."

"Then it must be Melanie you're worried about," she added in that same musing tone.

David kicked a rock. He knew very well that Melanie could have killed Kassandra alone. Or with Ken Laird's help. It alarmed him to see how damning the circumstances around her were.

"Holly Greg told me she convinced you that she saw Melanie outside. Apparently, on the nights of both murders," he said.

"Don't you believe her?"

"I'm not sure what to believe. I do know her main interest is keeping harm away from Theo. Who she'd knock down to achieve that, I can't say."

"Have you talked to Theo Greg?"

"Yes, if you call listening to one of his drunken tales talking to him, I have. And I've had a few conversations with Gerald, too. I'm in the same boat you are. Who's telling the truth? What has been left out?"

"But you've found out something you know is important, and you're not sure you want to tell me, haven't you?" Perez said.

"I haven't wanted to tell you anything! But since I had the colossal arrogance to believe I could help

Gerald's family by working with you, I find myself stuck in a hard place."

"Let's get back to Melanie. Which of those men would have been willing to help her, Laird or Blaine-Poole?"

He tried to keep from showing how unnerving her mindreading was.

"It's Laird, isn't it?" she persisted. "He's the likely one. An army officer. He's already trained to kill. I assume he and Melanie are lovers."

"You'll have to ask them," he said sullenly.

"If they are, what do you think that might suggest?"

David looked to see if the sarcasm in her voice was reflected in her eyes. They were bright, hard, hunter's eyes.

"What does it suggest to you?" he countered.

Perez continued to stare.

"Do you have any evidence against Melanie other than what Holly Greg imagines she saw?" he demanded.

Her lips compressed, drawing her skin taut over her cheekbones. With a slight jerk of her head, she made it clear she would not answer.

Opening the door again and swinging up into the seat, she said, "Here's one thing I can tell you. The ambassador is not helping himself or his daughter by lying to me about where he was the night his wife died."

She slammed the door and put the key into the ignition. Without looking at him she went on: "And Christine Moreland, too. Do they think I'm stupid? I know they were together sometime during that night."

She turned to look at him.

When he didn't respond, she made a sound of exasperation and leaned over to start the engine. "I'll be back here later this evening to interview Melanie and her father again. They'd both better be here." She revved the engine and put the truck into gear.

David turned toward the house. The sun was low on the horizon, the breeze strengthening and blowing mist in from the ocean. He felt an urgency to find Melanie.

Reenacting the scene in the meditation room had forced him to remember in detail the first time he saw Ellie in the pool, lying there so contemptuously defying Melanie. Melanie's face twisted in fury, Ellie's so confident. An idea he had not wanted to consider began to crowd his mind as he walked. He had to find Melanie before another night came to this place.

Chapter Twenty-Five

Ken Laird was sitting alone at one of the tables on the terrace, clutching a glass of beer.

"Melanie isn't back yet," he said by way of greeting.

David glanced at his watch. "Did you call the bar?"

"They didn't answer their phone."

"She and Blaine-Poole might have gone somewhere else—maybe into town for dinner."

Laird looked disgusted. "She was in one of her wild moods. When I saw her a couple of hours ago, she said she was getting out of this place and never coming back."

"There's going to be a problem if she isn't here by the time Perez and her crew show up again."

"Is Perez going to arrest her? Melanie didn't kill anybody. They're just looking for a scapegoat," he added, his voice truculent.

David wanted to take Laird into his confidence, but if

Perez was right, he might be shielding Melanie, too. "She might very well arrest her. I don't know. The important thing is that Melanie's out there with Blaine-Poole. I'm worried about her. I think we need to go and find her."

Laird looked as if he might argue; then, he seemed to catch the urgency in David's voice. He rose, grabbing a windbreaker lying on the chair next to him.

They found Gerald in the kitchen with Mrs. Sawyer, who was leaning over an oven rack, basting a turkey. Gerald stood in front of a large wooden salad bowl, his shirtsleeves rolled up, enthusiastically tearing romaine lettuce. In spite of the dark circles under his eyes, he did not look as agitated as he had before.

When they told him where they were going, he said, "I appreciate that. I doubt there's any real cause for concern, but I'd feel better if she were here." He cast a slightly embarrassed look at Laird. "Don't let Melanie's behavior bother you too much, Ken. She doesn't mean half of the things she says and does."

"Detective Perez is coming back this evening. She expects Melanie to be here," David said.

Mrs. Sawyer closed the oven door. "I wish Detective Perez would leave us alone. If she comes while you're eating dinner, I'll try to keep her from disturbing you."

David doubted that Mrs. Sawyer, or any of them, could deter Perez for long.

The wind was stronger when they went out to the garage, blowing gusts of mist in from the ocean. In the dim light remaining, the pine trees had taken on a gray tint, branches quivering nervously.

Wishing he'd put on a jacket instead of a sweater, he turned to go back into the house and caught sight of Ellie's white cat curled up on the steps leading to the apartment over the garage. Looking up at the windows, he saw a curtain move at the middle one, and he had an impression of a face. He hesitated, vaguely concerned, but Laird had already started Kassandra's Mercedes. He got in beside him.

They moved along the shadowy lane of eucalyptus at a sedate pace. At the highway, Laird accelerated, hunched tensely over the wheel, peering into the mist that lay across the road. "I just wish I knew what made Melanie freak out like this. She's gone crazy!" he said.

"Melanie's always loved to be dramatic," David said. Hoping to calm Laird down, he said, "I remember one time when she was a kid—maybe eleven. She manipulated Gerald's driver into taking her to a bazaar to buy some material for a costume. Then, she bullied the whole staff into watching her and a friend of hers act out a play they'd made up." He chuckled. "What a ham she was."

Laird seemed to relax a little. "She still is, once in a while."

"She told everybody she was going to be an actress. I wonder what happened to that ambition."

"Lost, along with a lot of other things, I guess," Laird said bitterly. "She's like so many Foreign Service and military kids. Living everywhere makes them sophisticated, but they never really find a place to belong in the world."

"Yes, I know. My father was in the Air Force," David said. He felt like adding, I have that same affliction. Instead, he said, "You've been taking care of her for a long time, haven't you?"

If Laird objected to the suggestion, he gave no sign.

"Melanie told me her flirting with Blaine-Poole made you jealous," David persisted.

Unexpectedly, Laird laughed. "She only says things like that when she's insecure or drinking too much."

"Then, you didn't mind her being in the hot tub with him?"

"I didn't say that." After a moment of silence, Laird said, "It's this situation that's got her so upset. She's scared to death that Gerald might have had something to do with Kassandra's death. And now that this girl's been killed—who's Perez trying to pin *that* on?"

David shook his head. "I think she's fishing at this point."

They came to a stop sign and Laird barely hesitated. "I thought for a while she was aiming at me."

"Why is that?" David said as casually as he could. He wished fervently that he were behind the wheel himself.

"They think Kassandra died around the time that I was outside walking. Perez kept asking me if I'd seen or heard anything. I said, 'Haven't you been out on the headland on a windy night? The wind does the same thing to your hearing that fog does to your vision.' I wish she'd quit hounding us. Kassandra was a monster, especially the way she treated Melanie. But none of us was ready to murder her."

"I don't disagree with you. Kassandra must have made a lot of enemies. Apparently, she had a practice of finding out things about people and using their secrets to pressure them for favors. I'm just beginning to understand how elaborate her network of manipulation was. I guess Perez assumes Melanie and Gerald were the main targets, but she probably thinks you're in it, too. Is she right? Did Kassandra know anything damaging about you?"

Laird glanced at him and then looked back at the road. "Perez sure picked the right guy to be her inside man."

David began to protest but then thought better of it. He waited. Finally, Laird said, "It seems almost funny now. Kassandra believed she was so subtle. She never actually made threats. One night at a party, she took me aside and told me that if I needed help, I could count on her.

"I didn't know what she was talking about until later. Then I realized she was just letting me know that she *knew*. She wasn't any run-of-the-mill busybody. She was an information-gathering machine. Her system put our intel methods to shame."

"Melanie said almost the same thing," David began, but Laird surged on.

"She couldn't resist baiting Kassandra. Then, after Kassandra dropped the bombshell that she wasn't going to finance her business, Melanie just stopped caring what happened." With a swift glance over his shoulder, Laird pulled into the left lane and accelerated to overtake a pickup. David braced himself for meeting another car on the narrow road.

"Didn't she tell you about that when you talked to her?" Laird demanded.

David clutched the seatbelt strap. "I could think a little clearer if we weren't doing road trials for the Grand Prix."

When Laird slowed the car slightly, David said, "She's still carrying a lot of resentment against Gerald. And she told me how much she hated Kassandra's influence over him."

"That's all?" Laird looked disappointed. "You haven't heard the whole story."

"Well, somebody should tell me. Perez isn't taking me into her confidence right now, but I'm reasonably sure she thinks either Melanie or Gerald is guilty."

"Melanie did not kill Kassandra!" Laird's face darkened with anger. "She was in her room. She didn't go back outside that night."

"You were watching the house?"

"No. But I know Melanie. Can you imagine her throwing a woman off a cliff? Can you?"

David thought about the fury he had seen in Melanie's eyes when she talked about her stepmother. She did have a distorted view of reality, one that might lead to violence if she were desperate enough. Then, there was Holly's story that Melanie was outside on the nights of both deaths. He just couldn't be sure.

They rounded a corner and saw a low cinderblock building perched at the edge of the bluff. Its signboard identified it as the Last Chance.

Laird swung the car into the parking lot and turned off the ignition but made no move to open the door. "She's hated Kassandra the whole time I've known her," he said as if he were musing aloud. "If she was going to kill her, I don't know why she waited this long."

"What's the other part of the story that I haven't heard?" David said.

Laird looked at him sharply. "Do you know what caused Melanie's divorce?"

Aware that he knew little about Melanie's adult life, David said, "I asked her why she left her husband, but she changed the subject."

Laird sighed. "That little brat. She said she'd told you the truth. She likes for people to think that she left Philip. But he divorced *her*. He was in Europe on a short-term assignment and ended up staying over there several more weeks following up on the negotiations. He knew the baby wasn't his."

"Baby?"

Laird swore softly. "How far is this going, Markam? Does Perez get a full report?"

"Come on, man. You know I'd never give her information you told me in confidence."

"Noble of you."

"Are you saying that Melanie got pregnant when her husband Philip was overseas? What happened to the baby?"

Laird's face became a tense mask. "She had an abortion."

"Why?" David said, startled. Then, he remembered the column in Kassandra's third ledger with the heading "P-Overseas" and a list of dates. The meaning became clear—these must have been the times Melanie's husband Philip was away from Washington on temporary assignments.

"She was trying to save her marriage, I guess. She was so confused. The marriage had already gone sour, but she couldn't stand for Gerald to know what she'd done."

"So that's the hold Kassandra had over her. By threatening to tell Gerald about the abortion, she forced Melanie to design the layout for her book."

"I don't think it was that blatant. Melanie wanted to open that shop in San Francisco so badly! She agreed to do the design work because Kassandra promised to finance the business. Then Kassandra reneged on the deal."

A powerful combination of reasons to kill, David thought. "The Fitzwilliams had already moved out to California by the time Melanie's marriage broke up, hadn't they? How did Kassandra even know about the abortion?"

Laird shook his head. "Phillip found out. He probably told her."

"The child was yours?"

Again the tormented look in Laird's eyes. "I begged her to keep the baby. But I've never had any illusions about Melanie. She is what she is. And I am what I am. Ten years older than she is and a long way from being able to afford the lifestyle she wants."

"Then, why—?"

"She always comes back to me. She knows I love her. I'm the one who'll take care of her."

David envied him that. He knew too well what it was to lose a woman and never stop wanting her back. Even after that fiasco of a marriage Layne had rushed into, David was sure he would have forgiven her if she'd come back to him. It was a galling realization, but he knew it was true.

The wind buffeted them as they stepped from the car. Through the fog, two fuzzy neon beer signs glowed orange and blue from the windows of the bar, and the parking lot lights were bright blurs. Throbbing, deep bass rhythm blared from the building, abnormally clear, as if amplified by the dense air. Near the entrance of the crowded parking lot, they saw Melanie's red Jaguar.

A blast of country music and smoky air hit them when they opened the door. They stood for a few moments, adjusting to the hazy light and scanning the crowd of people at small tables or hunched over the long wooden bar.

"I don't see them," Laird said. He went to the bar and spoke to one of the bartenders. When he came back, his frown was deeper. "He knows Melanie. He's the same guy who was making drinks when we were here last time. He says they left a few minutes ago."

"But her car's still in the lot."

They looked at each other. Laird's face was rigid.

"She and Blaine-Poole must be out on the headland together. I think we'd better go and look for them," David said.

"Together? Doing what?" Laird shouted. He punched the wall. "I'm sick of this shit! I'm through running after her. Let her go to hell!" He started out the door.

Realizing the man was ready to break, David grabbed his shoulder. "You can tell her that later. Right now, we've got to find her. You said yourself she's in a wild mood. Even if she is with Blaine-Poole, she might be in real trouble. We've got to find her, Ken!"

Laird's eyes narrowed, the angry lover giving way to the soldier. "Let's go." He plunged through the doorway. "There's a path that runs from the edge of the parking lot across the top of the bluff. They must be out there somewhere."

"Maybe they're down on the beach," David said as they crossed the parking lot. The mist began to break up and was drifting.

Laird surged ahead. "There's no beach below the bluffs. Just rocks down there. Follow me and be careful."

The pole lamps in the parking lot gave them enough light to see a few yards along a rutted path through the tall, dried grass, but as they moved away from the light, shadow closed over them, blinding them until their eyes adjusted to the deepening darkness.

"Just keep close behind me. Don't look at your feet. Try to feel the ground as you put each foot down,"

Laird said with authority.

The bluff sloped gradually, and the sound of the surf on their right side was louder now that they were closer. The throbbing bass from the bar still pounded behind them, distorted, as if it were a fitful heartbeat of the land itself.

A wail came from farther along the cliff and a muffled sound of running feet. "Melanie," Laird shouted. "Melanie, where are you?"

"No, Ken! Stay away! It's too late to save me," she shrieked.

Laird stood still. "Melanie! Stop running! We're close to the edge. I can't see you. Where are you?"

"Leave me alone," she screamed. Her voice seemed farther away, but Laird walked toward the sound without hesitation, continuing to talk to her as he went.

She was sobbing when they reached her. Laird lifted her gently from where she was huddled in the dry grass. He took out a handkerchief and began to dab the mascara-stained tears. Jerking it away from him, she covered her eyes, but she leaned against him, allowing him to pull her to her feet and help her walk.

Blaine-Poole was standing under a light when they reached the edge of the lot. He started toward Melanie, "What's all this fuss about, luv?"

"Don't touch me!" she screamed. She began to sob again.

Laird put both arms around her. "Get the fuck away from her, you son of a bitch!" he shouted at Blaine-Poole. He urged Melanie along. "I won't let him hurt you," he assured her.

When they reached the Jaguar, David turned to Blaine-Poole. "Can you take Melanie's car back to the house?"

Blaine-Poole pulled the keys from his pocket. "I drove it here; should be able to make it go the other way."

David would have liked to kick him. He told Laird, "Just take care of Melanie. I'll drive the Mercedes."

"Are you sure you can do it with that messed-up arm?"

"You've got to take care of her," David said, glancing at Melanie. As hysterical as she was, they couldn't be sure what she would do.

It had been several months since he had driven. Aside from an occasional short trip in a Consulate or Embassy car, he seldom drove overseas. As he had expected, the unfamiliar movements strained his arm muscles, but the big car made steering on the winding road fairly easy.

Melanie had stopped sobbing by the time they reached the house. When they got her into the living room, she sank down onto one of the couches and began to moan softly.

Mrs. Sawyer came in, and Laird asked her to bring blankets and pillows.

"I'll warm some milk for her, too," she said.

She was back with the bedding in a few minutes. As she was leaving, Gerald hurried in. She stopped him. "Sir, I just wanted to let you know. Mr. Blaine-Poole came in through the kitchen. He wants his dinner on a tray in his room, and he asked for a bottle of red wine."

"Give him whatever he wants," Gerald said grimly. He leaned over the couch where his daughter was lying and tried to take her hand. "Melanie, *ma petite*," he crooned. But his attempt to comfort her prompted a new burst of crying. He sat down in a chair across the room, looking baffled.

David went over to him and said, "Why don't we let Laird be alone with her for now? She'll be all right. Let's go into your study." He led the way down the hall and turned on the lights.

Gerald sat down and massaged his temples. "Why is she treating me this way? I just don't understand."

Bracing his back against the wall, David said, "I think she's trying to protect you, Gerald."

"From what? She can't possibly think I killed Kassandra." His eyes were anguished.

"She's probably been afraid all along that you did it to keep Kassandra from hurting her."

"Oh, I can't believe that. I've never in my life done anything violent. I never even so much as spanked her when she was a child. Why would she think I could kill someone? You've got to make her listen to me, David. We can't let this go on any longer."

"There's not much we can do until Laird gets her calmed down. Maybe he'll persuade her to tell him what happened tonight," David said. "While he's doing that, I'm going to talk to Blaine-Poole. He must be at least partly responsible for the state Melanie's in."

Jumping up, Gerald said, "I'll come with you. I've

been wanting to confront that bastard ever since I first saw him."

David shook his head. "It'll be better if I handle him first. You've got to talk to Perez when she gets here."

"I'll do that when I'm ready," Gerald said petulantly.

"You don't have a choice, Gerald. You have to tell her the truth. All of it. She knows you were with Christine the night Kassandra was murdered. No, she didn't hear it from me," he added when Gerald's expression hardened. "I'm not sure how much she's figured out, but you can bet the parts she has to fill in for herself are not going to be in your favor."

Gerald sat down again. He looked close to tears. "I'll tell Perez what I did, but I can't leave Melanie unprotected. She wasn't responsible. No matter what happened."

Chapter Twenty-Six

When David went back to the living room, Melanie was lying quietly, Laird sitting on an ottoman holding her hand. David pulled a chair closer to the couch. He was hoping to get some idea of what had happened on the headland before he went upstairs to tackle Blaine-Poole.

"You're with the people who care about you now, Melanie," he said gently. "If you tell us what's upset you, I promise we'll do everything we can to help you."

Even with her makeup gone and her face puffy from crying, she was a beautiful woman. Her usual expression of cynicism was gone. She looked vulnerable, much like she had that summer after her mother died when she'd tried so hard not to let a hint of grief show through the mask of rebellion she created for herself.

She shook her head, and David said, "Something happened. We can see that. Did Blaine-Poole hurt you?"

She turned her face away. After a few moments, she said, "It's all my fault, David."

"What is?"

"She's dead. I killed her," she wailed.

Laird seized her arm. "No. Don't say that! You couldn't."

David waited to recover his own equilibrium. Arguing with Melanie would clearly do no good. He brushed a strand of hair from her face and said, "What did you do to Ellie?"

"I gave her the sleeping pills!" Between sobs, she said, "The little pig came into my room. She said things about Père. How he would get sex now that Kassandra was gone. I wanted to strangle her!" She paused and then said in a rush, "She picked up my bottle of sleeping pills and said, 'I need these.' I poured almost the whole bottle into a tissue and gave it to her."

"Did she take any of the pills then, Melanie?" David said.

"No, but I knew she would do it. She was half drunk then. I knew she would get in the hot tub and drown herself. Then, when Michael told me she took something—" She covered her face with her hands. "I didn't really want her to die," she wailed. Her shoulders began to quiver as she sobbed. Laird drew her close, and she clung to him.

"Melanie, listen to me," David said. "I don't think Ellie took those pills."

She pulled away from Laird and looked at David incredulously. "How do you know? She must have. How else could she drown?"

"Nobody is sure how it happened, but we'll find out."
Squeezing her hand, he said, "I'm going upstairs to talk
to Blaine-Poole. I'll be back in a few minutes. In the
meantime, Melanie, you've got to get hold of yourself.
Detective Perez is coming back here this evening. Don't
try to hide anything from her. Tell her you gave Ellie
the pills and you're afraid she took them. That's all."

As he had expected, Blaine-Poole was in Kassandra's
bedroom, standing next to the display wall. He was
examining two of the South Indian bronze goddesses
under the light of a flood lamp that looked like one of
Theo's. The remains of his dinner and a half-empty wine
glass were on a small table nearby.

"Got her sorted out?" he said carelessly.

David pulled the desk chair out and sat down. "What
did you do to Melanie?"

Blaine-Poole flushed slightly. "That girl's barmy.
What's she saying I did?"

"You must have done something to upset her."

"It wasn't me! Melanie was well on her way when we
went off to the pub," he said angrily. "She kept going on
about how stupid Ellie was to go into the pool drunk. I
said the girl could hold her liquor. She must have taken
something else to make her pass out. Melanie gets the
wind up at that. She leaps out of her chair and flies
outside, shouting the place down."

"I haven't heard that you had any dealings with
Ellie. How did you know she could hold her liquor?"

Blaine-Poole drank a deep gulp of his wine and

turned away.

Suspecting what might have happened, David said, "Did you say that to taunt Melanie because you knew she had given pills to the girl?"

When there was no answer, he said, "Did you kill Ellie?"

Glaring indignantly, Blaine-Poole said, "Why would I do a daft thing like that? She was only the best shag I've had in years."

Even though he was not shocked, David was surprised. "Did Kassandra know you were having sex with her?"

"Know? Listen, Markam, before you ride that high horse 'round again, you'd better have a look at these chums of yours. It was Kassandra who set me up with this treat. The girl was keener than I was." He laughed. "She wanted to do it there in the hot tub, but the kid who was cleaning the place wouldn't shove off. So, we came 'round to my room."

"You spent the whole night together in your room?"

"I did. She was all for having another go in the tub after Kassandra went." Smirking, he added, "I must've fallen asleep."

"Ellie went out there alone, then. She was outside when Kassandra died?"

"Can't say. Only know I wasn't."

David saw again the girl's body in the murky water. He felt rage at both of them. Kassandra, the panderer, who offered Ellie as bait, and this arrogant bastard who obviously didn't give a damn whether the girl lived or died.

Remembering the wine and the expensive scent in the apricot-colored towel he'd found near Ellie's body, he said, "Just out of curiosity, did you give Ellie a bottle of perfume? Or buy her some special wine?"

"With Kassandra covering my costs, why not?"

"Did you get the wine from Theo's supply?"

Blaine-Poole shrugged.

"You're saying Kassandra paid your expenses and provided the girl for you as a bonus. This was in addition to what she paid for the antiquities you bought and delivered?" David said, not bothering to hide his disbelief.

Blaine-Poole slowly turned the bronze statue he was holding as if he were savoring its beauty. "We had an arrangement."

David watched him. He was beginning to see Kassandra's whole sordid plan, and it dazed him in its audacity and callousness. "She didn't pay you in cash, did she? There was never any money in that valise. Kassandra was just putting up a front—keeping her financial dealings a secret from Gerald."

"Let's say it was a bit of a trade," Blaine-Poole said smoothly. "I'm by way of setting myself up with a gallery. I wanted inventory and new clients. Kassandra wanted capital to fund that museum venture of hers. She pays my expenses to bring in a new piece now and then. I shop 'round a few pieces that she's willing to part with. I have a nice commission. She has funds for her project. Absolute win-win."

"That's why I couldn't find an updated list of her collection. She was waiting until you agreed on the pieces to sell before she finalized the paperwork for the donation."

"Very likely. Waste of time to bother with all that provenance for goods she no longer owned."

"This 'arrangement' sounds a little strange to me. You're saying she gave you no cash for the pieces you bought for her? Did you agree ahead of time which ones you'd be receiving in return for the new ones?"

Blaine-Poole took another sip of wine and pursed his lips. "We did a bit of negotiating. It's the way with these collectors, Markam. Like cocaine to them. They must have more to feed the addiction."

"So you were the pusher."

He grinned. "Never have to push hard if you choose the right clients. She was happy with what she got from me."

"She paid you for the Ganesh statue last year and nothing else? You didn't receive cash for anything after that?"

"Just a bit for the novelty—Gerald's present."

"What about the stone head you brought this time?"

Blaine-Poole put the statue on the table next to the other one he'd been handling. He stretched his arms and yawned. "No longer an issue. That masterpiece is going away with me. Along with a few others. Like these lovelies." He gestured toward the bronze goddesses. "There's a certain dealer in New York eager to get his hands on these two."

"Is Eva Dusant involved in any of your plans?"

He shook his head. "Far out of Eva's league. Eva's pretty well past it, anyway."

David watched him as he turned off the flood lamp and put his tools into a leather bag. The two bronze statues went into the bag as well. "You assume this deal still stands even though Kassandra's dead?"

Blaine-Poole gave him a long, complacent look. "I've got a contract. I expect Gerald will want to handle things quietly."

After he left, David stood looking at Kassandra's collection. Half a dozen of the niches were empty already. Gerald was going to be furious when he heard Blaine-Poole's terms. David felt the same way himself. It would be very satisfying to do this slime bucket real physical harm.

He started downstairs and met Melanie and Laird on their way up. "Perez isn't coming tonight. Gerald talked to her on the phone," Laird said.

Melanie reached for David. She pulled his face close to hers and kissed his cheek. "Please take care of Père," she whispered.

"I'm doing the best I can," he said.

Mrs. Sawyer called to him from the kitchen when he passed the door. "Thank goodness, we've finally got a little peace in this house now that they're all upstairs," she said. "Mr. Fitzwilliam's waiting for you in his study. Now, just a minute, sir. I've got a nice turkey sandwich already made for you. You can't go to bed hungry. I've been trying to fatten you up, you know, so you've got milk as well as tea."

David thanked her. She gave him the tray, and he took it to Gerald's study.

When he went in, Gerald jerked as though he'd been asleep. "We've got a reprieve. I took your advice. I called Perez and talked to her," he said when David sat down.

"What did she say?"

"Not much, but at least I'm not under arrest. I told her the state Melanie's in, and she said it didn't sound like anything could be accomplished tonight. She'll be here early tomorrow morning."

"Makes sense," David said, eating his sandwich.

"Perez did ask me to have you call her. I think she wants to hear your version of what went on tonight."

"She probably wants to find out what I got from Blaine-Poole. That guy's a piece of work. I'll tell you about it tomorrow."

When Gerald had gone, David closed the door and dialed the telephone number Detective Perez had left for him. As he expected, she wanted to know what Blaine-Poole had said, and she allowed herself a few pithy remarks after David told her.

"So, how do you think things stand now?" she said.

He outlined what he thought had been the sequence of events that led, first, to Kassandra's, and then, to Ellie's deaths.

"You know, I'm pretty unhappy with the direction this whole thing's going," Perez said.

"So am I. In fact, I'm worried about what might

happen tonight."

After a pause, Perez said, "Let me think this through. I'm not sure what I'm going to do yet. But one thing's for sure. I do *not* want you to do anything else on your own, Markam. You hear me, right?"

"I hear you," he said reluctantly.

Finishing the sandwich, he sat for a while thinking over what his options might be. He decided to go for a walk.

Chapter Twenty-Seven

The wind trailed shreds of fog across the dark lawn, making the path lights a string of glittering fuzz. Pulling on his jacket, David felt the weight in the right pocket of the stone carving Mrs. Sawyer had given him earlier. Now, he had an idea of how important this little piece of stone was.

When he passed through the opening in the tall hedges, he could see up close the effect of the garden at night. Pools of light illuminated the mounds of flowerbeds and walkways, creating an impression both elegant and cold, like all the beauty Kassandra had gathered around herself.

He was halfway through the garden, following one of the winding paths that eventually came out on the other side, when the lights went off. He stood still in the darkness, listening. No sound beyond the wind in the grove of trees at the far side of the garden. Then, as clouds began to clear the moon, he could see the path, and he walked on toward the headland. Rounding the curve of a hedge, he became aware of a presence in the shadows of an alcove.

"David?" It was Christine's voice.

He went closer and saw her sitting on a bench. "You startled me, Christine. I couldn't see you there."

"I often come here at night. The plant smells make me feel peaceful."

"Do you know what happened to the lights?"

"I can switch them back on if you want. Are you having trouble sleeping? Is that why you're out here?"

"I'm just decompressing from the drama with Melanie."

"Come and tell me about it," she said, moving to one side of the bench. There was concern in her voice.

Sitting next to her, he said, "I think she's having some kind of emotional breakdown."

"That doesn't surprise me," Christine said gravely. "She's been on the verge of a crisis for several days. What has she done this time?"

"She and Blaine-Poole went out to a local bar after Perez told them not to leave the house. When they didn't come back, Ken Laird and I went to look for Melanie. We found her out on the bluff, crying hysterically. It seems she let Ellie have some sleeping pills yesterday, and she believes they caused the girl's death."

"I'm sure she's upset. And everyone else is too. Poor Gerald. Melanie's narcissistic tantrums are all he's talked about this past week. He's worried sick. I'd like to find therapy for her, but I doubt she'd welcome my interference."

"Her concern about the pills seems to be valid. It's not certain that Ellie took them, but it's a possibility."

"Yes. It would be very much in character for Ellie. How tragic. That must have been what happened. But I'm sure Melanie won't be held responsible. Ellie's death was an accident, regardless."

"Detective Perez doesn't seem to be treating it as an accident," he said evenly. "Apparently, the bruise on the back of the girl's neck is similar to the one on Kassandra's."

"Oh? Well, she must have fallen against the edge of the pool and hit her head on the tile."

He was surprised at her dismissive tone. "Didn't Perez mention that when she interviewed you?"

Christine nodded, keeping her eyes averted.

Not certain he was taking the right course, he said, "I've just had a talk with Blaine-Poole about Ellie. Did you know Kassandra set her up as a bed partner for him?"

"That doesn't seem likely. How do you know?"

"Blaine-Poole was more than happy to tell me."

"He must be trying to impress you. Kassandra liked Ellie. I can't believe she would do such a thing."

"You don't think she would use Ellie as bait?"

"That's appalling."

"Kassandra was not a good person, Christine. As far as I can see, she did her best to destroy everyone who came under her control. It's generous of you to defend her, but I know she hurt you, too."

"Oh, David, you can't imagine." Her words seemed to surprise her.

"I can, at least I'm trying," he said, hoping she would trust him. "I found something I think is evidence of what Kassandra tried to do to you." He took the carving out of his pocket and unwrapped it. Even in the dim light, it was visible against the white cloth. "I want to help you, Christine, and getting at the truth is the only way I know how."

Her habitual calm seemed to slip away. "Oh, no!" she said. "How did you get that disgusting thing? It's like a plague rat, following me. It keeps coming back."

"Kassandra gave this to you, didn't she?"

When she didn't answer, he wadded the carving into the cloth and put it back into his pocket. Taking her hand, he massaged the back of it with his thumb. "Let's just talk about what happened. You don't have to deal with this alone anymore. Somehow, we're going to find a way to work it out."

She looked at him as if she longed to believe they could. Finally, she said in a weary voice, "She brought it to my house Friday night. On the way to her meditation ritual. She said it was a present, an ornament for my coffee table. She's given me things when she wanted something before. Beautiful things, like the Persian carpet. I wasn't prepared for this."

"It was her way of telling you she knew Gerald was coming to visit you?"

"I made the mistake of trying to deny it. Then, when I realized she really did know, I tried to explain. She said, 'Well, if Gerald won't be coming here to see it, I'll have to give it to him at the reception on Sunday. It will be so funny to see the look on his face, don't you think? And then everyone will know you're up to your old tricks of seducing husbands, won't they?'"

"Would she really have done it?" David said. "Something that crass would damage her own reputation. Not to mention Gerald's and yours."

"She was long past caring. You were perceptive when you said she was obsessed. It just wasn't in the way you thought it was."

Hoping she would explain the "seducing husbands" part, David said, "What could she gain by humiliating you?"

"The publication of her book. She'd been turned down by every publisher she contacted, and Kassandra didn't tolerate rejection well. She wanted me to use my influence with Stephen. We argued about it earlier in the week, and again Friday afternoon. No matter what I said, she would not let go of the fantasy that she could make whatever she wanted a reality."

David had begun to grasp the situation now. "Is Stephen someone you were close to?"

She was silent, and he wished he could see her face more clearly. "Is he a publisher?" he said.

"Yes. He came to me for therapy, but I never thought of him as a client. It was always something different."

"He was part of that bad time in San Francisco?"

"The worst time of my life! I was barely able to survive. It cost me my career and ruined Stephen's marriage. But afterward, I moved on somehow. What I've created in St. Judith has been good.

"Then, on Friday, Kassandra was standing there in my living room, demanding that I call Stephen and ask him for a 'favor,' she called it. It was insane. I'm the *last* person who could persuade him to do anything after what we went through."

"When did you realize she was responsible for what happened to your career?" David said.

Christine seemed uncertain. "I don't remember exactly what she said, but suddenly, I knew, in a flash, that it was *she* who had reported me to the Board! She was the one who destroyed my life, broke me. But then, later, she came to my rescue—put me back together.

"That repulsive little carving was meant to tell me she could break me again any time. That's why she brought it. She didn't care whether poor Gerald was coming to see me. I'm sure she's known all along. And gloated over the power it gave her. She said, 'All you have to do is contact Stephen. You can make him do this.' When I refused, she dropped the carving into a little bag she was carrying. She said, 'Then, you know what to expect on Sunday.'

"I pretended I didn't care, but I was so upset I was dizzy. When she left, the rage took hold of me again. I went after her and got the bag." Christine slumped against the back of the bench, as if she were exhausted.

"You must have been terrified," David said.

She looked up at him and shook her head. "No, I don't think I was. Not then. I wanted to hurt her, and my Tai Chi form came instinctively to me. Almost miraculously, as if my body were pure spirit. But when my foot struck her, I had more force than I expected. She just disappeared over the rim of the bluff. In an instant. I don't think she even made a sound. Then it was done and I was lost."

"You still had the carving? When did you put it back into her room?" he said gently.

"While Gerald was picking you up at the airport the next morning. I knew Michael Blaine-Poole had brought it. From the way he looked at me, I was afraid Kassandra had told him what she intended to do with the carving. But if it was in the collection, no one would know I'd ever seen it."

David found the calm reasonableness of her voice unnerving. "I suppose Ellie saw you struggling with Kassandra and tried to take advantage of that."

"Kassandra knew how to pick her minions," Christine said, the tone of her voice cynical. "Ellie was as good at spying as she was at the other things she was hired for. She only went wrong after Kassandra died."

"But you said she had problems from the very beginning. Didn't you try to counsel her?"

"What I told you was true. I did try to work with her."

"When you said she misinterpreted your intentions, you meant she turned on you, didn't you? She brought the carving back to you as a show of power?"

"Ellie's needs were crude. She wanted money as well as power. She called me on the phone and asked me to meet her in the meditation room on Monday night.

"When I arrived, she showed me the carving and said she had 'more proof' in her room. She demanded five thousand dollars. I told her I had nothing to give her. She said, 'I'm going to stay around until you and the rich ambassador get married. Then, I'll leave after I get a little going away present.' She was convinced that this fantastic plan would work. It was as if Kassandra had been reincarnated!"

Disturbed by a vision of Gerald caught up in such a situation, David said, "I saw someone in the apartment over the garage earlier this evening. You were looking for whatever proof she had, weren't you? What did you find?"

"Nothing. She must have been bluffing."

"Why did you bury the carving? Why not throw it into the ocean?"

"I suppose I was planning to do that. I had it in my hand, and I came and sat down here, trying to think of what to do. I heard a noise—I don't know what it was, and I just lifted one of the pavers and pressed it into the soil underneath. How could anyone know it was there? I don't understand that."

They sat in silence for a while, and then Christine pulled her hand away from his and stood up. "I'm tired, David. I'm going now. You were kind to say you want to help me. You're a good man. I wish I had known you before." She looked into his eyes and walked away.

"Wait, Christine. There still may be something we can do. Let's talk to Perez," he said, catching up with her.

"It's much too late for that, David. You've seen all of us. Ellie, Michael, Theo, even Melanie. Kassandra's *real* collection. When Ellie died, I admitted to myself that I was one of them."

They left the shelter of the hedges and walked out onto the headland. The clouds began to drift over the moon, and the darkness deepened. Christine started walking faster, apparently heading for the rim of the bluff.

"Christine, wait! Don't go too near the edge. Let me talk to you," David said urgently. "Gerald loves you. He'll do everything he can to protect you. And Perez wants—" She stopped, and he reached for her.

Ducking, she dipped her hand into his pocket and grabbed the dishtowel and carving. "I say we throw this into the ocean now! Then neither of us will ever come back," she said and laughed.

"No! That won't change anything!"

David had his hand on her arm when his foot slipped in the loose sand. Struggling for balance, he sensed rather than saw the movement behind him. The powerful kick caught him in the middle of his back, propelling him forward. His feet slid out from under him. His tailbone hit the ground, and he began to slide down the sloping bluff.

Flipping himself over, he grabbed at a clump of stiff,

dried vegetation and pulled its shallow roots away from the rock. His legs scraped over a ledge into nothingness. For an instant, he fell freely.

One foot landed on a small outcropping, jarring nerves all the way to his teeth. Straightening, he pressed his face against the cold, wet rock in overwhelming relief. Then the stone crumbled under his feet. He began to slide again. Frantically, he grabbed at rock ridges, tearing his fingernails.

Briefly, his foot found another ledge. It was wet and he slipped off, scraping his shin to the bone. Slowly, helplessly, he slid down to a lower ridge where decaying vegetation blanketed the rock. Plant tendrils broke off as he grabbed them, leaving him handfuls of slime. Precariously, he rested his foot against a jutting rock and turned his head, inhaling the slime into his mouth and nose. He rubbed his face against the sleeve of his jacket, and the wet nylon smeared the slime into his eyes.

A wave crashed in, splashing his back. He was very close to the surf. The deep sound and the magnitude of the wave told him there was no beach below, small hope of living once he slipped into that roaring maw at his heels.

Gripping a narrow shelf of rock, struggling to breathe, he tilted his head back slightly and saw only darkness. He thought he heard a woman's voice yell his name, but he did not dare to make a sound. Christine might throw a stone at him. Even a small one, if it hit him, could make him lose his grip. He pressed his body against the rock. For the first time in his life, he was physically afraid of a woman.

Chapter Twenty-Eight

His grip slipping from the rock shelf, David raised his throbbing left arm, feeling for another hold to keep his balance. His fingers closed over a pointed rock about the thickness of a baseball, wet but firmly anchored. The toes of both shoes were wedged into a tiny crevice.

Hanging there, he was amazed at how clear his mind was. He felt euphoric, as if he knew he would live forever. And he was equally sure, in a matter-of-fact way, that he would fall into the water in the next moment and die.

Looking up, he thought he could see a beam of light moving above him. Was it a flashlight? Had Christine gotten a flashlight? Was she walking along the rim of the bluff looking for him? Once again, he thought he heard a shout. If he yelled, she would hear him.

The light disappeared. Then, there was no sound but the wind and the waves splashing below. He waited, hoping his arm would keep its strength, his legs would not start to shake.

Suddenly, he saw a strong light almost directly above him. He heard the mechanical sound of a voice through a bullhorn. It was a woman's voice, and it sounded like Perez. A rush of hope strengthened his arms. He laid his cheek against the cold rock, willing himself to count seconds to stay calm. How could Perez be here? She didn't know what had happened.

The sharp, distorted wail of a siren cut through the roar of the wind. Then, there was a cacophony of shouts and the bullhorn rasping his name.

He tried to yell back. A huge, glaring light suddenly shown down on him. Directly above him, a man's voice yelled, "Jesus Christ! Let's get a harness down there."

Relief made David shift his weight, and his right foot slipped from its ridge. Adrenaline shot through his body, tingling in his arms and legs as he jammed his toe back into the crevice.

Perez yelled, "Hang on, Markam. We're lowering a rope to you. Try to grab it. I'm coming down to get you. Hang on!"

He waited, his nerves prickling, his mind in stasis. At last, he felt the whack of a knotted rope against the side of his head. Next, it hit his back. His fingers tightened on his handholds. He was frozen in place. Seconds passed as the rope moved in jerks and taps, threatening, promising.

A male voice shouted, "Can you feel the rope? Talk to us, Markam!"

David dared not draw breath to answer. They were surely not more than thirty feet above him, and yet it might as well be a hundred. The rope hit his back again. He forced himself to yell, "Yes!"

As he hung there, his relief began to trickle away. He could hear voices above, but they seemed unrelated to him. Had they forgotten or given up? The rope hung beside his cheek. To grab it he'd have to let go. Didn't they know he'd fall if he let go? What were they doing? Looking up, he saw a dark shadow moving toward him, silently. He had to look down, then, not breathing, he looked up again.

Suddenly, Perez was there next to him, familiar and real. She seized his belt in the back. "Okay, Markam. I've got you, but you have to help me get you into the harness. There's a big loop at the end of this rope. I want you to get your right hand through the loop and hold on," she said, lifting the rope to his hand level.

David pressed his cheek against the rock. Water, from the salt spray or his own sweat, trickled into the corners of his eyes, stinging. His legs were starting to shake.

"Come on, Markam. You're home free now," Perez urged. "Just open your hand so you can get your fingers around the rope. I will not let go of you. I promise."

She swung herself behind him and gripped his hips with her powerful legs. He slid his right arm into the loop and clung to the rope. Bracing her feet against the bluff, she gently pulled him a few inches away from the rock to get the harness fastened around his waist.

Swinging to his side, she yelled to the deputies above and said to David, "I'm going to hold on to you until we get a few yards higher." When the sheer rock gave way to a steep slope, she said, "Do you think you can walk up from here?"

Planting his foot against the rock face, he gripped the rope and leaned back, testing for balance. With the deputies pulling from above, his first three steps went well, but as soon as he took the next one, he knew he'd tilted too far. For a terrible instant, he fought to keep from tipping over backward. Adrenaline shot through his body as his feet slipped. His chest and face slammed against the slope of the bluff. He swore at Perez when she grabbed for him, but she managed to steady him until he got his footing again.

When he reached the edge of the bluff, hands hauled him up. His knees buckled and he sat down heavily on the hard ground.

What seemed like hours later, David was in the breakfast room where he had begun his stay in the house. He sat numbly, trying to keep his head clear while he waited for the painkiller to ease the misery throughout his body.

Across the round table from him, Perez sat with an empty coffee mug and her notepad in front of her. Her face was strained with fatigue.

Mrs. Sawyer, who had helped the other deputy clean

and bandage the worst of David's injuries, went to and from the kitchen, bringing tea and warm milk, fussing over him, until Perez asked her to go to bed.

When they were alone, she said, "I guess we've done as much as we can tonight." She looked hard at him. "Man, it's a good thing I didn't trust you. You did exactly what I said not to do. I hung up that phone, and I could feel in my bones you weren't going to leave it alone."

"So that's why you came back."

"I didn't know what to expect, but from what you told me, it seemed like a strong possibility that something else was going to happen. I thought it was likely to be out there in that garden or on the headland, so I left my vehicle outside the gate and walked back along the access road."

"You were just going to hang out and wait?"

She shrugged. "Whatever it takes."

"When did you realize what was going on? You couldn't see us. Could you hear our voices? We sat there talking for a while."

"No. I went along the other side of the hedge that blocks the view of the vegetable garden. The first thing I heard was you yelling at Christine out on the bluff. I took off through the trees, and when I got out on the headland, I heard feet running on the gravel driveway by her house. Then her car started and tore down the road."

"The keys were in her car? She must have been planning to leave. I was so sure she intended to commit suicide. I never even considered that she might have another plan," David said.

"Neither did I. For a second, I thought you might be with her, but for some reason, I flashed my light across the headland. If I hadn't seen that dishtowel on the ground, I probably would have started after her." She shook her head. "This one was too close for comfort."

David managed a smile. "How did you get that backup out here so fast?"

Perez looked pleased with herself. "I had put a deputy on alert, just in case. It was sheer luck that the one on duty was my partner in our Cliff Rescue Unit. We never go anywhere without ropes and equipment."

"You are truly an amazing woman!" David said.

She leaned closer to him. "By the way, I want you to know; I still could have gotten you to the top if you hadn't been able to walk up that bluff. I would *not* have let you go."

He had to look away to avoid letting her see how moved he was. "I guess I gave you a hard time," he said.

"Probably not as hard as the one I gave you during this investigation. I didn't want to let you know how much help you were giving me." Her eyes sparkled, and David liked her more than ever.

"I'm not as proud of my part in the thing as I'd like to be," he said. "I knew Christine was in trouble."

"I don't know how. I couldn't see it! She seemed like one of the sanest people I've ever dealt with."

"She was sane and very compassionate until she was pushed too far. Maybe she made mistakes like we all do, but if it hadn't been for Kassandra, she'd probably have had a good life."

"Looks like you knew a lot more than you shared with me. That stone carving, for instance. Why didn't you tell me about that? I never even saw the thing."

"I didn't realize the significance of it at first. When it disappeared, I assumed Ellie had stolen it, thinking she could sell it. It wasn't until I found out from Blaine-Poole that Kassandra asked him buy it as a 'treat' for Gerald that I began to see what it might mean."

"She got it to threaten Christine with? How did she know that would be necessary?"

David leaned back, beginning to feel the relaxing effect of the pill he had taken. "The threat to Christine was probably not the original intention. I think the carving was supposed to represent Ellie and Gerald. Kassandra planned to give it to Gerald as a way of suggesting that Ellie could be available to him sexually."

For the first time since he'd met her, David saw shock on Perez's face.

"She was pimping the girl to her husband?" She made a sound of disgust. "I thought that crap only happened in porn movies. It makes me sick!"

"It does me too, but that's the way Kassandra's mind worked. If Gerald had gone along with it, she'd have real power over him. It was also a way to derail the relationship she knew was growing between him and Christine. That was probably her biggest fear."

They heard a door closing in the hallway. Gerald came in, stopping just inside the room. His face was gray, his eyes swollen and red. He had the look of a man who had summoned the courage to take responsibility for a mistake he was ashamed of.

"I just wanted to tell you both how sorry I am about everything that's happened," he said. He hesitated as if he were searching for better words. Then he said, "I'm going to bed. I feel like the world's fallen apart. I'm so sorry."

Without waiting for a response, he left, and they sat staring at each other.

"Poor man," Perez said. "Life's too damned hard sometimes." She got to her feet stiffly. "I need to go home."

She came around the table and held out her hand. "Thank you, Mr. Markam—David. I'm glad you're all right."

David stood up. "Even if you are still on duty, Dita Perez, I'm going to hug you. I owe you my life, and I'll never forget it."

Chapter Twenty-Nine

It was Friday, barely a week since Kassandra Fitzwilliam had died of malice on a rock ledge near St. Judith.

Gerald and David sat at a table on the terrace. They had finished lunch and were savoring the afternoon sunshine. Gerald had dark circles under his eyes and the devastation of the past week was evident in his face. Even so, he looked like he was at peace with himself.

"You've decided to sell the house?" David said.

Gerald yawned. "If I can. The market isn't good right now, according to the realtor. He thinks leasing it as a B&B might be the best thing. It has a sizable mortgage, and it's hard to find anybody who wants to live in a monstrosity like this."

"I guess it would be. Melanie doesn't want to stay on with you?"

"No. She's leaving tomorrow. I doubt I could pay her

to live in this place after what she's been through."

David put his glass down. He had hardly thought about what would happen when they had all gone. Gerald would be here alone. "She's still planning to open her shop in San Francisco?"

Gerald shook his head. "She's just going down there to terminate all the arrangements she made. She's decided to go back to the East Coast to live."

"With Ken Laird?"

"Not immediately. He has to get back to Washington. I don't know whether she'll join him later or not. She doesn't seem to know herself. I hope so. I'd really like to have grandchildren someday," he said wistfully.

David said nothing. Apparently, Gerald did not know about Melanie's abortion. He was glad she had not told him.

The kitchen door opened and Mrs. Sawyer called to them. "Excuse me, Mr. Fitzwilliam. Detective Perez is here."

They both rose and shook hands with Perez, and Gerald pulled out a chair.

David thought she looked younger today, less pinched by tension, but something was definitely on her mind.

She sat down, and Gerald said, "I've been thinking about the Tai Chi classes. I hope you're planning to continue teaching them. Everyone would be disappointed not to have them."

"I am, but not right away," Perez said. "Before we get into that, Mr. Fitzwilliam, I have something to tell you. I wanted to see you in person instead of calling."

Gerald looked apprehensive, obviously preparing for news he dreaded.

"We found Christine Moreland's remains yesterday. The body was caught between some boulders, in a little cove just south of town. Not far from where we found her car abandoned." She laid her hand on his arm. "I'm sorry."

He patted her hand. "Thank you for coming here to let me know. I appreciate your kindness."

Having watched him struggle through the past few days, David knew how emotionally wrenching this news must be for Gerald. Christine had been such an appealing woman. It was hard, even after what she'd done, to think about how miserable and alone she must have been.

"Were you able to determine how she died?" David said, not entirely wanting to hear the answer.

"She probably jumped," Perez said matter-of-factly. "After this length of time, and with the tide washing in and out, there's really no way to tell much more."

Gerald made a comment, but David did not hear what he said. Perez's words had triggered a visceral memory of clinging to that slimy ridge, terrified of the churning ocean below him. Christine had sentenced herself to die as she must have thought he had died, plunging from one of those bluffs into the darkness.

"Well, sir, speaking of Tai Chi," Perez said to Gerald as she stood up to go, "I've made arrangements to hold the class in town. The trustees of Milstone House are letting us use a room. They've gotten funds to convert the space that used to be the kitchen into a community meeting room. I have a feeling you might have had something to do with that."

Gerald smiled blandly.

After she had gone, David and Gerald went into his study and sat relaxing in the wing chairs. "Since you're driving down the coast to Monterey with me, maybe we should stop and visit Theo and Holly when we go through San Francisco," David said, grinning.

He laughed at Gerald's incredulous look and said, "I suppose they made it home okay."

"They must have since we haven't heard anything to the contrary," Gerald said. "I've given that Vietnam picture issue a lot of thought, though."

"So have I. But I'm not inclined to pursue it. Theo's the one who has to make restitution for what he did. He's the only one who can."

Gerald flicked his hand dismissively. "I won't hold my breath waiting for him to do that. I guess we can say he's already done penance just living with himself."

"Well, at least we've put a dint in Blaine-Poole's operation," David said with satisfaction. "I think he's going to trip himself up when he starts doing business with that 'eager dealer in New York' he has lined up. From what Mary Beltran told me, that operation will soon be heating up. Blaine-Poole's not going to find those Customs agents and assorted ministries quite so easy to slide by anymore."

"It galls me that he got away with several valuable pieces, but he knew I wouldn't contest his claim."

"It really wasn't worth the stress that would cause you. The appraiser Chaney recommended should be able to dispose of what's left in the collection pretty cleanly. Without any legal entanglements, if you're lucky. I know it isn't the solution you hoped for," he said when Gerald frowned, "but maybe he can repatriate a few of the pieces."

"My God, it's such a relief to have them out of here. The statues, the pots, and the people," Gerald said. "Now, finally, you can have the peace and quiet I invited you here for."

He looked at David's bandaged hands. "Will you ever forgive me for putting you through this ordeal, David? I'll never forgive myself. How could I have been so blind to what Kassandra was doing? The lives she ruined. She drove Christine to madness." His features crumpled as he fought tears.

"You did love Christine, didn't you?"

"I must have. Yes, I did. Oh, maybe the relationship was mostly my own fantasy. A captivating daydream of being together in some exotic place. I think I imagined us married, but I'm not sure I would have asked her to marry me. Even I couldn't pretend the years between our ages didn't matter. But I did care for her deeply. I wanted her to care for me. For a while, I felt something I'd never known before. I felt—"

"Enchanted?" David suggested.

"Yes. That's it. I was, for a while, enchanted. I wanted to be. Those daydreams were a way to endure the torment my life with Kass had become. Perhaps it was even a way to revenge myself on Kass."

"I think Kassandra was aware of that. She tried to use the attraction between you to force Christine to do what she wanted. At the same time, she must have feared that she would lose control of both of you if you fell in love with Christine."

"Whatever it was, I can't avoid my share of blame for what happened," Gerald said.

"I'm not sure you could have done much to change things. Even showing Kassandra proof that Blaine-Poole was acquiring looted artifacts wouldn't have been a deterrent. Ambition and arrogance like hers are blinding. That's why she couldn't see that she was squeezing people too hard. I don't believe Christine really meant to kill her. I think she had been driven past endurance."

After a pause, he added, "Killing the girl was another story. That was deliberate. Even so, Kassandra's greed and ruthlessness were behind it."

Gerald wiped his eyes. "It was horrifying to hear what Perez just told us about Christine. But a relief to know it's over. Such an appalling waste of a beautiful life. And look what it did to you!" He shook his head miserably. "I have never been such a fool. I was so worried about Melanie that I didn't even trust *you*. After all these years!"

"Well, I'm not going to disagree. Just keep that in mind the next time we're in a desperate situation."

Gerald's face lit with hope. "Does that mean you've decided not to resign?"

David shifted restlessly. "I'm going to Washington next week, and I'm going back to work. That's all I know right now."

"Well, it's very likely that a chargé d'affaires position will be available in New Delhi after the election in November. You'll be in the right place to lobby for it. It would be one way to get another posting to India."

"I don't have the seniority for that job. Besides, if I get the India Desk at State, I'll be stuck in Washington for a couple of years."

"What about after that?" Gerald said.

"Who knows? I haven't even made up my mind what I'll do after next month."

"Are you talking about your career or something else?"

"All of it, I suppose. I don't want to let go of the freedom this job gives me. Being rootless suits me. I've been that way all my life. I've even gotten used to being an exile when I'm overseas and an outsider when I get back to the States."

"That makes you sound like a desperado," Gerald said.

"I guess. But I never wanted to live any other way."

"What's changed?"

"This past month has really messed me up! I've started wanting to find a place where I belong. Maybe I should buy a condo, actually own something."

Gerald looked at him with compassion. "But then you start thinking about living in that condo alone, don't you? Without Layne."

Turning away, David said, "That's another issue." In truth, Gerald had startled him by understanding him so well. Layne had been on his mind, in his dreams for months. When he found himself alive after the attack in Istanbul, a feeling of inevitability had started growing in him. Then, Mary Beltran's news that Layne was single again had roused a reckless hope.

Still, there were no guarantees. She might not want to come back to him. Once he was with her, he might not want to stay. Two things were certain. He was going to find her again, and if they were ever to have a chance of happiness together, both of their lives would have to change.

"Maybe this is a crossroad for me, and I need to take a different path," he said. "I could go back to graduate school. I'm not too old to start a new career."

"Doing what?"

"Probably archaeology, or maybe anthropology."

"Well, that's one way to make things work with Layne. Go into the same profession she's in. Of course, you'd probably miss the Foreign Service. And quitting three years before you're eligible for retirement might be a bit rash."

David shot him a warning look.

Gerald raised his hands. "I won't say another word. It's your life. When you're ready, you'll make the right decision. You certainly couldn't do any worse with yours than I have with mine."

Getting up, he went to the wall of photographs. "I do have just one more thing to tell you. This is fair warning. You may still be looking for your path, but I know where I belong. I called the State Department this morning to let them know I'm available for assignment."

He stood on tiptoes, took down his official ambassadorial portrait, and leaned it against the wall. "David, my friend, I'm going home."

ABOUT THE AUTHOR

Ann Saxton Reh, a retired educator and award-winning writer, spent her first 40 years living in six foreign countries and juggling family raising with an insatiable desire to experience the world. Now, she lives with her husband in Northern California and is planning her next adventure.

Made in the USA
San Bernardino, CA
07 March 2018